my adventures in rome

TESS RINI

ISBN: 978-1-7376372-9-5 (e-book)

ISBN: 979-8-9904586-0-4 (paperback)

Tessrini.com

Publisher: One Punch Productions, LLC

Cover design and interior formatting by *Hannah Linder Designs*

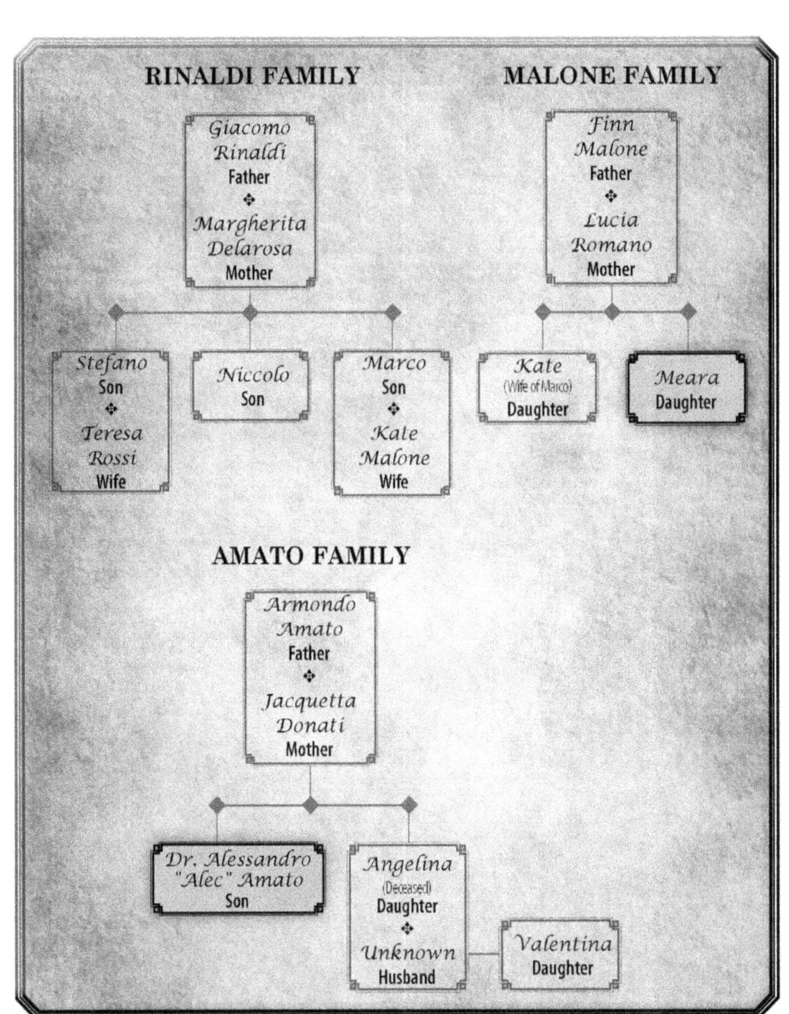

RINALDI FAMILY

Giacomo Rinaldi
Father
Margherita Delarosa
Mother

Stefano
Son
Teresa Rossi
Wife

Niccolo
Son

Marco
Son
Kate Malone
Wife

MALONE FAMILY

Finn Malone
Father
Lucia Romano
Mother

Kate
(Wife of Marco)
Daughter

Meara
Daughter

AMATO FAMILY

Armondo Amato
Father
Jacquetta Donati
Mother

Dr. Alessandro "Alec" Amato
Son

Angelina
(Deceased)
Daughter
Unknown
Husband

Valentina
Daughter

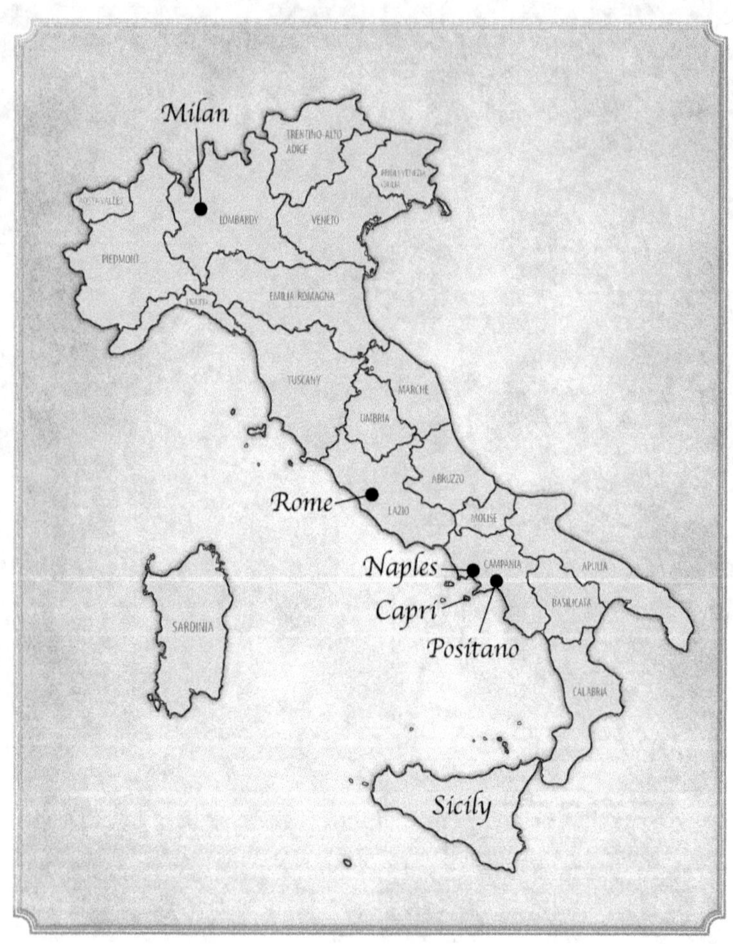

Where we travel in *My Adventures in Rome!*

one

Gelato. Lots of gelato. She was going to stuff her face with gelato. All different flavors. Pints and pints of the creamy sweet goodness for which Italy was known.

Meara Malone closed the door quietly behind her with a small click. It was tempting to slam the heavy mahogany door until it shook off its hinges, but that would display her temper. And Meara never showed her real feelings, especially in business. That would give her opponents a window into her emotions. As a woman in a corporate man's world, she had been forced to claw her way to the top. As she did so, she learned the game well. Early in her career, she naively thought people were promoted and recognized because of their hard work and success. It soon became clear to her that advancement was not always based on merit.

She squared her shoulders now and straightened up to her impressive height of almost six feet, even taller in her high-heeled Italian custom-made shoes. Impatiently brushing her long, wavy red hair back from her face, she strode out of what had been her executive suite for the past year.

She had just been fired.

There was no need to linger. There were no personal items in her office—no framed photos of loved ones, not even a roll of mints in the desk drawer. Watching how ruthless the corporate world could be, she learned a long time ago to leave as small a footprint as possible just for this reason. Though she had never been terminated, she had seen others' demise. She wasn't about to lose her dignity with employees watching their former Chief Executive Officer carry a box of belongings out the door.

Meara's phone buzzed, and her younger sister's photo flashed on the screen. She should probably take the call, but she had to mentally compose herself first. Kate would have to wait.

Walking out into the gloomy December day fit her mood perfectly. Rome was not as picturesque when the sun was not shining brightly. Not that she had noticed the Eternal City very much, considering she had worked most of the time during her tenure there.

As she headed to her hotel, Meara shook her head slightly at her driver who was standing at the door of a luxury black sedan, ready to chauffer her anywhere. He would find out soon enough that he was excused. She had an overwhelming amount to do, including packing and moving out of her place quickly.

Graham, the chair of the board, had a smug look on his face as he offered to allow her to stay in the company's penthouse in one of Rome's best hotels. He appeared to be inordinately pleased with his own graciousness, telling her she could continue occupying the apartment for thirty days. Though he was quick to point out it wasn't technically part of her significant severance package. While staying would make it easier for her, Meara was not inclined to take him up on his suggestion. That would mean being beholden to him, and that was the last thing she wanted to do.

She entered the hotel and rode the elevator, using her keycard to her apartment. After a brief moment of concern, she was relieved it still worked and that Graham hadn't pulled a sly one on her. Automatically, she kicked off her heels and walked barefoot across the exquisite carpeting to sit down on the plush sofa in the enormous room. Tucking her long shapely legs beneath her, she stared straight ahead. It wasn't that she had been fired; it was more that she hadn't seen it coming. She *always* saw what was coming. It was her strength. What had changed? She had gotten soft, letting herself slide in the last several months.

During the last decade, Meara had made a name for herself in Silicon Valley, working her way through the tech world. She was a rising star, a strong independent woman. While not vain, she acknowledged she was attractive. Unfortunately, in her world, it ultimately was a barrier that forced her to work even harder to be taken seriously. Now, in her early thirties, she felt like a failure.

Her phone on the coffee table buzzed, and she saw it was Kate again. She let it go to voicemail. She pushed down the guilt because she needed time to just breathe.

Meara had grown closer to her sister over the last several months, and now she lived in Italy as well. Kate had traveled to Italy on vacation in the summer and ran smack into a billionaire who had literally swept her off her feet after she injured her ankle. Marco Rinaldi was beyond handsome, charming and had just taken over as CEO of his family's dynasty. As the largest exporter of lemon products and olive oil from Italy, Oro Industries was a well-known powerhouse in Italy's corporate world. On the surface, Marco had seemed like the worst match for Kate. In fact, Meara had warned her repeatedly to stay away from him, believing everything she had heard and seen about the playboy billionaire.

Meara had even appeared at the family's estate in a vast lemon grove to show Kate photos of Marco with his ex-fiancé. They eventually learned the photos had misrepresented what was truly occurring. Meara still had a twinge of guilt about how easy it was to convince Kate to pack her things and leave abruptly.

It was only after their father's heart attack that the sisters—never very close—had formed a bond. Meara finally realized Kate had a fine-tuned intuition and possibly Marco could be trusted. On Kate's urgent appeal, Meara agreed to assist Marco and his brother, Stefano, unravel the complex corporate fraud by Sal, the company's Chief Financial Officer. Worse yet, Sal had been the best friend of their beloved late uncle. Meara had relished in watching the forensic accountants and lawyers expose his misdeeds. He was now awaiting trial in prison, and Marco was finding his way as CEO after Sal's constant undermining.

Meara had made good on her own interference and convinced Marco that Kate loved him just as much as he loved her. Marco had flown to San Francisco on the evening of Kate's book launch, and they had married shortly after. Kate had become pregnant quickly, and while the couple was thrilled about it, the surprise came at a time when they were still adjusting to their new lives. They were living in Positano but planned to move to Rome shortly to ensure Kate was near a modern hospital.

Her sister's photo appeared again on her phone, and it snapped Meara out of her stupor. Her heart began to race. Why was Kate calling her repeatedly? What if something was wrong with her or the baby?

"Katie, are you okay?"

She heard her sister's musical laugh. "I'm fine! Why does everyone ask me that all the time?"

"You called me three times! I was worried!"

"Well, if you're so worried, answer your freaking phone," Kate grumbled, but then her tone changed, sounding excited. "Didn't you get my text? We are in Rome, and Marco and I want you to come to dinner tonight."

"What's going on? You sound perky."

"I am NOT perky!" Kate said with an exasperated sigh. "I hate that word. I...we just want to talk to you."

"I already know you're pregnant," Meara said dryly. "What more news can there be? Twins? Triplets?"

"Oh God, bite your tongue! I think one baby is about all Marco and I can handle at this point. At least emotionally. We just want to discuss something with you. Marco is insistent that it be soon. And with all the wedding plans and Christmas coming, we thought it should be sooner than later. And tonight works well."

Meara sighed, leaning her head back on the sofa. Kate's best friend Teresa was getting married soon to Marco's brother, Stefano, in Capri. Kate was thrilled that Teresa would join her in Italy and also be part of the family. No one had seen this romance coming, as Stefano and Teresa were as different as night and day. Stefano, who had amazing culinary skills and loved fine dining, was an odd match for Teresa, who craved fast food. They had been brought together when Stefano had agreed to star in their cousin, Lucca's streaming television show about Italy's cuisine. Strikingly handsome like Marco, the resemblance stopped there. Stefano was quiet and withdrawn. Lucca had hired Teresa, a former television producer, to help draw Stefano out so he would be personable on film. While they had fallen in love, it appeared something must have happened to separate them. Teresa had remained in Italy because Kate was desperate to have her friend, who was now a nurse, close to her during the early weeks of her pregnancy.

Stefano and Teresa eventually made their way back to one another and decided to get married on Christmas Eve, which was now just weeks away. Meara had her doubts until she had seen them at Thanksgiving when Stefano had proposed. They were obviously deeply in love, and somehow it just worked. Kate was now in nonstop planning mode, helping Teresa with the wedding. Meara was happy for them and looking forward to it. All this romance, though, and finally establishing a closer relationship with her sister had distracted her. She had put her work second on some days. That was something she never would have done in the past.

"Are you still there? Can you come over?" Kate interrupted Meara's thoughts.

"Katie, it's not really the best time," Meara responded, examining her manicured nails. She didn't want to admit to her sister her plans were to change clothes and then pop down to the nearby *gelateria* where the staff knew her by first name.

"Why not? Do you have a hot date?"

"You know I'm not seeing anyone," Meara answered sharply. She swallowed and tried again. It wasn't fair to take her mood out on her sister. "I just had a horrible day. I was thinking of taking a bath and then going to bed."

"Meara, it's five o'clock," Kate protested. "Pull yourself together and head over in an hour or so. We're casual. You can wear sweats if you want."

"When have you ever seen me wear sweats unless I'm in a gym?" Meara asked incredulously. Even then, she only wore chic workout gear. Meara took a deep breath. Kate could be even more stubborn than she was, and it may be difficult to shake her off this idea. "Okay, fine," she said resolutely. "I'll change and come over. But only for dinner, and then I'm coming back home. It will be an early night."

"That's fine. I know how hard you've been working, and you're probably tired and want to get to the office early tomorrow as usual. See you soon!"

Kate hung up with what seemed like a satisfied click, and Meara groaned. She closed her eyes for a minute. If only she could cry. She hadn't been able to since she was younger. Somewhere along the line, she had convinced herself crying was a sign of weakness. It would help if she could release this energy.

Picking up a pillow from the sofa, she threw it as hard as she could. It bounced off the wall and slid to the floor with a quiet thump, a less than satisfying result. Reluctantly, she stood to go get changed and see whatever this mystery evening her sister had planned was all about.

Something was up, but she couldn't put her finger on it.

two

"What took you so long? And why did you take a taxi? Where's your driver?" Kate inquired as she stood at the door of their villa where an exquisite statue stood, surrounded by greenery at their circular drive.

Meara winced. She forgot it might generate questions when she had ordered the taxi to drive the fifteen-minute route from Rome's city center.

"Geez, Katie, let me come in before you start the inquisition."

Kate smirked in response, but her sharp eyes were busy looking at her sister. "Something's happened," she said quietly. "Just tell me and get it over with quickly. Is it dad? I just talked to him yesterday."

Meara smiled reassuringly. "He's fine! I didn't talk to him, but I texted earlier with Jimmy." Jimmy was the bar manager they had hired to help their father operate his famed San Francisco pub. "Jimmy said he's having a hard time keeping dad reined in. We may have to have a talk with Dad because he can't work like he used to. He needs to slow down."

Kate nodded, but her gaze was pensive as she carefully

assessed Meara in her perfectly pressed black jeans and forest green silk blouse. "Okay, sorry. You're just kind of pale."

Meara made a face. "I'm always pale." Her fair skin and green eyes meant a smattering of freckles across her fair-skinned face. She tried to stay out of the sun and used plenty of sunscreen, or she would burn immediately.

Kate led her into the expansive living room with its antique wooden furniture and big comfortable chairs with plush cream-colored cushions. The couple also had an apartment in central Rome, but they had loaned it to a friend who needed a place to stay. Besides, Kate said she preferred the villa because it felt homier. How her sister could think a 16,000-square-foot villa with nine bedrooms and eleven bathrooms could be homey made Meara smile. Kate was always positive, though.

"Meara, great to see you. We're pleased you could join us," Marco remarked as he walked into the room in a breeze of energy. He kissed her on both cheeks, as usual. "I was just about to pour a glass of wine. Would you like one or something stronger? You look like you could use it."

"What is with you two?" Shaking her head, she sat on the sofa, forcing a smile. "Wine would be great. I'm just tired, and it's been a long week."

"It's Tuesday," Kate pointed out.

Meara accepted the glass of Chianti that Marco handed her and chose not to respond. Her sister was sitting directly across from her, and Marco joined her, laying a casual arm across Kate's shoulders. She snuggled closer to him, and Meara tried to bat down a small spark of envy. Would she ever find someone who she could let her guard down with? Someone who she could relax with?

"What's so urgent that I needed to come over tonight?" Meara inquired, eager to have this night over with so she could go back to her plan for gelato and a lot of self-gratifying pity.

Marco leaned forward and looked like he was about to speak

when they heard a rustle in the entryway. "Maybe we should wait for our guest," he said. "Paolo is probably letting him in now."

Meara's eyes widened and looked around as if she could make a quick escape. Oh God, they weren't fixing her up, were they? She'd rather die than have a blind date tonight. Actually, a blind date *any time*. Paolo, their house assistant, was greeting someone. She sat up straighter.

"*Buonasera*," came a rich, soothing baritone voice behind her. Meara turned her head slightly as a tall, broad-shouldered man stepped into the living room. Marco and Kate both stood to greet him. He embraced Kate gently, kissing her on each check, before shaking hands and giving Marco a half hug. Meara sat up in interest.

The man standing before her sported a giant smile, with a deep dimple in his Mediterranean skin. His short, dark brown hair abundantly fell in natural waves. He had a slight stubble on his jaw as if he hadn't shaved in a couple days. It was only when he turned to catch her staring at him that she saw his soft brown eyes that were marred by dark circles under them. Despite that, his eyes lit up, and he walked toward her, obviously turning on the charm. It blasted her already, causing an odd stirring deep down. Good God, he looked just like that doctor on the hospital TV show Kate used to urge her to watch.

"You must be Meara. I've heard a lot about you," he remarked, clearly waiting for her to greet him. Mentally giving herself a shake, she finally stood, trying to show polite interest. She towered over most men, but even wearing her black high-heeled shoes, he still had her by a few inches. She thrust her hand out before he could do the customary kiss on each cheek. She ought to keep him at a distance—at least as long as her arm.

He stared at her outstretched hand and grasped it gently for a minute before pulling it up and gently kissing it with his perfect mouth. It was the last thing she expected, and she trembled at the spark she felt at the slight gesture. As she quickly yanked her hand away, he smirked a little. She realized the gesture was purposely performed to throw her off her game. This guy was like all the other charmers she had met along the way. Smoothing her hands on her jeans, she sat back down without saying a word or reacting further.

Marco was busy getting their visitor a drink while Kate made introductions. "Meara, this is Dr. Alessandro Amato. I know you've heard a lot about him, too."

It was everything Meara could do not to make a face. Certainly, she had heard nonstop about the famed Dr. Amato. He was Kate's obstetrician and was also working with Teresa on the medical foundation Marco's family had just created. The Angelo Foundation hoped to advance some of the country's medical facilities, especially in more rural areas that didn't have proper access to health care.

Meara nodded, still staying silent, but she surreptitiously gave Kate a speaking look. If this was a fix-up, she would claim a headache and leave. Not today of all days. Kate gave her a pleading look back, as if she was telling her to be nice. Meara took a deep breath. She would use a small amount of patience for her sister's sake. But very small.

Alessandro accepted the glass of wine and instead of sitting in the nearby chair, he opted for a seat alongside Meara on the wide sofa. Wow, he really was good at this. Even though there was a cushion between them, she could feel the heat from his body. She had to turn her head to look at him, which was something she refused to do. Out of the corner of her eye, she took in his faded jeans and creased, pale blue button-down shirt. He obviously spent little time getting ready for this blind date. She quickly turned her gaze back to her sister, who was sipping her lemonade, clearly letting her husband take the lead.

"Thanks for coming, Alec," Marco said with a smile, leaning back in his chair. "Meara's had a long day, and from the looks of you, you have probably been up since last night at the hospital. So, we're going to just cut to the chase and talk about why we wanted both of you here."

He looked directly at Meara now, his eyes glinting. "Meara, we want to hire you as the Executive Director of the Angelo Foundation. And we brought Alec here to help convince you."

~

MEARA SAT up and leaned forward, her eyes narrowing at Marco and Kate. Were they serious? She was met with determined stares by both. Opening her mouth to speak, she was stalled by Marco who held up his hand.

"*Per favore*, let me just finish," he requested gently. "We know you are at the top of your game right now and this may seem like stepping down to take a position such as this, but I can assure you it will challenge you just as greatly. We will exceed your current salary and executive package. We want you, Meara. We *need* you," he clarified softly.

Staring at him, she was once again surprised. She hadn't seen this coming either. What in the heck was wrong with her instincts? Though she felt Alessandro's eyes on her, she resisted glancing over at him. Marco and Kate continued observing her, Marco self-assuredly and Kate apprehensively.

She took a deep breath. "Um, wow, that's not what I thought you called me over here for. Thank you so much, Marco. It means a lot. Truly. But I don't think it's something I'm suited for. I have very limited medical knowledge and even less expertise in health care, especially in Italy. I'm not the right person for an esteemed position such as this."

Marco acknowledged her speech with a nod and a small smile, as if he had been waiting for her to say that. "You are exactly what we are looking for, Meara," he said with feeling. "I need someone I can trust. This medical foundation is in honor of my late uncle, and it is imperative that I have someone leading it who understands what I am trying to build in *Zio* Angelo's name. The idea of the Angelo Foundation was born out of a mere spark, and with Teresa and Alec's assistance, we are already on the way. They have helped lead a remarkable effort. Now it is a pivotal time, and I need someone who can seize this opportunity and make it a success. It can't fail, not with Angelo's name on it."

Marco's expression turned grim. "We need someone who can ensure everything is done ethically. I went through a dreadful time with Sal, and I am not going into this blind. There's a lot of people who could take advantage of this foundation, and I know you would not allow them to. You can hire people with the knowledge you don't have," he added, waving a hand in dismissal.

"Marco, I understand how important this is," Meara hedged. "But I can't believe that you just thought of me because you think I'm qualified. Respectfully, I know you and Katie want me to stay in Italy. Of course, I would love to as well, but that doesn't mean accepting a position from my brother-in-law so I can."

Marco opened his mouth to speak, but Alessandro turned fully toward Meara, and the abrupt movement made her finally turn her head toward him.

"Would it make you feel better if you knew it was I who suggested you?" Alessandro asked quietly. Meara found she couldn't look away from his penetrating gaze. "My time is very limited on this, and while we have made significant progress, I told Marco we need someone extremely savvy who can carry this load. I thought of you immediately."

"But how...?" she stammered.

"Do I know about you?" He smiled, finishing her sentence. "Meara, I read about you over the years in articles in several business publications. You are widely respected for your business acumen. I learned about your accomplishments. You have taken every company you've worked for to new heights. I know corporations are desperate to hire you. Kate told me it would be a long shot, but I convinced Marco to at least offer you the position."

"Why are you reading business publications? You're a doctor..." She trailed off. Perhaps that question was intrusive, but a part of her didn't believe him.

He smiled. "See? You cut down to the smallest detail immediately. I'm actually on the board of some of the tech companies that were part of my father's estate. And I like to read." He shrugged.

She nodded absentmindedly and finally tore her gaze away from his at Kate's voice. "Meara, I wanted Marco to ask you, but there's no pressure at all. I told them how many offers you have received even over the last year. You've worked so hard to get where you are, and it could be a mistake to leave that world. You might not be able to get back," she finished solemnly.

Meara took a deep breath and finally reached down and took a large sip of wine. Now was the time. She had to come clean. "You're right, Katie. I *have* worked hard. Remember how much I missed over the years? I've had no life and look where it's gotten me," she said bitterly.

"It's gotten you to the top of your field," Alessandro pointed out.

"Actually, it got me to the top and then dumped." She glanced around the room, seeing their startled expressions. "Today, I got fired."

Katie was the first to recover, standing quickly. "What? Are you freaking kidding me? Who would fire you? That's the stupidest thing I ever heard! You're the best thing to happen to that company!"

Meara smiled genuinely for the first time in the last few hours. "Down, Katie. Settle down or my nephew or niece is going to get a wild ride."

Marco pulled her hand, urging her to sit. "She's right, *amore mio*. Take a breath. Your sister can obviously fight her own battles."

Meara could feel Alessandro's stare again. "What happened?"

Shaking her head, Meara shrugged. "I should have seen it coming. I've been distracted lately."

Katie frowned. "Meara, you are not about to tell me you regret spending time with Dad in the hospital or helping me with the wedding and everything else. Because if you do, I'm going to slug you. You've finally had a life! And you've been able to spend time with me and relax a little. Well, as much as *you* can relax, that is."

Marco reached over with both arms to gently hold her down again, and Meara laughed. "Man, what is with you today, Katie?"

"Hormones," stated Alessandro matter-of-factly, before taking a sip of his wine.

Kate rolled her eyes. "Respectfully, *Doctor* Amato, not everything is boiled down to hormones for pregnant women." At Marco's raised eyebrows, she giggled. "Okay, maybe I am a little more feisty nowadays. But I'm not going to sit here while my sister, who has worked her butt off for years, gets trampled on."

"I agree. She can handle herself," Alessandro stated, looking at Meara with humor in his eyes.

Marco nodded in agreement. "Katie, let's allow Meara to tell us what happened."

Meara grimaced. "I've known for some time that some board members were underwhelmed by my performance. They made that clear. The chair is a real piece of work. I have never worked with such a condescending piece of..." She glanced at Alessandro and stopped abruptly. She should probably stay professional in front of a stranger.

"Let's just say I should have been more aware of some of the actions by my vice presidents. I'm not sure who was vying harder to take me down. Graham—that's his name. Graham, like as in graham cracker, told me the board didn't think I was living up to that famed reputation you talked about a few minutes ago, Alessandro. I'm not turning things around fast enough, and so they let me go. They don't want to hear the details regarding the barriers their decisions have made. Nor do they want me to make the difficult, but innovative changes that must be made to advance."

"I understand everything but the graham cracker part," Alessandro said with a smile. "However, I think the fact is that it boils down to one thing."

"What's that?" Meara inquired, turning to look at him.

"It was meant to be for you to become the Executive Director of the Angelo Foundation."

ALEC ALMOST LAUGHED out loud at the expression on Meara's face. She looked astounded at his audacity. He gazed back at her with a helpless shrug. "I'm just stating the obvious."

Her brows furrowed, and her emerald green eyes glittered at him. That shade of red hair was so unique. It was a dark, rich color. Longing to touch it, he fisted his hand. It almost looked like it would singe his finger.

He had never seen a more beautiful woman in all his life. The photos of her hadn't done her justice. She was stunning in person and even more so with her animated personality. He was drawn to her immediately. Maybe this hadn't been such a brilliant idea of his. They would be working closely together for at least a short time if she took on this new role, and it could get complicated. Complicated was not what Alec was looking for with his current situation.

Alec had almost called Marco to tell him he couldn't make it tonight. Working all night with a patient who had a complex labor, he was exhausted and dragging when he walked through the door. Now he felt energized. His heart had been beating faster ever since he saw her.

It was true that he had read about her. He might have been drawn to the articles by her attractive face, but once he started reading her accomplishments, he had been impressed. Meara Malone seemed to be a force to be reckoned with. He wanted to delve deeper. There were layers of complexity in her he could almost see, and he was up for the challenge. She was looking at him with wary distrust. Tonight, she hadn't been successful in hiding her emotions. It surprised him, but also made him realize how shocking the day had been for her.

Her words brought him out of his observations. "Well, it might be obvious to you that this was divine providence, but it's not to me."

"I think we should go see what our chef has prepared," suggested Marco mildly, and they both turned to see him helping Kate stand. "I don't know about you, but I think much better when I'm not so hungry."

They walked past the expansive formal dining area to a small sitting room with a round table that had been set for four. Over their dinner of *bruschetta* followed by *rigatoni all'amatriciana*, a mix of chunky pork in tomato sauce, topped with pecorino cheese, Marco steadily kept the conversation neutral. Kate started a couple of times to bring up the foundation, but Alessandro saw Marco shake his head slightly. Alec knew his old friend to be a savvy negotiator, and something told him Marco understood now was not the time to pressure Meara.

Meanwhile, Meara was quietly eating, answering the benign questions when they were directed toward her. Looking uncertain, Kate talked about her friend Teresa's wedding and the plans leading up to it.

"You're still coming the night before the wedding to the dinner and our little bachelorette party?" Kate asked her sister. Meara nodded without speaking, and Kate continued talking about how they would go to Stefano's villa for dinner after the rehearsal. She explained to Alec that they had planned to have some girl time at a luxurious hotel before the wedding later on the next day. Joining them would be the bride, as well as Ellie, who had just married Marco's cousin, Lucca. From her long-winded description of their plans, it was obvious Kate was looking forward to it.

As Kate finally exhausted the topic of the wedding plans, the conversation dwindled. Alec's fatigue set in. Meara also had tired lines around her eyes, and suddenly, he was inspired.

"Dinner was wonderful, Katie," he said, smiling and leaning back. "My compliments to the chef. I regret to say that I was up most of the night and probably need to take my leave."

Kate frowned. "But you haven't even had dessert yet."

He glanced toward Meara. "I couldn't eat another bite," he fibbed. Turning to his right, he smiled at the silent redhead. "I'll take you home, Meara." He purposely didn't make it a question but a statement, and she flashed him a defiant look. He could almost see the wheels turning. She wanted to escape as well, but her plans probably didn't include him.

"Thank you, no. I can manage," she said firmly.

"It's no trouble at all," he assured her, not giving her a chance to make further excuse. Already standing, he pulled her chair out. As he shook Marco's hand, they exchanged a look. Marco was clearly conveying to him to sell the idea on the way home. Alec only smiled. He had no intention of bringing the subject up with her. Right now, she needed to see him as an ally, not someone who was going to twist her arm into a situation she felt she was not ready for.

He waited while the sisters said goodbye and then quickly led Meara out into the cool night. Settling her into his Maserati, he ran around to the driver's side and quickly sped off, feeling like he was driving a get-away car. It was only then he took a deep breath, feeling like his luck had just changed.

three

Meara's voice cut into his thoughts, explaining where her hotel was located. Driving the car through Rome's traffic with practiced ease, he glanced over at her staring out the window. She clearly was not interested in conversing with him. Pulling the car abruptly up to a parking space seemed to spark her from her thoughts, and she glanced around. "Where are we? This isn't by the hotel. Please Alessandro, I just need to go home."

He took his seatbelt off and stared at her tired face that was lit by nearby streetlamps. "To do what? Mope? Go to bed? I doubt it. You'll be up half the night. You need to decompress, and you couldn't do that with your worried sister hovering over you. Come on."

He was out of the car and coming to her side to open the door as she continued to protest. No one probably ever told her what to do. That made him smirk a little.

"Alessandro..."

"My friends call me Alec."

"Fine, Alec. I'm not sure we're friends, though. Please take me home."

He was pulling her down the sidewalk but stopped to put his hands on her shoulders and look at her, his expression serious. "Meara, I know you just met me, but I promise I understand. Right now, just trust me," he appealed.

Staring at him for a minute, she finally nodded quickly. He bit back a smile, pleased at her acquiescence and put a light arm on her back to lead her down the street. They wove through the crowds, and once in a while, he grabbed her arm to keep her near him. Abruptly, he stopped, and she almost ran into him.

"Here we are."

Meara looked up and burst out laughing, the sound reverberating into the night. It was the first time he'd heard her laugh, and he stared at her, loving the sound. It completely transformed the serious woman he had spent the greater part of the evening with. He grinned at her in return.

"How did you know?" she asked, her eyes twinkling.

"I've been there," he responded softly.

MEARA FOLLOWED Alessandro through the street, not caring where he was taking her. He indicated a bench next to a fountain, and she sat down without taking a break from eating her massive cone of gelato. She swallowed and chuckled again, surveying her newly acquired treat. "Alec, this cone is as long as my arm.

He grinned. "That's one reason it's my favorite *gelateria*. They were able to stuff four different flavors into that cone. It seems more efficient to me," he told her earnestly.

She took a bite of the top flavor, a luscious dark chocolate chunk. "I always just go to the place down the street from my apartment," she said with a shrug. "But this tastes so much better! It's creamier and somehow more delicious."

He nodded seriously. "Not every *gelateria* is created equal. You have to pay attention."

Taking another bite, she savored the chocolate. "How can you tell a good one from a bad one?"

He was busy licking his cone, and she was fascinated by his handsome face so focused on his gelato. He was concentrating like a small child. Finally, when he drew his mouth away, it was ringed with white cream.

She smiled a little. "You have a little..." She waved her finger at his mouth and then snatched it away. She almost touched his lips. Quickly putting her hand back with the other one on her cone, she decided it better stay there. It was safer anyway to hold the gigantic cone with both hands. Still, those lips looked so soft. She realized he finished wiping his mouth with a napkin and was explaining gelato to her.

"Well, of course, you can try them all to figure out what is the best," he teased. "But then there are also some obvious giveaways that it is mass produced for tourists."

"Like what?" she asked before taking several bites.

"Well, first, gelato should be in metal containers. Not plastic. And if you see it in mounds way above the container, that is a clue, too. Gelato needs to be kept at certain temperatures. If it is piled high, it's probably filled with a bunch of chemicals."

She was fascinated. "This is probably the most important information that anyone has told me about Italy," she said sincerely. "Go on. I need more info."

He laughed, taking a few more licks. "Well, you must look at the colors, too. It shouldn't be shiny. And *gelato artigianale*, artisanal gelato, is made with fresh ingredients."

"But how can you tell?"

He took several bites before answering. "Here's my biggest clue. Most places offer pistachio flavor, since it is something Italians often eat in foods. Pistachio gelato has to be white. If it is green, you know it's made for the tourists."

Her eyes widened as if he had just given her insider trading information. "I never knew. You've blown my mind." She continued to eat, mulling over his gelato wisdom, and then finally glanced around. "Where are we?"

He looked at her quizzically. "The *Piazza Navona*. Haven't you been here?"

She shrugged, carefully not looking at him. "I haven't really been anywhere."

He rolled his eyes. "*Mamma Mia*. I cannot believe it." He began to tell her about it, and his quiet voice lulled her turbulent senses. Explaining about the three fountains in the *piazza*, he seemed to know as many details as a tour guide.

"And this fountain we are sitting next to is the *Fontana dei Quattro Fiumi*," he explained. "Fountain of the Four Rivers. The four statues in it represent the rivers where Christianity had spread."

Meara listened to the rich, smooth tone of Alec's voice, which oddly soothed her. That was incredibly strange, considering no one's voice ever affected her that way. For now, she wouldn't analyze it. It was nice to just sink into that voice and avoid thinking about anything else.

"Am I boring you?" he asked, breaking into her musing.

"Not at all," she answered honestly. "But for once, I think this gelato has won. I don't think I can eat anymore." She looked regretfully at the giant cone, which was now half its original size.

He laughed. "We'll get you into gelato eating shape in no time."

Meara's heart gave a little extra beat. Did that mean they would be spending time together? Well, of course it did if she took this proposed job. Did he feel the pull, too? It was as if a spark had ignited as soon as he had turned those beautiful brown eyes on her. How wonderful it would be to reach up and draw her hand through his thick hair and see if it fell back into the natural waves that made it so enticing. Then she'd lean up and kiss him to find out if those lips were as soft as they looked. He would be a great kisser. She could tell.

Meara realized he had been speaking to her. "I'm sorry. I kind of drifted off," she apologized, trying not to look embarrassed.

"You're tired," he remarked gently. "So am I. Let's wander through the *piazza* to make sure we're physically tired, and then it will be easier to sleep."

She followed him to the trash can where he tossed the rest of their cones and was surprised when he took her hand. She felt an electrical sensation running down her spine, but willed herself not to react. The *piazza* had gotten more crowded, and she told herself it was practical so she could follow him. This was so different for her. She usually did the leading. Meara had never followed anyone in her life.

"One more story," he commented with a small smile. "It's rather ghoulish, but an old tale. See that small tavern? Legend has it that in the 1500s there was a pope named Sixtus the Fifth. He liked to dress in civilian clothes and wander the streets. One night, he entered this tavern and ordered a glass of wine. The proprietor found him pleasant to talk to, and let's just say he talked too much. He freely gave his opinion, even about the pope. The next day, the proprietor looked into the square to see a platform. It would turn out to be his execution platform."

Meara widened her eyes. "This story took a turn!"

Alec laughed, throwing his head back, showing his deep dimples. He put his hands on her shoulders and turned her around, her back to him. With his chest pressed behind her, his face came down close to hers over her shoulder. He pointed, and his breath brushed her ear. "Look up there."

Meara strained to see a white face, almost like a mask affixed to the wall.

"The other restaurant owners and innkeepers put up that

symbol there to remind themselves not to talk too much to strangers."

Meara chuckled and resisted the urge not to lean into Alec's arms. "That didn't happen!"

He turned her and stared with humor in his eyes. "Are you sure? Rome is filled with all kinds of similar stories. Its rich history vacillates between gory to glorious. I'll have to tell you more."

Meara tried not to read too much into his statement as she followed him to the car. Alec seemed lost in his thoughts, and she stayed silent as well. They drove past monuments lit up against the cloudy sky, and for the first time, she wished to explore the city. Working long hours, she had always been too tired or admittedly unmotivated to sightsee on her own. Alec made it exciting and fresh and told her fun facts that brought the history alive.

As he pulled up to her grand hotel, she felt a wave of disappointment. The fatigue had hit her, and all she wanted to do was lay her head on a pillow. However, these last two hours had been an unexpected reprieve from her current situation. Turning to thank him, she realized he had already gotten out and come around to open her door. She wasn't used to being catered to.

"Alec…"

"I'll walk you to your door," he told her firmly.

"Can you leave your car here?"

He smiled and tossed his keys to the valet, shouting something in Italian. The young valet only nodded and grinned.

Meara followed him into her hotel and suddenly the memory returned of her entrance just a few hours ago. The waves of humiliation and shock washed over her once again, and her shoulders stiffened.

Alec stopped at the elevators, eyeing her closely. He pushed the button and ushered her into an elevator. She had gotten her keycard out, and he wordlessly took it from her to use it. The elevator glided to the top and opened into her apartment.

She automatically kicked off her shoes, like she did every day. He smiled. "I don't know how you can wear those heels on Rome's cobblestones. You'll have to get a pair of walking shoes if you're going to survive sightseeing."

"I don't know if I will be doing much of that. I may leave soon."

He stared at her. "Can I give you some advice?"

She nodded and stayed silent.

"You have endured a shock. I have seen many people in my professional life and in my personal life, who have as well. I always tell them to take things slowly. No decision-making for a time."

"It's just a job, Alec. I'm sure the people you are talking about suffered tragedies."

He shrugged. "You can't compare your experiences to anyone else. It's still been something that has deeply upset you, though I hope it's only temporary. Take some time, enjoy the city, and explore your opportunities."

She looked at him with a narrow gaze. "You aren't going to try to persuade me to take the position at the foundation?"

He shook his head. "That's not for me to do. My only suggestion was for Marco to offer it to you. Of course, I did not know that your day would play out the way it has."

She gave him a grateful smile because he was not adding pressure to her awful day.

He glanced around. "Nice place. Are you going to stay here for the time being?"

Meara shook her head. "They offered to allow me to stay for a month as part of my severance package, but I want to make a clean break."

"Don't you have a saying in your country about cutting off your nose to spite your face?"

She gave him a speculative gaze. "You'll find I'm a straight shooter. Just say it. You think I should stay?"

He smiled a little. "I am not about to tell you what to do, Meara. I will say, though, it's beneficial for one to take what is owed."

She looked away from his steady gaze. It unnerved her. "I know you're probably right. But I'm..."

"Stubborn?" he interrupted softly.

She gave a small laugh. "I thought the word you were going to use was foolish. But yes, I am stubborn, too. I'll think about it, though."

He turned as if to depart. "*Bene.*" Turning back toward her, he continued staring at her, as if trying to decide something. Finally shaking his head, it was almost as if he was telling himself not to do something.

"*Buona notte*, Meara," he said softly.

"*Buona notte*," she echoed. The elevator's door opened and he entered, giving her a small wave. After the doors closed, she remained standing in the same spot. For someone she had just met, he had understood her remarkably. Now she felt oddly alone.

four

Meara threw her phone down in disgust. It had been ringing nonstop all morning. While she ignored the calls, she glanced over the texts and emails from so-called friends. They most likely were fishing for her next move, so they could be the first ones to have the scoop. Too bad she had zero idea. She punched a pillow, still feeling anger and shame from the day before.

When her phone beeped again, she almost hurled it across the room. But it was a text from Alec. Her heart beat a little faster. Last night she had been so exhausted she had simply eased into a deep sleep. She owed Alec for that. He had been right to keep her out, distance her brain from her job and stuff her full of gelato. It was only this morning when she woke that her heart felt heavy again.

She glanced at his text: *Come downstairs, per favore*

Frowning, she typed. *Why?*

He didn't answer her question but responded quickly. *Bring your purse and a jacket*

Meara never followed orders from anyone unless it was at work or before that, school. Biting her lip, she wavered. Well, why not? She was sitting alone wallowing in self-pity. It was better than watching the nosy, inquiring messages fill up her phone.

Giving a thumbs up emoji, she ran into the bathroom. She wore black pants and a navy silk sweater. Though she should probably change into jeans, he'd have to take her as she was. Fluffing her hair, she applied a little makeup and shrugged. The dark shadows underneath her eyes and her pale complexion didn't add to her appearance.

If Alec was taking her somewhere, there would probably be cobblestone streets involved. Last night she had to admit she was weary of teetering on heels. Compromising now, she walked into her massive closet and chose a pair of black booties that had a lower heel than she normally wore.

Descending in the elevator, she applied her game face, the demeanor and expression she'd perfected over the years. When the door opened, she took a deep breath. Alec stood there waiting, jiggling his car keys. Today, he was dressed a little more formally in dark pants and a brown cashmere sweater that went well with his hair.

"*Buongiorno*," he said, kissing her on each cheek.

"*Buongiorno*," she responded, hating that her voice sounded faint. She tried again, with a stronger tone. "What do I owe the pleasure of this morning's visit?"

"Remarkably, I have the day free. I'm leaving for a medical conference in Florence tonight, and my secretary decided I needed some time off," he said and smiled. "One of my partners is taking my patients while I am away. This rarely happens, and I looked at it as fate."

Meara raised her eyebrows. "Fate? For what?"

"For spending the day with you," he answered. "It's about time you saw a slice of Rome. It's not very warm, but the sun is out and we need to go have an adventure."

"Alessandro," she said, trying to look stern.

"Alec."

She gave him a little smile. "Alec, I know you're trying to be nice. But I'm okay. I promise. I was going to start packing, and my day is full. Thank you anyway."

He laid a gentle hand on her arm. "Has anyone ever helped you before?"

She looked confused. "Helped me do what?"

He sighed. "Exactly. Just what I thought. Helped you with emotions. Gave you a shoulder, or took you on a silly adventure. Let you obsess over every minor detail of what is troubling you."

A wave of feeling was running through her, and she wasn't sure what it was. Definitely, she wasn't about to show it to Alec. She smiled as serenely as possible. "I don't need anyone's help. I never have."

He shook his head. "*Mamma Mia*," he teased. "We all need help from time to time. Come, let's go."

Waffling, she stood, twisting the handle of her purse, not knowing what to do. It was very rare that she had moments of uncertainty. This man seemed to knock her off her even keel. Biting her lip, she gave in. "Well, I guess I could go out for a bit and pack later."

"That's my girl," he said approvingly, and her heart fluttered. It was only a few meaningless words, but it made her feel an odd trickle of pleasure.

Following him through the lobby, they walked out to the hotel's opulent doors and over to a green Alfa Romeo. He held the door open, and she got in.

"You have two cars?" she asked when he slid into the driver's seat.

He didn't look at her as he checked his mirrors and pulled out. His wayfarer sunglasses hid his eyes. "Uh, yes. Actually, a few more than that." He glanced over at her and smiled. "I like cars," he said hesitantly.

"What's on the agenda?" Meara asked, sensing his discomfort. She got out her own cat-eye sunglasses.

"Today, I thought we'd see a little of the known and even more of the unknown."

Meara waited for him to explain, but he didn't. He drove silently until they pulled into a car park, and he quickly dealt with the parking attendants. Grasping her hand casually as he did the night before, they walked down the street. Suddenly, he stopped and glanced down at her booties. "Well, I guess those are an improvement. Though next time you need to wear trainers."

Meara felt laughter bubble up. "Trainers? You mean tennis shoes? I wear them to work out in, not to be seen around Rome. Look around you." She waved dramatically. "These Roman women are gorgeous. I will not be caught dead plodding around in tennis shoes."

Alec threw his head back and laughed. "Okay, okay, you can't blame me for trying!"

"SO WHY *IS* THE COLOSSEUM BROKEN?" Meara asked, peering up at it. She turned to look at Alec. "I should have warned you that history was not my strongest subject. It was always boring for me."

He smiled gently at her. "You must have had terrible instructors. Or maybe you just needed to be a part of it by seeing it, smelling it, and absorbing it."

As they walked, he began to explain. "The Colosseum is actually one-third its original size for lots of reasons. Of course, age and natural things like earthquakes. But in the Middle Ages, the popes or wealthy families pilfered it. If you walk around Rome, you can see many churches or palaces that are made from the stone from the Colosseum. It's pretty incredible."

Walking near the wrought-iron gates, he told her he already bought tickets online. "It's funny when you think about it. In ancient times, the Romans still had to buy tickets to see the shows. See those Roman numerals?" He pointed to above the arches where the gates stood. "That's how you knew which gate to enter."

They got through security quickly, with Alec remarking how less crowded it was on a fall day in Rome. Tours were passing them with the guides stopping every so often to give their carefully rehearsed speeches. Meara didn't have time to wonder if they should have taken a tour because Alec explained every fact she could ever wonder about the Colosseum. He made the gladiators come alive by describing their heavy helmets, swords, and how they fought. She gently touched a wall, in awe that she was seeing something so iconic and rich in history. They were standing on the top level where he said servants, slaves and women were allowed to watch the shows.

"Am I boring you?"

Meara widened her eyes in shock. "Absolutely not. I was just feeling...overwhelmed in a way. I've just never cared about history, and now I want to know more."

He grinned. "Oh, there's more! Someday we can go underground here. But for now, let's do more exploring. We only have the day, and I want to get as much in as possible."

Hours later, Alec proved he had meant every word. They had explored the nearby Roman Forum and parts of Palatine Hill, where she had absorbed all Alec's remarkable facts. As she followed his purposeful strides down streets and stairs, she was surprised when he abruptly stopped. "Are you claustrophobic?" As she shook her head, he grinned. "Fabulous. Come on."

They entered the Basilica of San Clemente, and they descended the stairs. "There is a church from the Fourth Century down here," he told her quietly. Pointing to a wall that looked like colorful, ancient hieroglyphics, he smiled. "Apparently these are ancient swear words, at least that's what I've been told. There is an entire world underground, more temples and buildings. Even Roman houses." Meara walked through, taking in the large arches, the porticos, and crumbling stone. They walked slowly around, and a tingling sense ran through her, as if there was a lingering presence of the spirits among the stone. "Alec, this place gives me the creeps," she whispered. He laughed, the sound bouncing off the stone.

"Okay, we'll move on. One more church for today, I promise. It's near here, and you have to see it."

They climbed the stairs and emerged outside, blinking in the sunlight. He grasped her hand again, leading her through the streets. "Here we are," he said, as they came upon a building. "This is the Church of *Santi Cosma e Damiano*—the Saints Cosma and Damian," he translated while holding the door open for her.

Meara gazed at the massive oval fresco on the ceiling. "It's amazing," she breathed, taking in the vivid colors of angels and saints. They walked slowly toward the altar, with its gold and striking blue colors. There was a scene of Jesus and his apostles.

"This is breathtaking," Meara told him, turning to see the arches, the gold and the artistry.

"Yes, but that's not why we're here," he remarked as he led her toward a window. "This church was erected in the 1600s, but it was actually built on the Temple of Romulus. When the Roman Empire fell, the temple was abandoned. Eventually, the Pope at the time made it a Christian church. It was the first one in the Roman Forum."

"How do you remember all these facts?" Meara asked with a small laugh.

"All part of my tour guide service," he answered with a smile. "This church has a bit of my heart. It was named after twin brothers who were doctors. They were persecuted and killed by the Romans because they were Christians. I wonder what their practices were like. Apparently, they didn't charge for their services," he said, his eyes dancing. "They are the patron saints of doctors and surgeons."

Pointing out the window, he told her, "That's the real church down there, but because of floods, they built this new one. There's a gate over there that we can use to go down to see the temple, but I think you've had enough underground tours for a day."

He led her out the door. "Let's go find some lunch," he said, swinging her hand companionably.

They entered a modern market, strolling past vendors selling local produce, a vast assortment of cheese, breads, desserts and meats. "After all that ancient history, this is the part of our tour that focuses on the new," Alec remarked. "This market hasn't been open that long. At least it is from this century! I want you to try some of the street foods of Rome."

Alec went stall to stall, examining the offerings and eventually putting orders in. He pointed to a table nearby and told her to make herself comfortable while he fetched lunch. Apparently, they were going to be trying everything. She watched in amusement as he brought several baskets and containers over until finally, he sat next to her at the round table.

They slowly worked their way through a variety of food, with Alec telling her about each of them. There was *supplì*, his favorite. Rice balls rolled in breadcrumbs were filled with stringy mozzarella, deep-fried, and dipped into a delicious tomato sauce.

"Aren't these called *arancini*?" Meara asked. "I had them once in Positano with Katie."

Alec shook his head. "No, those are Sicilian and are similar, but different. Romans know the difference," he told her smugly.

They moved on to a *trapizzino*, a triangular-shaped sandwich made with focaccia and wrapped with brown paper. Inside it was fried eggplant, rich tomato sauce and *parmigiano*.

"This is like a little pizza pocket," Meara said, wiping her mouth with a napkin. "Messy, but delicious."

"Time to try *carciofi alla giudia*," Alec said. At her confused look, he translated. "It's an artichoke. They are one of my favorites as well."

Meara bit into the deep-fried, flower-shaped bundle and chewed. "That's delicious! I wasn't expecting it to be soft inside."

Alec had only bought one, and he took it from her to sample a bite. Chewing for a minute with a contemplating look, he finally swallowed. "Just what I thought. A little early for them. I'll have to bring you to the Jewish Ghetto to get one in the spring. That is where they are the best."

"I'm not sure I can eat anything else," Meara said, eyeing a long piece of fish and ignoring his comments about the future. It was better to just let it ride.

"Just try a bite," Alec urged, squeezing lemon on to it. "*Filetti di baccala*. It's salted codfish, and though it's fried, it's not greasy.

"I could eat that whole thing, but I won't," Meara said, after sampling it. "That's amazing."

Comfortably full, they sat quietly, watching people go by. It was easy to spot the tourists, who mostly wore an array of tennis shoes. Alec was right.

"It's nice to see you smiling," he commented.

"I've been smiling all day," she protested. "Some of those stories you told me I swear you made up."

He chuckled a little. "Roman history does not need my creativity. There are countless legends. Many of them end with someone dying tragically." He gave her a sideways smile. "Hardly cheering you up."

She concentrated on taking another bite of the fish. "It doesn't matter. It still took my mind off everything."

"I'm glad it did, but do you want to talk about it?" he asked quietly. "I'm a good listener."

Meara shrugged. "I told you most of the story last night."

"But there's more," he added in his soft tone.

"You're right," she agreed grimly. "There's so much."

"Start at the beginning."

Meara wasn't sure what made her confide in him or even how long she talked. Pouring her heart out to Alec was not on her to-do list for the day, and she marveled that he could get it all out of her. She told him about the years of sacrifice, working harder than most people for little reward. Then there were the struggles of constantly having to prove her intelligence while supervisors stole her ideas and presented them as their own. She had learned quickly how to navigate that terrain. Finally, there was the frequent late night where inevitably she had to extricate herself from an unwanted embrace, an inappropriate touch.

Alec frowned but only nodded for her to continue. She explained that when she began to get media attention, it made things worse. The men became more insecure and consequently worked to undermine her. Looking around most boardrooms, she found very few female counterparts. Disheartening as it was, she was determined to prove herself. Her latest job had been a hard-earned victory, and she was finally at the pinnacle of her career. When she got to Rome, she had dived in like usual, but it was more difficult this time. She had underestimated the vast number of issues that she needed to fix. Yet, the board continued to thwart many of her ideas for improvement. Unfortunately, there was the chair and a handful of others, including a father and son who had made it a sport to get enough votes to tie her hands. In hindsight, she wondered if they had other motives. The father most likely thought his son should lead the company.

Abruptly, Meara stood and stretched. Alec had thrown their lunch away a while ago. "I'm tired of hearing myself talk," she said wryly. "Thank you for listening, Alec." Before he could respond, she pointed to a *gelateria*. "Come on. I'll buy you some gelato. That is, if that place over there lives up to your standards!"

Smiling, they entered the gelateria and put their heads together, enthusiastically debating flavors. Egged on by him, she tried the appropriately white-colored pistachio, and he got his favorite, chocolate.

Taking a bite as they exited the shop, she smiled at him. "Just chocolate? Not chocolate brownie? Not chocolate and vanilla?"

He was busy licking his cone, his face intent. She watched him, mesmerized. But when he looked up, she quickly turned her attention to her own cone.

"Nope. Chocolate. Not just chocolate. Chocolate does not need a qualifier. It is singularly fantastic."

They walked down the now crowded streets, eating their cones while Alec pointed out small alleyways, and told her of more undergrounds and secret passages. "Rome has so many secrets. I have more to show you."

They wandered through the streets until they reached the Trevi Fountain. Even Meara knew what it was, but enjoyed Alec, standing behind her, telling her about its artistry, architecture and how long it took to build. Though it was crowded, they found a small spot to take a few photos.

"Am I supposed to throw the coin over my left or my right?"

Alec reached into his pocket and found three coins. He put his hands on her shoulders and turned her around so her back was to the fountain. "Sit and toss them with your right hand over your left shoulder."

Meara took all three coins and tossed them, turning around quickly to see them plop into the crystal green water. "Why three?"

"Oh, it's a tradition," he said absentmindedly. "Throwing coins into water was an ancient practice to grant safe travel."

Thousands of coins already rested in the fountain. "What happens to all the money?"

"It's vacuumed up each night and given to charity," he told her, leading her through the crowds. "Let me show you the real interesting part, though. See those windows right there? I'll show you what's behind them."

She followed Alec, who heaved a giant wooden door open. "There are usually tours in here. I'm not sure why it's so quiet today. See those windows? They used to be open, and water flowed out of them. It's Rome's largest fountain, but the water comes from an ancient water aqueduct that was built in Nineteen B.C. They use modern pumps now and it is recycled, but it is mind boggling that it all stems from something built so long ago."

Meara smiled at him. He really was so sweet. She didn't care in the slightest about some old rusty aqueduct, but he did, and that made her conscious of her heart swelling.

"Why are you smiling at me like that?" he asked suspiciously.

"Because you're the best tour guide in all of Rome," she said honestly.

He grinned, and their gazes locked. For a minute, she thought he might kiss her, but he drew back. Glancing at his watch, he winced. "We have time for just one more attraction. It's close by."

They walked through the crowds into an opulent indoor Art Nouveau courtyard. The coolness rose from the marble floor, and brilliantly colored frescoes led up to the wrought iron ceiling where the sun was peeking through. "What is this? It's beautiful!"

He smiled at her expression. "It is the *Galleria Sciarra*. Breathtaking, isn't it? It was built in the Nineteenth Century for a wealthy family."

They stood for a moment among the frescos and the curled floral designs. Alec moved again to place himself in back of her. He bent, speaking into her ear and at his warm breath, she felt the familiar sensation go down her spine.

"Notice all the women in the artistry. It was painted by Cellini. We call it the *glorificazione della donna*. Glorifying and unifying women was his theme. He wanted to show all female virtues: justice, fidelity, patience, and strength. It is believed to be the greatest celebration of women in Rome."

She turned around slowly to see him staring intently at her. "I just thought you should see this today, especially after all you told me at lunch. That's you, Meara," he said, pointing to the frescos. "You have all those virtues, and you can never forget that. You are remarkable and do not let this graham cracker guy tear you down."

She smiled a little at his reference to Graham but was touched. It meant a lot to have Alec so confident in her abilities after the humiliation the day prior. She nodded, swallowing the lump in her throat. He leaned down and this time, he gave her a small kiss on the cheek. His soft lips grazed her face, and disappointment passed through her. The moment was gone, and he was now leading her back outside. The sun was setting.

"I wish we had time to drive up a hill. Sunset is my favorite time in Rome," Alec remarked as they walked toward where he had left the car. He turned to smile at her. "I promise to take you up to see it one evening."

Meara didn't respond. She undoubtedly would be relocating soon, but she didn't want to discuss that now. It had been such a wonderful day, and it would be a shame to have reality seep in.

It felt like heaven to sink into the soft leather of his car. Her legs were tired from all the walking, but she was not going to admit he had been right about the shoes. Comfortable and pleasantly fatigued, they raced through Rome's terrifying streets. It didn't faze her at all, as Alec drove with quiet competence. People cut him off or motorbikes weaved around him, and he just steadily drove on. After months of having a driver and listening to him swear madly at others on the road, Meara was reassured by Alec's calm. Quietly, she sighed. Rome had not disappointed and neither had Alec. He was quick-witted, entertaining, and full of facts. It was impossible how much the man kept in his head about Rome. He had also been a good listener. She had abnormally shared a lot, and a knot grew in her stomach.

He looked inquiringly at her, like he might have misinterpreted her sigh. "I'm sorry I can't take you to dinner. I need to get to Florence, and I have a small stop on the way at my mother's."

"Does she live in Rome?"

"No, she lives in Frascati, about twenty kilometers away. Have you heard of it? It's a charming town famous for its wine. She and my father adored the views from their villa. But sadly, he died two years ago. She still struggles with her grief, but she is showing more interest in living. Especially because..."

Right then two motorbikes swerved in front of Alec, and he had to quickly apply the brake. This time he showed a little emotion, his brow furrowed.

"*Mi dispiace,*" he said, apologizing for their sudden lurch.

Meara opened her mouth to ask him to continue telling her about his mother. It seemed she barely knew him. Focusing on information about Rome all day, he had barely told her anything about himself. She monopolized the afternoon with the story of her career. Now, sadly, their day was coming to an end, and she was disheartened she didn't know more about him. After parking, he walked her into the hotel, calmly held out his hand for her key card and used it to travel up to her apartment.

Meara was trying to gauge his sudden quietness. "I had fun today, Alec," she said. "Thank you. And thank you for last night. I seldom say this, so it is a compliment. You're really a nice man."

He gazed at her before shaking his head. "Nice? Such a milk toast word. We must change your opinion of me."

Suddenly, his head swept down, but despite the abruptness, his lips were gentle. She responded uncertainly, but then moving her lips against his, drawing him in. He leaned in and put his arms around her, and the kiss deepened. The pressure of his mouth increased, as if he was inviting her to give more. Alec was taking, and she was to do the giving in what was quickly becoming the most searing, passionate kiss of her life. She had been right. This man could kiss. It curled her toes, and surprisingly he ended it just as swiftly as he had started it. He looked down at her with an unreadable expression before giving her a small kiss on each cheek.

"*Buonasera,* Meara."

He walked away from her and pushed the button for the elevator. Striding into it, he turned and intently stared at her until the elevators closed. Meara stood where he left her, her hand on her mouth. And for the third time in twenty-four hours, Meara Malone experienced something she didn't see coming.

five

"Marco said I shouldn't bring it up, but I can't help it. Have you thought about the offer?" Kate asked, hopping on to Meara's bed with a flourish. She was wearing a white luxurious hotel robe and intently eyed her sister.

Meara tied her own robe tighter and sat down next to her sister. She had avoided this conversation during Teresa and Stefano's rehearsal dinner the night before in Capri. It had been easy with so many people milling around Stefano's gorgeous villa that overlooked the crystal blue water. Afterwards, Meara, Kate, Teresa, and Ellie had come back to their hotel. The women had toasted the bride, ate more gelato, talked half the night, and laughed. It had been a good old-fashioned sleepover. Meara, who had never been to one, wondered if life would have been different for her if she had let anyone get close to her in school. Always competitive and disciplined about her studies, she had avoided close relationships her whole life. She marveled at Kate, who seemed to collect friends wherever she went. Meara was more comfortable in a boardroom than she was spending time with women, yet she unexpectedly had enjoyed herself.

Now, after treating themselves to hours in the spa where they had gotten massages and facials and all the pampering they could ever desire, she was truly stress-free. Kate's topic of conversation was already bringing back that tight muscle in her neck that the masseuse had finally gotten to subside.

Meara sighed, looking at her sweet sister's beautiful face, devoid of any make-up. "Oh Katie, I don't know. I've thought about it, but things have been just so strange for me. You know I thrive on routine, and I haven't had one these past few weeks. It's been difficult for me."

"Don't say that," Katie protested. "We had fun! It's been wonderful having you in Positano. I thought you enjoyed it."

"I have enjoyed it," Meara acknowledged gently. "Almost too much. It's not what I'm used to. I'm losing my edge."

Kate smiled a little, and Meara laid back against the pillow. Truthfully, her thoughts had been scrambled ever since her day with Alec. That day. That kiss. She still thought about it, since it had thrown her so off-base. It was hard to admit that she expected to hear from him. Yet, there had been nothing. Feeling remarkably vulnerable, she had stuffed her feelings down to her core. He was Italian, after all. Italian men probably kissed everyone like that and were always charming. Teresa had casually mentioned last night that Stefano called Alec a player. They had all laughed, but Meara had felt a little wrench to her heart. Here, she had spent so much effort trying to divert Kate because of Marco's reputation. And then she had stepped into spending time with a man who had a similar one.

Wanting to put some distance between her failed job and even Alec, Meara left Rome and willingly traveled to Positano to spend time with her sister. Kate was right in that they did have fun together. They had helped Teresa choose her bridal gown along with Kate's fashionable friend Francesca. Meara had eaten her weight in gelato, giving away to Kate's cravings as an excuse. They had extensively explored Positano. By now, all the shopkeepers and restauranteurs knew Kate, and it was a fun for

Meara to see her sister so beloved. They ventured all over the Amalfi Coast, including Sorrento, Amalfi and Praiano. Watching Kate put her energy into her Italian social media business and begin outlining posts on Rome had been fun. Meara had finally opened her computer and ran more numbers for her after researching potential advertisers. Just a few tips had brought in even more revenue streams for Kate, who was thrilled to have her sister's sage advice.

Meara had felt like she was intruding when Marco came home and she offered to make herself scarce. Marco had been kind, insisting on having her around, even asking her opinion every so often about a business deal he was involved in.

Now Kate was staring at her innocently. "Maybe it is time you lost your edge," she remarked quietly.

Meara raised her eyebrows, and Kate continued nervously. "Look, there isn't anyone who is going to say this to you but me. You've always had an edge—lots of edges if you want the truth. Maybe it's time you thought about what life would be like if you let your guard down."

Meara shook her head in horror. "What are you suggesting? That I just become a big pile of mush?"

Kate giggled. "Because that is likely to happen. No, of course not! I just mean that you have spent your whole life so guarded. You occasionally let me in. Maybe it's time you let yourself in. Take some time to do something different. Do something that would allow you free time to actually have a life."

"You are clever, Katie. That is a unique way of getting me to think about this job offer. I'll give you that."

"I don't even care about that anymore," Kate said earnestly. "These last couple of weeks have been wonderful. It just gave me a whole new view of you. Let's just say you *can* have fun, Meara. You have actually relaxed. I know the R word has negative connotations for you. But you *did* relax even if you won't admit it. It's just disappointing to see you go back into the rat race."

Meara played with a few threads on her belt. She knew deep down what Kate was trying to say. "It's all I know," she finally said. "I'm not sure how to do anything else."

Kate sat up and looked at Meara intently. "What if you compromised? I don't care if you take this foundation job or not but take something like it. Do something where you can enjoy your life. I know that you've made a ton of money over the past few years and probably not spent a cent on yourself except to buy more business clothes. You have poured a lot into dad's business. But now he's in the black, and you can scale that back. The only reason to take another high-powered tech job is for your own ego. I'm just saying you might not need that anymore. And this is an opportunity to do something meaningful."

At Meara's raised eyebrows, Kate looked uncomfortable. "I'm not trying to say that what you have been doing isn't important," she quickly continued. "But this role could really help so many people. Maybe you can make a difference in this world and that might help you in your own life."

Meara laughed at her sister's intense expression. "You have been spending way too much time reading inspirational quotes on social media. But I get what you are saying. Point taken. I will make some decisions soon."

"Have you heard from Dr. Amato?"

Meara took a breath and deflected Kate's attention. "Why do you call him that? Why don't you just call him Alec?"

Kate looked embarrassed. "He's, you know...my doctor. I would rather see him as a doctor right now until I get this baby out. Then I'll call him Alec."

"Oh, I kind of get that," Meara said with a laugh, stalling for time. "No, I haven't heard from him. Would you expect me to?" She tried to appear casual.

Kate shrugged. "I don't know. I guess I just thought he'd try to persuade you. Did he talk about it when he took you home?"

"No. We...uh, talked about other stuff." Meara shifted

uncomfortably. It was difficult not to tell Katie about spending the day with him. She had been about to several times but felt embarrassed when he never contacted her afterwards. Telling Kate would lead to more questions.

"Did he tell you much about his life?"

Meara shook her head. "No, we didn't really talk about personal stuff. Why?"

"Oh, I don't know," Kate said nonchalantly, examining her nails with an odd expression. "I just wondered. He'll be at the wedding tonight. Maybe you can talk with him then."

"Katie, don't get any ideas," Meara said firmly. "The last thing I need you to do is matchmaking like some Italian mother."

Kate patted her now growing stomach. "Well, I'm not one yet, but I will be. Okay, I'll leave you alone. He is really attractive, though, you have to admit."

Meara rolled her eyes. "You are married to an extremely handsome billionaire. Isn't that enough for you?"

"It doesn't mean I can't appreciate swoon worthy. And he's definitely swoon worthy."

"It just means he has more experience with women," Meara said dryly. "I'm not interested in being one more adoring female in his life."

"Why not? Now that might be the fun you need. Sorry, just kidding." Kate giggled as she stood and stretched. "I have time for a small nap before the hair and makeup people get here."

Meara watched her sister depart, knowing she was purposely going to nap with her sexy husband. She nestled down into her comfy bed and allowed her thoughts to go back to Alec. Maybe Kate was right. And there could be a good reason he hadn't called her. How bad could it be to have a small fling with an extremely handsome, funny, and intelligent man? She might work on that tonight. Smiling at the thought, she drifted into a gentle sleep.

MEARA CLAPPED and cheered with everyone else as Teresa and Stefano ran down the aisle of their makeshift wedding venue in the *Piazzetta,* followed by Kate and Marco, who had been their only attendants. Teresa looked beautiful in her Italian lace dress with its short train.

Meara shivered in her thin, but fashionable coat and glanced behind her casually. The guests were filing out, and she joined them, as people remarked about the emotional ceremony. Each of Teresa's five brothers had joined her at some point to walk her several feet down the aisle. There hadn't been a dry eye in the place. Stefano had been completely transformed. Once withdrawn and remote, his love shone brightly, and he couldn't have smiled wider watching his bride.

While Meara had been charmed by the ceremony, she had waited for the prickle at her neck to alert her that Alec was somewhere in the crowd. She never felt it. Glancing around surreptitiously, she didn't see him and slipped into the nearby restaurant for the reception.

Teresa's brothers were making their presence known, and Kate came over to grab her to say hello. Stefano had flown them all over to surprise Teresa at Thanksgiving, and Meara had gotten reacquainted with them. Growing up with the family as neighbors, the boys had been familiar faces, but that was all. Like others, Meara had never gotten close to them, though she remembered vaguely competing with one of them at some school debate competition. Was that Anthony or Bennett? She couldn't remember.

Silently, she accepted the prosecco someone pushed into her hand and tried to look like she was interested in mingling. It was then she felt cold air from the door and the tingle of awareness that she had been waiting for. Marco was greeting Alec, and she strained her ears. Damn, why hadn't she learned more Italian?

She had lived in the country for more than a year. They now switched to English as Kate said hello. Apparently, Alec had gotten tied up with yet another delivery and was regretful he had missed the wedding.

Meara pretended to be absorbed in a story Marco's brother, Nico, was telling the group. Nico, the youngest of the Rinaldi's, was a smaller version of Marco, and was charming and sweet. The consummate younger brother, he loved to tease his siblings and had a great sense of humor. He greeted her like an old friend and immediately continued telling a story to Teresa's brothers. It was something about his recent trip to Sicily. Meara was having a difficult time focusing, with Alec's laugh somewhere behind her. She felt a very light hand on her bare back. "Meara," that rich voice said softly.

Turning, she looked at him with a polite expression. "Oh, hello, Alessandro. It's nice to see you again."

She could see the laughter in his eyes, but his face remained solemn. This man seemed like he could see into her soul. "It is also *nice* to see you," he acknowledged, kissing her on each cheek. She felt his warm breath and his soft lips linger. "But why am I being greeted so formally? My friends call me Alec."

"Are we friends?" she asked, raising her eyebrows intently.

"I would hope we are." He grinned charmingly.

"I am not sure we are," she said lightly, her eyebrows raised. She wanted to add that friends kept in touch, but that would be presumptuous. Their gazes locked for a minute.

Lowering his voice, he bent toward her. "I am certain we are. I have been thinking nonstop about our day together. Most of all, the kiss." His lips were hovering near her ear. All she would have to do was lean over and...

"Alec, there you are!" Teresa exclaimed, coming up behind them. Always exuberant, Teresa gave him a big hug, punching him on the shoulder. "You missed the wedding! There is probably another baby in this world, right?" He laughed and told her she looked beautiful, and she accepted the compliment graciously. "Meara, you don't mind if I steal him, do you? I want to introduce him to my brothers. Though I might regret it!"

Meara only nodded with a slight smile, but Alec's penetrating gaze stayed with her for a moment as he drew back and let Teresa begin the introductions. It was only then that she exhaled.

ALEC GREETED each one of Teresa's brothers. They were alphabetically named and yet, he already forgot who was who. He doubted it would matter as they all talked at once, with Teresa bearing the brunt of their teasing as they called her by a nickname. Slinky? He'd have to ask about that later. "Hey you guys have to be nice to me! I'm the bride!" she teased, as she playfully swatted at one of them.

Alec smiled, but he felt a lump in his throat. He missed his late sister so much his heart ached. Just seeing the interaction between the siblings in front of him ripped at his heart. He envied large families.

Now his thoughts went back to Meara, and he glanced around to see her across the room, talking with Stefano. She looked absolutely gorgeous tonight in her emerald green gown, held up by the wispiest straps he had ever seen. Its neckline dropped into a deep V and gathered at her slim waist, a deep slit showing her long legs. She simply took his breath away, not just for her beauty but for all the complexities of her character he was looking forward to uncovering. He felt like an inexperienced teenager around her. It had been true that he had thought a lot about their day together, but had berated himself. Why in the world had he spent the day in tour guide mode? Stating facts and figures and telling her gory stories was hardly romantic, yet he couldn't stop himself. He hadn't been that nervous for a long time. Memories of his awkward years washed over him.

Admittedly, he had eventually learned how to talk to women, or at least listen. Though he had once had an active social life, he hadn't been out with a woman recently, and it showed. Deep down, he knew it was more than the hiatus from dating. Meara Malone was the first woman who truly intimidated him. He found her highly intelligent, witty and yet so guarded. He constantly wondered what she was thinking. There had been brief moments where he felt her relax just a small amount. She had opened up at lunch, but then withdrew. At least until he kissed her. Smiling at the memory, he recognized his own impulsiveness. The word "nice" to describe him had infuriated him, and he had acted. When she responded, he had been surprised and then thrilled.

Tonight, he planned to spend as much energy as possible to see if he could at least peel away one or two more of those layers. She intrigued him and intoxicated him. He couldn't wait for the evening to unfold. That is, if he could at least not act like some fumbling amateur. Smiling, he took a sip of his prosecco. Meara was glancing at him across the room. He raised his glass slightly and smiled. She did not alter her expression, but turned back toward Stefano. It would be an eventful night.

MEARA GLANCED at the seating chart and sighed. Alec's seat was right next to her own seat. Besides the printed seating chart at the entrance to the dining room, there were also place cards at each seat. She had no hope of switching them. Glancing around, she looked for her sister. She might have to wring her neck later. While she had earlier entertained the idea of flirting with him, she was now a ball of unexplained anxiety. The man kept her guessing.

Squaring her shoulders, Meara walked to her seat, only to have Alec appear out of nowhere. He graciously slid her chair out, and she sat, placing her glass of prosecco down on the table. She smoothed the folds of her gown, wondering why her hands were clammy. Over the years, she had found herself in a lot of situations that would have been nerve-wracking to a regular person. Most of the time, she was able to bypass nerves. Why did this man have this effect on her? Shaking it off, she tossed a polite smile his way and pretended to be studying the printed menu at their plates. Stefano and Teresa had long debates over the food, which were Stefano's only real specifications for the event. They had compromised, and the menu was a wild array of both Italian and American cuisine. They also had a more informal vibe about it, which was strictly Teresa's personality. The assigned seats had been Kate's doing, as she told Teresa it would help the guests meet each other.

Meara smiled politely as some of the Rinaldi family joined them. Lucca and Ellie sat down, and Meara was about to introduce them when Lucca interrupted that he knew Alec already. Instead, Lucca introduced Ellie to Alec, who gave him a bright smile. "I've heard all about you, Dr. Amato," she said. At Meara's intense stare, she rushed to clarify. "Katie just thinks the world of you." That led to questions about his practice and profession. A world-famous actor, Lucca was used to being in the spotlight, but Meara noticed he often seemed more comfortable asking questions of others. He was now lightly boasting about his wife's artwork. Ellie was an amazing artist, and Meara would love to buy one of her pieces someday if she truly ever had a place she called home.

"Excuse me?" she asked, realizing Ellie had said something to her. Ellie smiled and leaned in to whisper in her ear. "Alec seems really sweet."

Meara glared at her. "Not you, too. Did Katie put you up to this?"

Ellie raised her eyebrows innocently. "All I said was he was sweet, Meara." She nudged her. "Give the guy a chance. I'll keep Lucca occupied so you two can chat."

Ellie turned and captured her husband's attention with practiced ease. The seats next to Alec were still empty, and soon Nico and Alfonso joined them and Meara beamed at them. They both blinked a little, not used to seeing her so friendly. Alfonso had grown up around the Rinaldi Family and was a de facto cousin. He ran a nearby ceramic shop that Meara had visited several times with Kate. He was also a local soccer player, or *calcio,* as it is called in Italy. Now he and Nico immediately launched into a discussion of the sport.

Alec casually put an arm on the back of her chair. "This looks like quite a menu," he commented with a chuckle. That led to a discussion of foods, and soon, Meara found her resolve slipping a little. Alec told her about some of Rome's best restaurants.

"I heard a little about some of them from Teresa," Meara said, "But to be honest, I usually just ordered something to go. Teresa and Stefano ate their way through half the country as part of Lucca's show."

At the mention of his name, Lucca turned and launched into a story about the upcoming series. Ellie threw her a helpless look, but Meara gave a small shrug, accepting the situation. She and Alec had all night to talk. The food began arriving, and Meara smiled despite her attempt to remain cool. Katie had been right. This was a fun table, and she let Alec fill her wineglass with Pinot Grigio while dining on an entertaining mixture of food that showcased the couple's favorite cuisine. They indulged in sliders, fries, pizza, caprese ravioli, bruschetta and *risotto alla pescatora.*

When the men launched into some debate about soccer again, she and Ellie laughed about their slumber party. "Did you see Katie fall asleep with her spoon in her gelato? She looked so cute," Ellie said with a giggle. "We are so happy for them. A little baby," she said wistfully.

At Meara's raised eyebrows, she laughed harder. "Oh, don't start. My parents are bad enough! We aren't even close to thinking about it. Lucca and I need some time together, and I'm enjoying painting so much right now. In fact, we are going to Puglia after this so I can paint for a while. Lucca will probably be on the phone or his computer half the time," she said and rolled her eyes. "But the post production is nearing the end of his show, so he needs to keep a tight handle on it before it launches and makes Stefano a star."

They both laughed at that idea and talked about the show for a little while before she felt Alec turn back to her. "Are you going to eat that?" he pointed to her remaining slider.

She smiled and shook her head and let him grab it from her plate. His closeness and demeanor made them appear to be a couple. She glanced over at Nico and Alfonso who gave her knowing looks. Well, earlier she thought about a fling. Now her doubts were slipping away. When Alec whispered in her ear about being happy he was at her table, she turned her head a little. It was just enough for her lips to be millimeters from his. His intense gaze almost burned her. Drawing away, she put her hand on Alec's leg and felt him almost jump. Letting it rest there, she felt him relax and then tighten his arm around her.

"We should dance," he whispered, and she felt the familiar tingle go down her spine.

The next couple of hours were something Meara would never forget. She and Alec had developed a closeness she hadn't expected. Alec danced with her most of the time, except for a few laughing cut-ins by Nico, Alfonso, and a couple of Teresa's brothers. They stopped to toast the bride and groom several times with clinking glasses that demanded they kiss. The dancing only stopped to sample an array of desserts, including the wedding cake decorated by Ellie. As the evening wore on, Marco and Kate stopped by to say they were going to their hotel. Marco, with his arms around Kate, explained she was getting tired while Kate protested she was feeling fine. Still, it was obvious they wanted to be alone as they quickly exited the room.

As others departed and things quieted down, Meara sank into Alec's arms. He had taken off his tie, and she had lost her shoes somewhere. She came right up to below his shoulder and felt the wide breadth of him. He was warm, and she snuggled deeper, feeling his hand traveling the length of her back, touching her smooth, fair skin.

"You look exquisite tonight, Meara. I haven't told you before now because I didn't want you to think I was hitting on you."

She pulled back to look at him teasingly. "Are you? Hitting on me?"

He laughed a little and pulled her closer. "I must be losing my touch if you don't know it by now," he said softly in her ear. "Do you mind? All I can think about is getting you out of here and explore kissing you again."

"That's all I can think about, too," she said honestly. Her heart began to pound erratically. She was putting herself out there like Kate told her to do, and it was terrifying and exhilarating at the same time. His lips began traveling from her ear across the cheek.

"Alec," she drew back. She had to know something first, and it was important just to be direct. "Why didn't you call me or text me these last few weeks?" Looking him in the eyes, she saw a careful expression cross his face. His hand traveled up and down her back soothingly while the other gripped her waist tighter.

"I wanted to," he told her, his expression sincere. "But Meara...we have to talk. I am very attracted to you, and I'd like to explore that. But my life is very complicated right now. It's only fair that you know about that going in. Marco told me you were in Positano, but I was still in Rome. I thought it was better if we spoke in person."

She felt reassured by his honesty, and the vulnerability she had been feeling melted away. He was worth the risk. "I like complicated," she murmured, wondering if he was going to tell her he was devoted to his job or traveled a lot. He seemed so busy. She snuggled close to him and felt his body tense a little. But the music had already ended. She pulled back awkwardly.

"Let's get out of here," he spoke roughly.

Nodding, she agreed, despite the small inkling she felt. They would have to talk first. "Just let me go find my shoes and get myself together. I'll join you by the entrance."

Walking back to the table, she sat and put on her shoes before going to the women's room. Touching herself up was just an excuse. She needed a minute to pull herself together. Was she really doing this? Sure, she had boyfriends over the years, but it was always on her terms. Where they went, what they did. Everything was carefully controlled by her. She had a feeling Alessandro Amato was not to be controlled. It made her heart skip a beat, and she smiled tremulously at the mirror.

The door swung open, and Kate's mother-in-law entered. "Hello, dear, I have hardly spoken to you tonight," she greeted her with a smile.

Meara smiled widely at her. Margherita was a treasure and someone she respected. "How is the mother of the groom holding up?" she teased.

"Relieved, my dear. Relieved. I cannot tell you how it does my heart good to see Stefano so happy. He's always been one I've worried about and now..." She snapped her fingers. "I have no cares."

Meara laughed. "What about Nico?"

"Oh Nico. That boy brings me joy. And someday he'll bring a woman the same joy. For now, the weddings of my two sons and a nephew, are enough for me. But I sense there's more romance in the air," she said, eyeing Meara speculatively.

Meara opened her purse and carefully applied her lip gloss, avoiding Margherita's gaze. The older woman was known to cut to the chase, something Meara admired. They were one and the same when it came to that.

"Well, I don't know about that," Meara replied with her best poker face.

"Hmmm," was all Margherita replied, touching a hand to her carefully coiffed black hair. "Sergio and I will be leaving soon," she said, referring to her boyfriend. "But I hope you continue to stay and have fun." Meara turned to see the twinkle in her eye and remained silent.

After hugging Margherita, Meara went out the door quickly, eager now to join Alec. She descended the stairs to the lobby area where the bar and cocktail hour had been and saw him standing at the entrance as promised. He was talking on the phone. Retrieving her coat from the coat check, she walked slowly toward him. He was running his hand through his hair and seemed agitated. She wondered if it was a patient. Would he have to leave to go to the hospital? Hoping that wasn't the case, she stood right behind him. Suddenly, she heard him shout an expletive in Italian that made her jump. She could understand that much. He then switched to English, speaking in an angry, condescending tone. "I will not repeat myself. Olivia, you will leave immediately! Do you understand me? You are fired! Security is arriving to escort you out. Do not even pack! Someone will retrieve your things. Do not return to my house or ever contact me again. You repulse me! You are nothing. Do you hear me? Nothing!"

Meara stepped back automatically. The ruthlessness in his voice, and the anger and resentment that was directed at whoever this poor woman was, alarmed her. She didn't know this Alec. Frankly, she really didn't know Alec at all. He was so different from the man who had waxed on about Cellini celebrating women.

The walls were rushing in, and a coldness swiftly washed over her. Was she out of her mind? What had she been thinking?

So this was the complication he had talked about. She felt physically sick.

His back was still to her, and he was taking great heaving breaths. Abruptly turning around, he saw her, at first seemingly not even recognizing her, his eyes still full of rage. He blinked, and she watched the dawning realization on his face that she had overheard his conversation.

Finally he spoke. "I have to go home," he told her flatly. Staring at her, he gave no further explanation.

She stared back, her face expressionless. Stepping past him, she pulled open the door and stepped into the dark night alone.

six

Meara sat stiffly at the mahogany boardroom table. She concentrated on the luxurious carpet, the enchanting view of Rome in the distance and the exquisite artwork while she tried to control her breathing. She crossed her long legs and once again ran her hands down her best navy blue suit and white silk blouse. She needed to have her armor on today, and she always felt the most powerful in certain work clothes.

"Meara, I'm sorry to keep you waiting," Marco said apologetically, as he hurried in. She stood in greeting, and he kissed her on each cheek before giving her a gentle hug. "You know, we could have met at our villa," he teased, as he sat down. "We didn't need to be so formal."

Meara smiled at her brother-in-law's sincere expression. "I know, Marco, but I wanted everything to be on the up and up. If this is going to be a professional relationship, then I want this to be formal."

He nodded, looking at the large leather portfolio in front of him. Putting on his wire-rimmed glasses, he opened it and took several papers out and began to examine them.

"I was able to study these a little bit last night. I trust you found the foundation's lawyers accommodating?"

Meara smiled a little. She was sure she had given them a little of angst. "Is Alec, er, Dr. Amato, going to join us?" she asked as nonchalantly as she could.

"No, he's at home today. He texted that something came up," Marco explained absentmindedly, still reading. He finally straightened and regarded her thoughtfully. "You seem to have really thought this out. Your modifications to your contract are very...interesting."

Meara had been expecting this. "Yes. I wanted clear lines of direction."

"You also wanted Alec's role very formalized," Marco prompted. Taking off his glasses, he narrowed his eyes. "Meara, I must ask. Did he say or do something to make you uncomfortable? Alec is usually not that way." Now Marco was the one who looked uncomfortable. "We, er...saw both of you dancing at the wedding. You seemed like you were getting along."

"We were. But not the way you think. Please, Marco, don't worry that Alec offended me or anything. No matter where I work, I always have certain guidelines for consultants or contractors," she told him and hoped he would not see through her fib.

"You didn't put any restrictions on Teresa's involvement," Marco noted. Meara tried not to wince. He *would* point out the obvious.

"That's because I've known Teresa all my life, and believe me, we can pound it out like the best of them. But obviously, I don't know Alec that well. I understand he's one of the medical consultants on a particular part of this project, and I want to ensure we don't step over each other. I wanted it explained clearly so he understands my role, and that ultimately, with the board's support, I am the one making the decisions."

Marco gazed at her speculatively. "I have no problem with it.

I just wanted to make sure there were no underlying reasons." Shifting the papers, he began signing them.

Meara willed herself to keep her expression unreadable. There were plenty of reasons, but she wasn't going to tell Marco that.

Just then, Marco's executive assistant, Dominico, hurried through the door and whispered in his ear. Marco sighed, taking his glasses off. "Meara, I need to go make a call to our Milan office. I may have to fly up there later."

"I hope everything is okay."

"Just one of our daily crises," he said and grimaced. "With Stefano minimizing his role, we are making changes. We are reallocating his work, but there are things I still must take care of personally. Kate said I have trust issues after Sal's fraud."

Meara smiled understandingly. "Of course. I think we are finished here. I have signed everything, and Dominico already showed me the foundation's new offices, so I'll be ready to come to work tomorrow. I'm really excited about this opportunity, Marco," she said earnestly. "I won't let you down."

He grinned. "Meara, I have 100 percent faith in you and not because you are my sister-in-law. One last question before I go. What made you change your mind about accepting it? You seemed as if you had decided this wasn't for you."

"It was actually something Katie said. She just told me it was time to do something that mattered." At Marco's raised eyebrows, she hurried to defend her sister. "No, she didn't mean it badly. She just told me this was an opportunity to change lives, and well, I don't think I've ever changed anyone's life."

"My wife is very intelligent," he said proudly and smiled. Standing, he gave her a quick hug. "I really am sorry to have to leave. I was looking forward to introducing you to the small staff we have already hired."

Meara shook her head. "No, actually, it's better I do that myself anyway. I don't want the nepotism to be that blatant."

"You are right, of course!" he said, before giving her a brief hug. "*Ciao, mia sorella*," he called as he departed.

Meara gathered up her copies of the legal documents and put them in her briefcase as Dominico returned. "*Signorina* Malone, do you need anything else?" he asked, looking frazzled.

"No, Dominico, I'm fine. And please call me Meara. Is there anything wrong?"

He winced, his eyes wide with dismay. "It is my fault. Please don't tell Marco! I was to send Dr. Amato's documents to his *casa,* and I forgot. He has to sign them today or else we have to reprint everything and start over with the right date. The attorneys gave me strict instructions. But now Marco needs me to fly to Milan with him. I'll have to go convince someone else to take them to him."

"Can it be done online?"

Dominico shook his head. "The government requires paper copies with the foundation's imprint," he said. "Things are a little stricter because of the rules governing a foundation such as this."

Meara paused for a minute and then quickly made up her mind. "Dominico, I'll take them to Dr. Amato. I'll watch him sign them. As the new Executive Director, I can sign them after he does. I'll bring them in with me tomorrow."

Dominico looked horrified. "*Signorina*, I can't ask you to do that."

Meara put out her hand. "It's no problem. Alec…er, Dr. Amato and I need to talk anyway."

"You're certain?"

She nodded, ignoring the growing knot in the pit of her stomach.

〜

MEARA LOOKED OUT THE WINDOW, not focusing on any of Rome's beautiful scenery. She settled into the soft leather in the backseat of the luxury sedan. It was nice to have a driver again. Cosmo was wonderful, and luckily Marco had insisted he be part of her executive package. He had also thrown in an apartment in Rome, but this one was in a private building. She had moved all her things last night, and the view was even better. While she guessed he was paying for it himself to spare the foundation, she had no way of confirming it. She had stopped asking after witnessing Marco's stern expression. After all, it was critical to Marco to have someone he could trust. If he had to pay for it, then so be it.

Why had she decided it was a good idea to take the papers to Alec? With a sinking feeling, she realized that she needed to get this initial meeting with him over with. Since he had been invited to the meeting today, she had been prepared with her game face intact. It was a waste since he was a no-show. Part of her seethed. If this was going to be his carelessness with this project, she was even happier she had formalized his role. There was no room for someone who wasn't fully committed. He hadn't even had the decency to call or text her since that night in Capri. Her cheeks burned thinking about how close she came to running off with him in the night to do God knows what. The man seemed to be able to persuade her to do things that were out of character for her. It was time she established herself as the one in control. He would soon learn that when he read through the documents.

Her plan was straightforward. After getting him to sign them, she would set a time for a more formal meeting with others on the project to review the details for the clinics they were building and remodeling on the Amalfi Coast. Then they would finalize the equipment list they had for the hospital. Everything in this phase of the project was related to obstetrics and neonatal care. After that phase was done, she wouldn't even have to see Alec.

While the scope of the foundation was still being outlined, that was the only phase that would require an obstetrician/gynecologist as a consultant.

That had been the final factor in her decision to take this job. She accepted once she realized it was only a few months of possibly having to see Alec. Kate had been right. It was time to break out of the methodically planned life she had carved for herself. Throwing caution to the wind, she was launching herself into a new sphere. She reasoned the things she excelled at as a savvy executive transcended across most fields. While she would have some health care knowledge to attain, she would rely on experts and keep her focus more at the 20,000-foot level.

Meara glanced out the window at the expansive white luxury villa they were pulling up to. It looked to be three floors with an iron gated balcony peeking out from the top. Windows outlined with brown trim seemed to be everywhere, glinting in the setting sun. It had modern, clean lines and almost looked like it belonged on a California hillside. The villa was unique and fresh looking. Darn it, he would have a cool house.

She went to get out and her driver, Cosmo, was already there to help. He frowned at her, telling her with his expression yet again that it was his job to assist her with everything. She appreciated the fatherly attention of the older gentleman and smiled at him. Grabbing her briefcase from the seat, she told him she would be a few minutes. He nodded and tipped his cap, getting back into the car to drive the car off to the side.

Bringing herself to her full height, she walked purposely toward the door. She was pleased she had worn her highest heels. Growing up, she had always felt like an Amazon, towering over most people, even men. But after realizing it brought her strength, especially in negotiations, she now relished in it.

Using the ornate door knocker, she quickly pounded before she lost her nerve. Tapping her well-shod foot, she looked around at the expansive manicured lawn that looked like it led to more gardens. After waiting a couple minutes, she rapped sharply again. It may have been prudent to have called first. Biting her lip, she remembered Marco saying he was at home today. No other excuse was given. Oh God, what if he was with a woman?

Before she could digest that disconcerting thought, the door opened with a flourish, and her mouth dropped open a little. Alec stood before her in well-worn jeans and a gray T-shirt that showed his muscular chest. He was wiping his hands on a kitchen towel, and his abundant brown hair was ruffled. He looked harassed at first and then surprised to see Meara standing before him.

"Meara, I didn't expect you. I told Marco I couldn't make it today. I'm sorry," he said, nervously glancing quickly over his shoulder.

The hair on her neck stood up. Let her just die now rather than see who he was with. Her mind had already flown to an image of a famed Italian model. That would be his type. Probably blonde. Her heart was thundering so loud she almost couldn't speak. She tried to recover.

"Yes, I know." She retrieved the envelope from her bag and thrust it at him awkwardly. "Dominico forgot to send these over, and we need you to sign them today. I can, er...wait in the car while you do so."

Suddenly, banging began coming from somewhere in the house. What in the world was happening in there? Meara took a step back as Alec glanced again over his shoulder.

"He could have sent them by courier," Alec pointed out.

Meara tried to keep her face impassive, even though his words were spot on. "Yes, I know. I offered to as I thought we could determine a few things about this project, but I can see you are busy. I apologize."

He winced a little, running his hands through his hair. "No I should apologize. It's just not the day to...."

BANG!

Something sounded like pots and pans hitting the floor and then a wail. Alec's eyes widened, and he turned and sprinted down the hall. Meara looked down at the envelope he inadvertently dropped. She bent and picked it up, and something propelled her inside. It was time she faced reality. Maybe that would shake her out of this odd behavior. She closed the door and followed Alec's path. Glancing around, she quickly admired the exquisite entry with its ornate Italian vases and eclectic artwork on the wall. The lines were clean and almost not lived in.

She turned the corner and saw the gleaming white kitchen and its stainless-steel modern appliances. The wailing noise was growing louder and she walked through the kitchen to the other side of the large island to see Alec sitting on the floor rocking a small child. Flour was strewn all over the floor, and pots and pans with spoons in them were scattered about. Chocolate dripped from an overturned bottle that was still on the island. The child, dressed in tiny jeans and a T-shirt, was sobbing into Alec's shoulder. His hand was cradling her head as he made small comforting noises, rocking his body.

Abruptly, the child straightened and noticed her. Meara saw the messy brown ringlets then, the inquisitive eyes and the chubby pink cheeks. The little girl was eyeing Meara from head to toe, her eyes wide. She had been sucking on her chocolatey fingers, and now she pulled her hand out with a plop. She gasped and said one word that was distinguishable in any language.

"Mamma!"

seven

Alec looked up frantically and scrambled to his feet. "Meara, this isn't…"

"Papa!" shrieked the small child.

"Shh, Valentina!"

"Mamma!" The little girl struggled to her tiny feet, clad in purple high-top tennis shoes. Her entire shirt was covered in chocolate sauce. She ran to Meara and threw herself in a hug around Meara's legs.

"Mamma," she cooed happily.

Meara stood frozen. She wasn't sure what to do: pry the child off of her legs or wait for Alec to do so? She felt sticky wetness on her legs and then almost visibly shuddered when she realized Valentina was now reaching up, grabbing her fine wool skirt.

"Alec," Meara pleaded softly, not sure what to do. She swallowed. "Can you pick up your daughter?"

"She's not…"

"Papa!" Valentina laughed and hugged Meara tighter. She chattered happily in Italian, and Alec was answering her. He bent down and attempted to detach her from Meara. Finally, he was able to scoop her up, but she promptly ran her hands down the front of Meara's white silk blouse as she tried to hug her.

"*Mi dispiace!*" he said to Meara and then reverted to English. "I will make this right. I promise. But now I better get her into a bath." He looked at her, his gaze traveling the length of her. "And we better do something about you as well."

Meara continued to stare at him in shock. He's a father. That's what he meant about complicated. Was that his wife or the mother of his child that he had ordered out of his house? Immediately dismissing that idea as Marco would have told her, she tried to wrap her head around this sexy doctor being a father. He was busy slinging a laughing Valentina over his shoulder and murmuring to her in Italian.

He turned suddenly. "Come this way, Meara," he instructed. Not glancing behind him to see if she was following, he continued to walk down the hallway, almost whistling.

Meara shook her head, trying to clear her tumultuous thoughts. She would leave the papers and tell him to have a courier bring them back to the office tonight. Glancing over her shoulder, she looked back at the way she had entered. It was time to get out of there.

"Meara!" Alec called.

She bit her lip. She might as well see this through. This was the other woman, a tinier one than she had assumed, and definitely not a blonde. However, she was almost more threatening and foreign. Meara didn't do small human beings. She had never been around children, and they were as daunting to her as the most formidable opponent. Standing tall and holding her head up, she followed him down the hall. Entering a luxurious bathroom, she admired the most enormous shower she had ever seen in her life, lined in Italian marble with several shower heads. Alec was filling up a giant modern slanted bathtub with water while holding the squirming child. Meara stood awkwardly as he undressed Valentina, tested the water, and plunked her into a child's seat that was perched in the tub. The child cried out in Italian, and Alec reached over to grab a bag of toys to sprinkle in the bubble bath. Kneeling beside the tub, he finally turned and looked at her.

"I'll apologize again, Meara, for your clothes getting damaged. You need to get cleaned up as well. There are some washcloths in the cabinet behind you if you want to wash off. And then I can get you a change of clothes. My housekeeper is out today, or else I would ask her to get the stains out."

Meara glanced down, thinking there was a slim chance of the stains ever coming out of her clothes. She found her voice finally. "That's okay, Alec. I'll just get some of this chocolate off me, and then if you can just sign these papers, I'll go. My driver is waiting. I can head straight back to my apartment."

He turned away from her to look at the little girl. Valentina was happily making noises and playing with her toys. Turning to stare at Meara thoughtfully, he stayed quiet for a minute, watching her dab the chocolate from her legs. "You missed a spot," he said softly. She glanced down to see one giant blob of chocolate near her ankle and quickly wiped it, placing the washcloth on the counter.

"Can you watch her a minute?" he asked, as he stood and left the bathroom quickly, before Meara could muster any words. She would have clarified what she was supposed to do. Watch her do what? She certainly wasn't going to bathe the child. Maybe her sole responsibility was acting as a lifeguard. Almost giddy with relief when he reappeared, she glanced down to see him holding a pair of sweats and a shirt.

"Go put these on. I told your driver we'd call him back when we need him," he said calmly.

"You did what? Who do you think you are? I could have plans tonight!"

"Do you?" he asked, his head tilted with a knowing smile.

She glared at him, trying to come up with a terse reply.

Finally, she shook her head. "Well, no, but I *could* have. You had no right to do that. I just came to discuss my new position and how we are...how you..."

Meara frowned darkly. She never had problems articulating herself. It was only this man who affected her. Now her business and personal life were intertwined, and it illustrated why it was a bad idea to mix the two.

"You came here to put me in my place and make sure I understand what my role is," Alec finished for her. "Because of our personal relationship, you don't want any misinterpretations. You're making sure everything is in black and white because that's how you like things. That way you are in control."

Her frown grew. She could swear he was laughing at her behind his bland expression. Stomping her foot would be childish, but right now she wanted to do just that. Before she could utter her thoughts, he walked over and put a hand on her shoulder.

"Meara, you are right. We *do* need to talk. That probably can't happen till this *angioletto* goes to bed. I am sorry about your clothes. I promise I will take care of getting them cleaned or replaced. And you're right, it was high-handed of me to release your driver. But *per favore*, let's have a little dinner after I get Nia to bed, and then we can talk and...clear the air. Is that alright?"

His gentle, persuasive tone seemed to take over her anger. How did he influence her in a way most people could never achieve? She glanced down at the casual clothes for a minute.

"Do you have anything that's more...fashionable?" she asked resignedly.

His laughter rang out in the expansive bathroom. Valentina looked up, shocked at first, and then joined him in laughing, splashing merrily with her small hands.

~

ALEC SIGHED in relief as he turned back to the tub. Meara had taken the clothes and gone into a guest bathroom to change. He hadn't been sure she would agree to his plan and was surprised when she acquiesced. Meara was unlike any woman he had ever known, and when he geared up for a battle, she seemed to back down. When he didn't expect her to retort, she did. He wasn't ever sure what was going on in that fiery red head of hers.

The last couple of weeks had been a whirlwind. Knowing he needed to explain to Meara what happened in Capri weighed on him. He owed her that, at the very least. There was a part of him that had wondered if she would be better off just thinking the worst of him. It would avoid a future entanglement between them. The problem was, he really wanted to be entangled with her. He was intrigued by her and wanted to get to know the real Meara Malone. Had anyone ever done that?

Smiling tenderly at Valentina, who was busy lining up her toy boats, he wondered if his life would ever become simpler. The last two-and-a-half years had certainly been rocky. He kept waiting for things to normalize, but just as he became confident that things were evening out, disaster would strike. Capri was an example of that.

"I haven't worn sweats since I played sports in high school," came a dry voice behind him.

He turned around and was glad he was almost sitting down. Meara stood looking at him, wearing his black sweats and T-shirt he had gotten at some medical conference. Her feet were bare, and she was rubbing one ankle with a perfectly pedicured foot. "Um, can I borrow some socks? It seemed ridiculous to keep my shoes on."

He smiled and nodded, thinking how beautiful she looked in his clothes. Grabbing Valentina from the tub, he draped a towel around her as she fought him off, insisting in her childish babble that she was not finished. He told her they were going to read her beloved books, and that seemed to distract her.

"Let me just get her dressed, and then I'll find you a pair," he told her.

Carrying Valentina out of the bathroom and down the hall to her room, he was surprised to find Meara following him. Automatically, he got pajamas out of an extensive wardrobe and began to dress the little girl. Out of the corner of his eye, he saw Meara wandering around, occasionally picking up a stuffed animal or book. She was now staring at a photo in a frame before moving on. The room had been carefully decorated with a mural on the wall showcasing cartoon-like animals. Valentina's toddler bed was covered in an animal print as well. A miniature table and chairs were in the corner. The rest of the room was in complete disarray. Books, toys and other items were scattered all over. It looked like a small toddler bomb had gone off. Alec winced, wondering what Meara thought of the upheaval. Valentina had a playroom as well, but somehow all her toys ended up in her bedroom. His housekeeper, Rosalie, had been watching Valentina and hadn't had time to clean. He certainly never had enough time in his day.

"I'll meet you back in the kitchen," he told her with a smile. "Just give me a few minutes to read her a story, and then she'll be off to dreamland." Valentina was protesting in Italian about hugging Mamma again. Alec knew a long explanation would be required in the morning. Meara had heard it obviously because he saw her eyes widen and she backed out and nearly ran down the hall. He took a deep breath and flew Valentina to her bed in his arms like he always did. The airplane move distracted her enough to divert her thoughts about the lovely woman who had appeared out of nowhere. Reading stories he had read a hundred times to her made it easy for his thoughts to travel. Tonight would be interesting and pivotal for any relationship between them, but probably not in a good way. All he could do was tell the truth. Hearing a gentle snore, he smiled and kissed the cherub's pink cheeks. Slumber was achieved after a very busy day. There was something so gratifying about watching a sleeping content child. He doused the light, leaving the night-light shining stars on the ceiling and made sure the baby monitor was on.

Grabbing a pair of crew socks from his large wardrobe, he changed his own shirt before walking into the kitchen. Meara was sitting awkwardly at the large white modular table. She was thumbing through a book he had left there on parenting, frowning as she turned the pages.

"Here you go," he said, trying to appear cheerful and keep the growing dread he felt dampened down.

Throwing the socks to her, he watched her reach up and catch them easily and then bend to put them on those adorable feet of hers. He glanced at the mess on the floor, but decided to leave it. Meara must have up righted the jar of chocolate, but most of it had poured out anyway. Pouring two glasses of Chianti, he carried them over to the table and sat down to see the wary look in her eyes. Shutting the book, she pushed it on the other edge of the table, almost as if she didn't want it too close to her. She regarded him with a tense expression.

"Why didn't you tell me?"

He should have anticipated she would cut right to the chase. Staring at his wineglass, he finally looked up to meet her gaze. "Can I explain?" he asked in an even tone.

There was a growing anger in her eyes. "You think the fact that you're a father. A *father*," she emphasized, "would have come up somewhere in the conversation."

He shook his head. "Let me explain, *per favore*" he repeated. Taking a deep breath, he nodded. "Yes, I could—I *should* have told you about Valentina, but I am *not* a father. I am Nia's uncle." Blowing out a breath, he looked at her with a sad expression.

"It's a long story and one that I'm not fond of telling, but I owe you that." He stopped and looked away before continuing. "My sister, Angelina, was an amazing person. Light seemed to come from her. She walked into a room, and people turned to notice her. It wasn't just her beauty, but she just radiated kindness and goodness, I guess. She was eight years younger than me. Enough years that we weren't particularly close, but I always wanted to be there for her. It was difficult, though, as I was gone so much, first to university and then medical school and residencies. I lived in the States when she was a teenager, and I missed a lot. When I came home, I found her to be a little lost. She didn't know what she wanted to do with her life and was floating from job to job."

He looked at her grimly. "I rarely discuss this as well, but it's important to the story. My family has extreme wealth. My grandfather and his father before him were very smart. They invested in land and waited until it was worth millions. Our fortune grew tremendously and none of us needed to work, but my father insisted on it. My parents ensured we were educated, taught us to be good people and to help when we could. I guess that's what attracted me to become a physician; the opportunity to help people."

"More than three-and-a-half years ago, everything changed. My father became angry at Angelina's casual lifestyle and insisted she spend time helping those less fortunate so she could appreciate the blessings she had."

Alec rubbed his neck and then looked off into the distance. "She was so stubborn, but I think she even questioned what she was to do in life. She was gone for a while with a missionary group in Eastern Europe. When she came home, she was very pregnant. She told us the father was a soldier who had been killed shortly after going to war. My parents were very upset. As traditional Catholics, it was difficult for them. They tried to accept it, but Angelina felt it would be easier on them if she left. We had no idea where she went. Unfortunately, that was the night she went into labor. She was on her way to the Amalfi Coast, where we have family. Her driver pulled into a small town, nervous and worried for her. There was a small rural clinic."

He sighed and looked at her. "Italians can be very old-fashioned, especially the older medical establishment. Giving birth is as old as time, and so complications are sometimes overlooked. One ultrasound would have told them so much. They didn't have one, and neither doctor was an obstetrician. They were just doctors tending to the local community. Angelina had a problem called placenta previa."

At Meara's confused look, he explained. "It's where the placenta attaches lower in the uterus, sometimes covering the opening. Depending on the position, it can make a delivery unsafe. It can cause bleeding, low blood pressure, and other complications for a mother. In most cases, a doctor would probably have the mother deliver by Cesarean section. Since they did not know, they went ahead and tried to deliver the baby. The baby survived, but Angelina did not."

He wiped tears from his eyes. "I blame myself. I was too busy, and though I asked her if she had seen a doctor, I didn't ask many questions. It was all such a shock. I wasn't even in Rome. I was down south myself. I could have gotten to her if I had known where she was. By the time I found out she had left, she was already dead."

He smiled and wiped his eyes. "And so, there was Valentina. I named her that because it means strong one. The moment I looked at her, I could feel my sister's strength in her. I also knew she would need that strength to grow up in this world without Angelina. Without a mamma."

Looking at Meara now, he shrugged. "I am sorry about tonight. She has one picture book that has a red-haired woman in it. I think she confused that with a mamma. There's a photo of Angelina in her bedroom, and Nia knows that's her mamma."

"And so, you are a full-time father—rather, uncle to her?"

He shrugged again. "I decided it was easier to refer to me as her papa. As soon as she can really understand, she will be told the truth. My mother and father had agreed to care for her following Angelina's death, but my father soon became ill. Some would say he had a broken heart. He died only six months after Angelina, and my mother called and begged me to take Nia. My mother had lost her husband and daughter in such a short span. She was torn with grief."

"You lost both your father and sister," Meara stated softly.

He nodded, but spread out his hands. "But what was I to do? My mother couldn't even function. I had to get her help to just prod her out of bed, make her eat. It wasn't a positive environment for Nia. I brought her here. As you can see, it doesn't much look like a child's home. But I've tried to make adjustments, and then I hired nannies and assistants because my work still means a lot to me and I have commitments. And sometimes I travel and must be gone for longer periods. It's not ideal, but it is what I can give her right now."

"Alec, I'm sorry I was so angry. It was just not what I expected. But listen, you can bow out of your duties at the foundation. You don't need that on top of your work, and now that I know about Valentina, I'm convinced you have enough on your plate."

He looked at her and raised his eyebrows. Shaking his head, he frowned. "No."

With that, he stood and walked out of the room, angrier than he had been in weeks. In fact, probably at least since the last time he saw her. For once, he didn't care if she followed him.

eight

Alec left the room. Where did he go? Should she follow him? Was he coming back? Honestly, this man was so frustrating. His voice had been filled with heartache as he'd told his story. Losing a sibling and then a parent was beyond comprehension. He had been through so much. However, his mistaking her empathy as an excuse to eliminate him from the foundation was irritating. She was trying to be considerate despite the fact of how he had acted in Capri. No matter what, his niece needed him, and Meara was simply trying to give him an out regarding the foundation.

Standing, she went in the direction he had gone. He had been right about the house. As she traveled through the rooms with white sofas, striking artwork and modern furniture, she wondered how he was going to keep a small child from destroying it. She peered out the French doors into the inky night. He stood outside on a stone verandah, illuminated by a small light.

Opening a door, she stepped out into the cool night. Beautiful greenery and well-placed furniture flowed around them Below was a massive pool, covered and surrounded by lights. She thought about apologizing, but she was annoyed. He had just walked away from her rather than discuss things like a civilized human being.

Staring at him now with a frown, she was almost speechless. "No? That's all you have to say?"

He turned to give her a grim look. "You're not getting rid of me that easily by using Nia as an excuse."

"I'm not. I'm pointing out the obvious!" Meara said, frustrated. "You don't have time for this project. You should be with her. I am trying to be compassionate, Alec. It may not look like that, but I *do* have a heart."

He continued to stare off into the darkness. Finally, he took a breath. "I know you do, and I apologize. As I told you, this is hard for me to talk about. My sister died because of poor medical care. I want to change the course for other women. It's what keeps me going in my own work, and what the foundation could accomplish brings me some sense of hope. Maybe I can help some other family from ever experiencing this kind of loss. While our country has excellent health care in many places, it is not always equitable. You'll find examples of this from one end of the country to the other. That's what we need to change."

Meara's heart ached for him, and she didn't know how to respond except to explain she wasn't trying to dismiss him. "Alec," she began.

"Please understand," he interrupted roughly. "This is very important to me. The most important work I can do. When Marco told me about it, and that it was named after his *Zio* Angelo, I saw it as a sign. I look for signs of Angelina every day, and here was one hitting me in the face. I asked Marco immediately to let me come on board."

Meara reached out her hand to touch his arm, trying to show him that she understood. "Alec," she said, softer this time. "I get it. Really, I'm not trying to dissuade you."

He turned, his brown eyes glittering in the small light that was coming from the verandah. "I believe you. But that envelope in there contains papers that are designed to minimize me. Marco called me to go over them. He knew how I would respond. You intentionally wanted to make sure I had a very insignificant role."

Meara shook her head. "No, I didn't," she explained impatiently. "I needed to know that I was in charge. It was more about *my* role."

He stared at her wordlessly, and she continued. "Look, let's just tackle the elephant in the room. The last time I saw you, I heard you on the phone with a woman, your girlfriend or whoever she was. The way you spoke to her was incomprehensible. The way you treated her was even worse. You literally threw her out of your home. It was the most misogynistic moment I have had since my firing. I had to make sure that you were not seen as my boss or allowed to override my decisions."

She shivered, remembering that day in the boardroom and how diminished she had felt, as if she was nothing, just like Alec had spoken to that woman. He reached out and rubbed her upper arm. "You're cold. Let's go in the house. Obviously, we need to clear that up as well."

He led Meara back inside and gently propelled her to the kitchen to sit down. "I'm sorry I got so angry. Most of it was reliving the story. I go outside when I lose my temper. It's just a coping mechanism for me. The fresh air always calms me."

He took a deep breath. "However, I will not apologize for my behavior on the phone that night. I was alerted that Olivia, the woman I had engaged as a nanny, was in bed with my personal assistant. They were too *busy*, shall we say, to even have the baby monitor with them. Apparently, they had gone swimming earlier and left the gate to the pool open and unlocked. I had the fence constructed when Nia came to live here."

Staring at her steadily, he continued. "I have a great security team. Marco's cousin Lucca helped me in hiring the company he uses. They called me when they saw Nia going through the open gate to the pool. Fortunately, she had triggered the alarms. The ninety seconds it took for them to run down and sweep her up to safety was still too long. I finally was able to rouse Olivia out of bed. I fired both her and my assistant. I know how it sounded, but Meara, I was angrier than I have ever been in my entire life. I promise you I do not make a habit of speaking to women—or anyone—in that way. In this case, I lost it. It was like a blinding rage and a fear that I cannot explain."

Meara's mind was whirling. She was going over his words on the phone, telling the woman that someone would pack her things. She had assumed it was a lover he was throwing out. Now it was as if the pieces were all coming together. What did she do with the finished puzzle?

Meeting his eyes, she smiled in what was her first genuine smile of the day. She asked the only question that she really cared about at that moment.

"Got anything to eat?"

MEARA SAT BACK, twisting her wine glass. Though the food was excellent and she was starving, it was already churning in her stomach. Alec had re-heated a lovely dinner his chef had prepared for him. He insisted his chef always made too much, and he had evenly divided the insalata and *pasta carbonara*.

They had kept the conversation light. It was easy to talk about Kate and Marco, a little about the foundation, and nothing more about Angelina or Valentina. Alec had asked some small probing questions about her life, but she had deflected. There was no use in sharing anything else personally.

"I'm sorry, what were you saying?" Meara asked, aware that she had let her thoughts wander.

He smiled a little at her, his eyes still wary. "I was wondering if you wanted to talk about the next steps for the foundation."

She shook her head. "I need to come on board, read the reports Teresa submitted from the work you two did, and start hiring more staff. I also need a lot of time to evaluate the financials, including some appraisals and estimates that have been submitted. Then we can move ahead once we have crafted a strategic plan."

"I am just impatient to get some of this done," Alec explained. "I feel I should have started something like this myself. I let my grief cloud me."

Her heart tugged a little at the look on his face. She wanted to cover his hand with hers, but she purposely kept one in her lap and one on her wineglass. She smiled gently and tried to reassure him. "Alec, it sounds like you did what you could to take care of your family. It was more important that you ensure Valentina was cared for. Plus, this is not a one-person job. Marco was right to build a proper foundation. It needs to have structure so it can continue for years and be a thriving resource for people. This shouldn't just be a onetime project. Anyone can construct a building or buy some equipment. This is more than that."

He leaned back, smiling a little.

"Why are you looking at me like that?" she asked uncertainly.

"I was right," he said smugly.

"Right about what?"

"That you were the perfect person to take this over. That you would dive in and create something amazing."

Meara twisted her wineglass again nervously. "No pressure or anything. I'll do my best, and I am committed to this for at least a year. But I don't have a magic wand. I have a lot to learn and even more to uncover before I can create anything. I know you're eager for things to progress, but you, Marco and everyone else have to be patient. Things are only going to move ahead when I say so," she said firmly.

"I will be patient," he promised. He stood and picked up the envelope, opening it. Scanning the documents briefly, he left the room for a minute. Coming back with a pen in his hand, he started signing the papers.

She frowned a little. "Don't you want to read them?"

"I know what's in them after my conversation with Marco," he said and shrugged.

"But Alec..."

He pushed the signed papers aside and looked at her seriously. "I understand my role. I am to be an adviser only. Just so you know, I am also now an investor and board member. But I won't hold that over you. I just wanted to be a part of this financially, and I have pledged funds for it. But you should know that, so you didn't think I am keeping that a secret, too. It doesn't matter in the least. I will stay out of your way, Meara."

Why did she feel like such a heel? Outlining their respective roles in the organization was important. When he phrased it like that, she felt guilty.

"Alec, you don't need to..."

He shook his head. "I understand. Please don't bother explaining further." He stuffed the papers in the envelope and then handed it to her.

"Thank you," she whispered. Her throat felt dry. She was used to the flirty Alec, the informative tour guide Alec, charming Alec. This firm, yet calm man sitting across from her was unfamiliar.

"I guess I should be going," she muttered.

"I feel badly about your clothes. I can have new ones sent over by tomorrow."

Texting her driver to return, she played with the envelope. "That isn't necessary. I'll get these back to you when I can. At least I can go home in the cloak of darkness wearing this outfit," she said, trying to joke.

He nodded and stayed silent.

"Cosmo isn't too far away. He's been waiting," she told him, feeling awkward. Standing, she walked down the hall, hoping she was going in the right direction toward the front door.

"Meara," he said softly. She felt the sensation run down her spine at his tone. Almost scared to look at him, she turned around slowly. His gaze searched her face, as if he was trying to gauge her emotions. He put a hand around her neck, under her hair. The other brushed wisps away from her face. His hands felt warm and solid, and she wanted to close her eyes and drink in this secure feeling.

"What about us?" he asked quietly.

"There is no us," she said quickly, keeping her eyes averted.

"But there is. We can't ignore it. I know you felt the magic in our time together. And if things hadn't turned out the way they did in Capri, there would *definitely* be an us."

She swallowed hard at the memory. He kept her so off-balance. No man had ever made her feel like that. His lips moved closer to her ear. She felt a tingling as they traveled down her jawline in a whisper soft caress.

"But it happened," she said firmly. "And now, I know about Valentina."

"And?

She pulled back. His lips were so close it would take just a few millimeters to reach them. It was so tempting yet she must stay strong.

Giving him a small smile, she disengaged from his arms. "I don't do complicated."

With that, she turned and exited, walking toward the car. Cosmo got out and opened the door for her. She didn't glance back, but out of the corner of her eye she could see Alec still standing at the front door, leaning against the doorjamb, watching her. It was only then she realized she had done something she had never done in her life. She had forgotten her shoes.

nine

Meara punched the pillow and peered through the opening in the curtains. From the small amount of light she could see, the sunrise was another gorgeous one. For the last week, she had worked late into the night and went to bed exhausted, only to wake in the early morning hours. Her mind would then take her back to Alec.

Seeking to define what feelings were deep in her heart had kept her tossing and turning. How could it be a sense of loss? She didn't know him that well, for they hadn't even spent that much time together. Yet...she missed him. At night, she wondered what he was doing and with whom.

It didn't matter that he had been in touch a couple of times to inquire if she needed any more information for the foundation. Putting him off, she focused instead on learning her new role. It seemed overwhelming some days, but she had gradually made progress. She now held regular meetings with her small team to carve out tasks, learn the financials, and get an accelerated course in the Italian health care system. Leaning on the experts, she had absorbed as much as she could. She had stayed up late at night reading the reports Teresa and Alec had assembled.

Though her strategic plan was not complete, she felt it was wise to move ahead on projects in southern Italy. That would mean meeting with Alec. Her heart tumbled at the thought, but she had finally told her assistant, Nicoletta to set it up.

Today was the fateful day. Getting up, Meara went about her normal morning routine. Setting habits and routines had always helped her through the challenges in life. It was important for her to keep things in balance. Working out in the building's deluxe fitness room was first, followed by a shower, breakfast, and then selecting one of her power suits.

Standing in her closet, she fingered her new navy suit. A few days following the evening at Alec's villa, her assistant had brought in a garment bag with an insignia from a well-known designer. Nicoletta had been curious, but Meara had dismissed her to open it in private. Sure enough, there was an exact replica of her suit and blouse. She was confused, knowing that the suit was a few years old and not sold anymore, but ultimately, was pleased to have a replacement. Peering into a small, attached shopping bag, she had grinned when she saw her shoes.

Wearing that suit today was out of the question. It might send a signal that could be misinterpreted. Looking at it now, it was hard to even think of those little chocolate handprints. Yet it still brought back her feelings of betrayal thinking Alex had a wife or girlfriend and then child to boot. It was heartbreaking when he told her the tragic story. Though she felt deep compassion, it wasn't enough for her to become involved with him. For her, kids were not part of her future. Meara had drawn her life plan when she was in her twenties. Over the years, she had redrawn it on her computer, along with spreadsheets of expectations for herself. Reviewing it often gave her confidence that she was on the course she had set for herself. And while this new position wasn't exactly on the same path as her previous jobs, she had made peace with it. A slight deviation to lead a nonprofit, especially something high-profile, still fit in the square boxes she had drawn. By committing to this for a year and making significant contributions, she would carve out a new area of expertise. Acquiring this kind of medical knowledge would be helpful when she returned to the U.S. Leadership opportunities were plentiful in companies related to insurance, medical supply or drug companies.

As she chose a burgundy suit, Meara smiled, remembering the deals she had brokered wearing it. This suit was definitely one of her good luck pieces. She wore a cream-colored shell and slipped her feet into some of her highest heels. Fluffing her hair, she made herself taller by raising her shoulders and arms. There was some movie or television show where the character had done that for confidence, and it seemed to work. She had never struggled with confidence before, but this was unknown territory. Shrugging, she silently wished herself good luck. She was ready.

Arriving at her office, Meara spent just a few minutes asking questions of her new employees. They all seemed a little intimidated by her, and she liked that. Never one to befriend those who worked for her, she led by ensuring they knew who was boss.

After spending an hour answering emails and drinking two cappuccinos, she sat back and let her mind wander for a moment. She had purposely invited Marco to this meeting on the guise that they were going to have action items he should approve. They would add equipment to the hospital and current clinics in the rural areas. The construction of one new clinic and the extensive remodel of the other were complicated, but the plans were thorough. Marco really didn't need to be present, but she had assumed he would want to know what was occurring and he could act as their buffer.

Grabbing her laptop and phone, she went into the conference room. Marco's offices were upstairs, taking up most of the building except for the small area they had given to the foundation. As the foundation grew, they would look for a separate location. For now, it fit their needs.

"*Buongiorno, mia sorella,*" sang Marco's voice. He came in with a bright smile, wearing one of his usual custom-made dark Italian suits. Meara smiled at him. He appeared so much more relaxed than when she had first met him. Kate had told her he was finally comfortable in his role as CEO of Oro Industries, and it showed.

"*Buongiorno, mio fratello,*" she responded automatically. "Just don't call me that when people are around, or else the nepotism will be pretty obvious." She gave him a stern look, which made him laugh.

"Your staff will only sympathize. They all seem to be afraid of me," he said. "Nicoletta already runs as soon as she sees me. The other day she dropped her laptop." He winced. "I hope it was okay."

"I don't think it's fear. She's a little in awe of you. She told me she had read a lot of articles about you."

Marco shook his head wryly. "Just remind me to keep my famous cousin from her! God knows what we'll have to replace then."

He turned serious. "You updated me the other day on what you've been doing, but I have a question that you didn't address." At her raised eyebrows, he continued, looking at her speculatively. "Are you happy?"

"Am I happy?"

"It's a reasonable question, Meara."

She shook her head. "No one I've worked for has ever asked me that."

"Technically, you don't work for me. You work for the foundation's board. No one has ever wanted to know if you were at least comfortable in your position?"

"No."

He laughed. "Let me be the first, then."

She looked at him suspiciously. "Why?"

"Meara, this should not have to be a back and forth. It's a simple question."

She frowned. It was never supposed to be about her. This was business. "Yes, thank you, I'm happy, Marco. I'm pleased at how much I've been able to learn. I think we have hired some excellent people, and I'm excited about what we can accomplish."

Shaking his head, he smiled wider. "Katie warned me I wouldn't get much," he said, without explaining. Meara stared at him for a minute before deciding not to pursue the topic any further. Opening her laptop, she filled him in on some of the next steps.

He interrupted gently. "Shouldn't we wait for Alec to go over this schedule?"

Meara bit her lip. In her excitement to share all their work, she had almost forgotten about him. Now her heart raced a little. According to her watch, thirty minutes had gone by. When she mentioned that to Marco, he frowned. "Let me text him. There's a chance he just couldn't get away from work."

Meara went back to her laptop for a minute, opening files and getting ready to discuss more. For a few minutes, they were both silent.

Marco finally set his phone down. "He hasn't answered. I'm wondering if we should just continue."

She nodded with a strange twinge of disappointment. Getting herself all pumped up to see him had taken a lot of thought, and now she felt deflated. Squaring her shoulders, she turned her laptop toward Marco. He put on his glasses, and she went over some of the project timelines.

An hour later, the two of them still sat in the same spot. They had made a few adjustments, but overall, things were in good shape. Meara was finishing up explaining one possible delay when there was a rustle at the door. They both turned to see Nicoletta opening the door, her face flushed.

"*Mi dispiace, Signorina*, but *Il dottore* is here."

"Well, send him in," Meara said a little more sharply than she would have normally. Annoyed that Alec had missed the entire presentation, she waited.

Nicoletta looked anxious. "It's just that…"

"She's trying to tell you that I'm not alone." Alec breezed past her, smiling and holding Valentina. "I brought company."

"Mamma!"

Marco turned to look at Meara with surprise. She tried to keep her face neutral. "I'll explain later," she muttered.

Marco stared at her for a second and then recovered, springing from his chair. "Valentina, *topolina.*"

The child giggled and eagerly grabbed at Marco's legs, who picked her up and swung her around, speaking softly in Italian to her.

Alec walked toward Meara and set a backpack down on the boardroom table. "I apologize for being late. My mother was supposed to come to pick up Nia today for a few days. She called at the last minute to say she wasn't up to it." For a moment, a solemn look crossed his face.

Marco paused in playing with Valentina to glance at Alec. "Where's your nanny?"

Alec sighed and slumped into a chair. He glanced at Meara briefly. "That's a long story."

Meara's eyes narrowed. "You haven't replaced her?"

"Oh, I did. But that was three nannies ago. I can't seem to find anyone I can trust." He made a frustrated shrug. "I thought I could have some time to find a new one while my mother took her, but that's not to be."

Marco frowned. "How are you going to manage, Alec? I know your schedule is erratic and you get called out at all hours."

"I have been relying on my housekeeper, Rosalie," he admitted. "But she had to leave to take care of her mother, who fell this morning."

"I can call Katie and see if we can help. I can pitch in. It will be great practice," Marco told him sincerely.

Alec smiled. "*Grazie,* Marco. I may have to take you up on that. Though I don't want to put any stress on Kate."

"I don't either, but I will speak to her about it," Marco said sincerely as he tucked Valentina over his shoulder and let her hang down his back, giggling. "

"I brought some toys," Alec said. "They might occupy her while we meet."

Meara tried to keep her professional cool. "Actually, Alec. We were pretty much finished when you walked in. What if I just email you the information?" At his frown, Meara softened a little, so he wouldn't think she was purposely excluding him. "Wouldn't that be easier? You can look at them when you're not... busy. And call me with questions."

Marco put Valentina down and began taking out some toys and books from the backpack. She was sitting on a blanket with a small bag of snacks and chattering to herself. He stood abruptly. "Why don't I leave and let you go over it with Alec? I'm sure you can cover it more quickly with him. You won't have to explain all the medical stuff, and it's based on the reports he and Teresa worked on. He should be able to grasp everything. Thank you for updating me." Turning to Alec, he shook his hand. "Alec, I'll get back to you. I can also loan you some staff if needed. I mean it."

Marco departed, closing the door softly. Meara's heart sunk. Things had not turned out at all as she planned. She had lost control, and Alec was so close. Turning around, her gaze met his.

"Hi," he said softly.

"Hi," she squeaked. Her voice didn't even sound like herself.

"Shall we get started?" he asked with a small smirk.

Flustered, she sat back down and tried to bring up the right window on her laptop and ended up closing two. She impatiently yanked the laptop nearer to her and got settled. Taking a deep breath, she turned it so he could see the screen. She automatically started going over the figures and timeline with him. This was her comfort zone, her power. She could do this. Growing more comfortable, she was nearing the end about thirty minutes later when his phone buzzed.

"I apologize, Meara, but I have to take this."

He quickly put the phone to his ear, listened for a few minutes, and then spoke sharply into it.

Concluding the call, he looked at her uncomfortably. "A patient of mine has just arrived in the Emergency Department. This was completely unexpected. I need to go and quickly take Nia back to my villa." He ran his hands through his hair. "Rosalie's daughter, Alice, is my back-up and I can call her on the way."

Meara stared at him. "Um, I'd offer to help, but I don't really do kids."

"Yes, you told me," he said, his expression unreadable. "I completely understand." He picked up the backpack and they both glanced over at the floor. Valentina had been unusually quiet. Now they knew why. Curled up, using her stuffed turtle as a pillow, she was fast asleep. He smiled gently.

Meara's heart softened a little. She felt his frustration and made a quick decision. "She's asleep, Alec. Why don't you leave her. I can ask Nicoletta to watch her for a while. She comes from a big family. I can't remember how many younger siblings she has, but it's a lot! I'm sure she'd rather do that than the spreadsheets I asked her to get prepared for me."

He looked uncomfortable, and ran his hands through his hair. "I might be gone for some time."

Meara slowly nodded. "We can figure it out. Why don't you call Alice and have her go to your villa? Better yet, text me her contact info. I'll let her know what's going on. Nicoletta can watch Valentina until she wakes up and then my driver can take them to your villa. Then Nicoletta can come back."

"Valentina will need a car seat," he explained.

"Oh, I didn't think of that," Meara said, feeling foolish.

"I can send my driver, Mario. But that's a good idea. If Nicoletta can accompany her home, Alice will know what to do. And then Mario can bring her back. Hopefully that won't interrupt her work for too long."

Meara tried to look confident. "We'll manage. Text me his info, too. You better go. I'm worried about your patient."

He smiled a little. "*Grazie.* This is a big help. You have no idea how much I appreciate this. She may sleep for a little bit. I better go," he said quietly. Walking back to Meara, he leaned over. Her startled gaze met his, but instead of her lips, he kissed her gently on the cheek. "Give her this kiss for me," he said. "And tell her I'll be back soon. *Ciao.*"

Meara watched him depart, still in shock. She stroked her cheek for a minute like a sixteen-year-old girl in love. She stood to go get Nicoletta. It was only then she remembered her young assistant had planned on running the many errands that Meara had asked to be done. Maybe she would be back by the time Valentina woke up.

She looked at the sleeping cherub. How hard could this be?

ten

Thirty minutes later, Meara glanced at her watch. It couldn't be that Alec only left a half-hour ago. It seemed like several hours. Truth be told, Valentina was still sleeping. But Meara had been watching her the whole time, worried that if she made a move, the little girl would wake up and be frightened.

Meara continued working on her computer, but she couldn't focus with having to glance at Valentina every few seconds. She finally pushed the laptop away and her mind went back to Alec. Though he was frustrated about his current situation and lack of a caregiver, he seemed happy. Had he lain awake at night and thought about her? Doubtful. Meara grimaced, even thinking about it. She needed to move on and realize this wasn't happening between them under any circumstances.

Fabric rustled, and Meara was met with Valentina's wide-eyed gaze. She was sitting, her entire hand in her mouth, sucking gently on her fingers. They stared at each other for a minute, as if each were contemplating their next move.

Valentina apparently made a decision and pushed herself to stand. She toddled over to Meara and immediately reached her chubby arms up to be picked up. Meara winced at the wet hand on her skirt and reached down to awkwardly pick her up. The little girl snuggled into her lap, and Meara grasped her tightly, afraid she was going to drop her. Taking a deep breath, she inhaled the smells of baby shampoo and cheese crackers.

Meara's stomach grumbled a little, and she looked at her watch and realized with a sinking heart it was lunchtime. It was doubtful Alec had packed much of a lunch for Valentina since he hadn't planned on staying. Holding on to the squirming child who was chattering in Italian, Meara reached into the backpack and came across two small containers. Both were empty.

Standing and trying to adjust the little girl on her hip, she opened the boardroom door and walked out into the shared office space. Three male heads turned to stare at her. They were standing, pushing their chairs in. One was slinging his backpack over his shoulder.

"Does anyone know what a toddler likes to eat?" Meara asked, frowning a little at the growing suspicion that her new employees were trying to hide their laughter. One of them recovered slightly to offer, "My little sister eats pasta."

Meara smiled a little. "Of course, pasta. Can one of you go pick up some?"

They looked uncomfortable. "*Signorina*, we are all only working a half day today, remember? It's an Italian holiday tomorrow."

Valentina was staring up at her, her hand in her mouth again. Meara had begun to realize that was a nervous signal. The little girl took out her hand for a moment and said emphatically, "*Ho fame!*"

Meara looked at the staffers helplessly. "What does that mean?"

They all looked amused. "She's hungry."

"Hungry," Valentina repeated. She twisted in Meara's arms. "Mamma, hungry."

Meara began to walk away with Valentina now chanting, "Hungry, hungry hungreeeeee."

Hearing snickers behind her, Meara didn't dare look back. With her current temperament, she might not be able to resist firing them all.

Walking into her office, she set Valentina down on her feet. Distracted, Valentina began to explore a little. Meara bit her lip, trying to figure out what to do. If Valentina was hungry there was no way they had time to wait for Alec's driver to arrive. They would then have to travel all the way home before Alice could feed her. Valentina would likely be in full meltdown by then.

Marco said he was flying up to Milan. She took out her phone and called Kate. She could help her figure this out. It went to voicemail.

"Can I call you later?" Kate texted. "I'm treating myself to a spa day today." It was followed by emojis that described her bliss.

Meara wanted to hurl her phone down. "Spa day? Are you kidding me? When's my spa day?"

She must have spoken louder than she should have because Valentina was now standing, staring at her. Tears welled in her eyes. Meara rushed over and bent down. She still loomed over the little girl. "Nia, let's go find you something to eat!"

Valentina continued to stare, blinking through tears. Meara realized the language barrier was one more issue between them. She tried again. "Pasta?"

Valentina smiled at the magic word. "Pasta. Pasta. Pasta," she chanted.

Meara blew out a breath. Now to just find her some pasta. They'd have to go to a restaurant. Nodding, she grabbed a coat and her purse. Maybe she should also take the backpack just in case. She wasn't sure what was in it, but she had better grab it. She ran into the boardroom, scooping it up along with Valentina's toys and blanket. Stuffing everything inside the backpack, she hurried back to her office. No Valentina. Swallowing panic, she called her name. Nothing. Running out into the hallway, she called again. Suddenly, she heard a tiny giggle. She saw Valentina's small tennis shoes under a desk.

"Oh, Valentina, not funny." She picked up the little girl in one swoosh and was met with laughter. Meara had to crack a weary smile. "Okay, maybe a little funny," she acknowledged. Valentina threw her little arms around Meara's neck and held on tight.

"*BOLOGNESE*?" the waiter asked, his eyebrows raised.

Meara had walked to the closest *piazza* and had chosen a restaurant where she thought she had seen families dine. Though no other children were in sight, there must be something there for Valentina to eat.

"*Si,*" Meara nodded.

"*Ne sei sicura?*" The waiter asked her if she was certain.

As Meara wondered why he was questioning her, Valentina showed her impatience. She was sitting in the highchair that had been found for her, and suddenly began pounding her spoon on the top. "Pasta, pasta, pasta."

"*Bolognese, per favore,*" Meara repeated, trying to sound authoritative.

"And for you, *Signorina*?"

Meara had only glanced at the menu. Now with Valentina making a ruckus, she was eager to get the food and feed her before she evolved into tears.

"I'll just have some of hers," Meara said with a sigh. "Please hurry."

The waiter departed, and Meara gently lifted the spoon out of Valentina's hand, as people sitting nearby gave her annoyed glares. Valentina frowned, and Meara glanced around for something to replace it with. There were only more utensils. Digging into the backpack, she found a few of the child's books and placed them on the highchair. But rather than looking at them nicely, as she had done in the office, Valentina picked them up and dropped them over the highchair and chortled.

"Well, that wasn't cool," Meara muttered, bending to pick them up.

She placed them on the highchair again, only to have Valentina repeat the action.

"Valentina, this is getting old," Meara told her, but the child just laughed.

Meara looked inside her purse. Did she have anything to entertain a child? Wallet, lipstick, package of tissues. This was the world's most boring purse. Picking up the books yet again, she automatically placed them on the tray. Now Valentina was squirming. "Mamma," she wailed. "Pasta."

"They are coming," Meara said. Oh, why didn't she know more Italian? What was soon? *Presto*?

The books were promptly thrown over again, and Meara groaned. Leaning over to pick them up, the sunglasses fell from her head.

Picking them up, she had an idea. She put them on and then took them off. "Peek-a-boo," she said in a singsongy voice. Valentina laughed. Encouraged, Meara did it again. The game went on for a few minutes, and Meara sighed with relief.

It began to get old, though. Valentina reached out a hand, trying to grab the glasses.

"No, not my vintage designer ones. They don't make these anymore," Meara told her matter-of-factly.

Valentina stuck out her lip as if she was going to wail. Meara shook her head. "No, Valentina," she said softly. "Mine."

"Mine!" wailed Valentina.

"Well, there's a word you know," acknowledged Meara dryly.

"Mine," repeated Meara firmly, slipping them into her purse. "That's not going to happen, little girl," she said. Valentina stopped crying and sniffed. She seemed to be focused on Meara's words, so Meara began to talk again, telling her how she was going to have a delicious lunch and they would bring it soon. She talked nonstop, and Valentina was transfixed. Meara began to breathe easier again.

"*Bolognese con penne, Signorina,*" the waiter said, setting a large bowl down. "I have brought a plate for the child," he said matter-of-factly.

Meara smiled a little. "*Grazie.*" Shrugging her jacket off, she took the spoon and ladled the sauce and penne pasta on the smaller plate. She placed the plate on the tray in front of the child. Should she give her a spoon or fork? The fork seemed too big for the child's mouth, yet the spoon might work. Deciding, she turned back to hand Valentina the spoon, but the little girl had already taken matters into her own hands. Grabbing the pasta with both fists, she was now stuffing it into her mouth. The pasta was slippery and only one in about four was actually getting in her tiny mouth. Meara looked at her alarmed. She watched the pasta with its deep red sauce sliding down the child's front. *Bolognese.* Meat sauce. She hadn't even thought about that.

"I guess I should have ordered you the carbonara?" Meara told her sarcastically. Valentina, not understanding, stared wide-eyed and kept shoving.

Meara took a fork and speared a few from her own bowl. "I might as well join you," she muttered.

VALENTINA WAS APPARENTLY FULL. Squirming in the chair, she was demanding something in Italian that must mean she wanted down. Meara swallowed another few bites quickly and then turned to her. Valentina was rubbing her small hands through her hair. Sauce was now mixed in with the brown curls. One piece of penne pasta was dripping off her hair, near her ear. Her face was red and white, and her small pink overalls were covered in sauce.

Meara's eyes widened in alarm. She grabbed the backpack to look for a package of wipes. She found a toddler's cup, and when Valentina saw it, she grinned and yelled, "*tazza!*" Meara handed it to her to occupy her and continued to search. Perhaps Alec had brought a spare outfit. Reaching in, she pulled out a cotton dress. At least that was something.

Assessing the damage, she was at least grateful it had been penne and not spaghetti. She signaled to the waiter to bring the check, shrugged her jacket on, and immediately paid the bill. Now looking at Valentina, who was happily finger painting in sauce, she sat back, trying to assess what to do next. It was obvious she'd have to change her.

Standing, she grabbed her purse and the backpack and then struggled to find the latches to get the tray off the now impatient child. She unbuckled her and held her away from her as she put her on the ground to walk. Valentina refused to stand, keeping her legs bent, she put her hands up to be carried.

"Oh, not now, girlie. Not in this suit, you don't," Meara cautioned. She tried to hold her hand, but Valentina was not having it. She wailed, wanting Meara to lift her up, screaming, "Mamma!" Everyone in the restaurant was probably looking at her, thinking she was the worst mother in the world. Meara quickly slid the backpack on. She probably looked ridiculous in her power suit, wearing a backpack. Grabbing Valentina under her arms, she carried her as far from her as she could, skirting the tables. Was her phone ringing? There was no answering it now.

The waiters, grinning, pointed to the toilet sign. She ran into the restroom and frantically looked around. There was no changing table, and there was no way she was going to kneel on the restroom floor. Putting the child down, she ran over and frantically grabbed paper towels. Getting them wet, she tried to wipe Valentina's hands and face. It was almost as if the red sauce was regenerating. The more she wiped, the more it spread. The hair seemed to be a lost cause. Unbuttoning Valentina's overalls with wet fingers was more difficult, but she managed to get it off as well as her shirt. Meara's phone began ringing, but she ignored it. This was more important.

Valentina danced around at the ringtone as Meara tried putting the dress over her, but the little girl was squirming. Meara ran back to the napkin dispenser and grabbed a handful. Spreading them out on the floor, she knelt on them. Finally, she was able to successfully pull the dress over Valentina's head. The child grabbed Meara's hair to steady herself. Meara could only imagine the penne or *Bolognese* now in her hair. Hopefully, it would just blend in.

Finally, Meara straightened. Valentina was far from clean, but she looked a little better. Swiping her hands and face again with a wet paper towel, Meara took another layer of sauce off and tried to pick bits of pasta out of her hair. Valentina was singing softly, not minding Meara's attempts to clean her. Meara smiled a little at the childish song.

Sitting back on her heels, she assessed the situation. She wasn't going to even try getting her shoes back on. That would mean sitting Valentina down on the floor. Standing, Meara retrieved the backpack and then looked down at the tiny girl, who was rubbing her eyes tiredly.

Meara's phone rang for the third time. Answering it, she heard Alec's frantic voice. "Meara, is everything okay? I called you a few times. Neither Alice or Mario have heard from you."

"We just had lunch," Meara responded, trying to sound self-assured.

"Really? Thank you! I hope Nicoletta didn't mind watching her."

Meara bit her lip. She would explain that later. "I was just going to text Mario to come," she explained. "I think Valentina's tired again."

"I can't thank you enough," Alec said quietly. "I have to go, but please extend my thanks to Nicoletta as well. I will make this up to you both."

After a quick *ciao*, Meara glanced down at Valentina, who was looking up at her anxiously. Meara felt an odd tug at her heart. It seemed they had already been through a lot together. Meara might as well see this through.

Meara washed her hands and leaned forward to ensure she didn't have pasta in her own hair, she turned to go. She quickly texted Mario, who promptly responded he would be in front of her office in fifteen minutes. Meara put the backpack on again and picked the child up without thinking. Too late, she realized the little girl just wanted to snuggle. She rubbed her head and face all over Meara's suit and blouse.

Glancing down, Meara saw the red stains already appearing. "We lost another one," Meara told Valentina softly. "It's okay, though. I have others."

She carried the small girl through the *piazza* and toward her building. Just as they arrived in front, Nicoletta arrived, looking flustered.

"*Signorina*, I got everything delivered. I..." She stopped in shock, watching Meara adjusting Valentina on her hip.

"Nicoletta, I know you're supposed to be off now," Meara said matter-of-factly. "But I need a quick favor. I'll pay you myself because it's a personal favor."

She proceeded to tell the young girl what she needed. Nodding, Nicoletta ran off and returned just as Mario pulled up. He held out his arms for the child and strapped her into the car seat as if he had done it many times. Meara took a bag from Nicoletta and gave her a calm smile as if this was a regular day before getting into the vehicle and joining Valentina in the back seat.

ALEC PULLED up in front of his villa and stopped the car abruptly. His patient was still not doing well but was stabilized. He was hopeful they could buy a few more weeks before he was forced to deliver the baby. It would give the pre-term baby a fighting chance if he could just stay with his mother longer.

Rubbing his tired face, he got out of the car quickly. All the way home, he tried to figure out what he would say to Meara the next time he saw her. She had made it extremely clear that she did not want anything to do with a child and what had he done? He had dumped one on her all afternoon. Of course, she had offered, but that was because she had a kind heart. When he called, it had been good to hear that she sounded like herself. Though he could only imagine what a long afternoon it had been for her, even with her assistant taking charge. He had sealed his fate undoubtedly since she was unprepared to oversee the care of a toddler. He was sure this afternoon ruined everything.

Opening the door, only silence greeted him. Walking into the kitchen, he put his medical bag down. He still was wearing his scrubs, not wanting to waste time to change. His stomach rumbled. He had skipped lunch, and he was dying to grab something. But where were Alice and Valentina?

He went to Valentina's bedroom, and in the hallway, he finally heard soft voices. Nudging the door open more, he looked into the room and leaned on the doorjamb. Meara was stacking books and toys in multi-colored bins. Wearing yoga pants and a sweatshirt, her hair was tied in a high ponytail. Valentina was standing with her hand in her mouth, watching as Meara appeared to be sorting toys.

"So, you see, this way your toys stay organized," Meara told the confused child.

Valentina glanced his way and grinned. "Papa!" she

exclaimed. "Mamma" she pointed at the bins. "Orized," she tried repeating slowly, trying out the word.

Meara turned around, showing her surprise and then smiled slightly. "Organized," she repeated. Nervously, she adjusted the tie on her ponytail. "Hi."

He grinned at her. "Hi yourself. Uh, where's Alice?"

She shrugged. "I didn't call her." She glanced down at the little girl. "Valentina and I—well we just figured we'd stick together."

She lifted her head to stare at him, and he felt uncomfortable. "What's the matter? You're looking at me funny."

"You just look…er, different," she stammered.

He raised his eyebrows. "How?"

She shrugged as if she felt embarrassed. "I don't know," she muttered. "I guess you look like a doctor."

He laughed, entering the room. "Well, that's a relief. I'm sure my patients appreciate that I at least *look* like a doctor," he teased.

His eyes slowly appraised her. "You don't look like yourself either."

He watched the color rise in her cheeks. Glancing down, she grimaced, "You're right. I asked Nicoletta to go find me something to wear that was more suitable for hanging out with Miss Sticky Fingers."

Bending over, he picked up Valentina who had been jumping with her arms in the air. "I can only imagine," he said with a smile. He turned and looked closely at Valentina. "Um, Meara, is that pasta in her hair?"

eleven

Meara wandered around the comfortable room, admiring the overstuffed gray sofas, the built-in bookshelves lining the walls and a flat-screen television on the wall. Glancing through the books, she saw a varied selection from history to science fiction to romance. Seriously? He read romance? She smiled at the thought.

Of all the rooms, this was the warmest. The rest of the house seemed cold and bare, as if an interior designer was the only influence. There was nothing personal. This room seemed lived in, and she smiled at some photographs on a table in the corner. Picking up a frame, she looked at a photo of what she presumed was Alec's family. His father was tall and distinguished, his mother petite, but fashionable, and his sister looked like she could have been a model with abundant dark wavy hair. It must have been a happy moment for the family, evidenced by their smiles. Meara put it down, thinking about the loss Alec had endured. They had that in common. She had a similar photo of her sister and parents taken at her college graduation. It had been such a nice moment. Losing her mother was enough for her. She shivered at the thought of anything happening to Kate, especially now that they were finally closer.

Down the hall, small childish chatter still came from Valentina. Meara had explained the *Bolognese* mishap, and Alec's lips had twitched. He was trying his best not to laugh at her. She knew he wanted to, but his eyes had also held a sense of gratefulness. He had asked for a few minutes to get changed and then returned in his worn jeans and T-shirt to calmly go bathe the child.

Afterwards, he set out a prepared dinner for Valentina, who ate it dutifully. Alec explained a chef made them up for him and all he had to do was ensure she ate it. She watched him help spoon applesauce in her mouth when her uncoordinated movements didn't quite make it. It seemed as if his movements were automatic and fluid, and Valentina behaved for him. Meara almost rolled her eyes, remembering how she just plunked the food in front of the little girl. As he cleaned Valentina's face and hands, he told Meara to make herself comfortable while he put her to bed.

Meara thumbed through the large selection of magazines and journals on a table. He was right about reading a wide variety of stuff. She saw what appeared to be a stack of resumes. Picking one up, she scanned it. "Well, you won't do," she muttered, frowning.

"Who won't do?" Alec asked from behind her.

Meara jumped and turned around, feeling guilty. "Uh, sorry. I didn't mean to snoop." She held up the paper. "Are these prospective nannies?"

He nodded. "I haven't been able to get to them yet. My secretary printed them out from the agency."

"May I?" Meara pointed at the stack. "I've hired hundreds of people."

"Go for it," he said nonchalantly. "You should be able to read them. I asked for resumes in English because I wanted to know their proficiency of the language. I want Nia to grow up speaking Italian and English. Bring them into the kitchen while I heat up dinner."

"I wasn't going to stay…"

He rubbed his neck tiredly. When he looked at her, his eyes were sincere. "Please stay for dinner, Meara. I owe you that, at the very least."

The truth was, she wanted to stay. Nodding, she followed him, clutching the resumes. Everything within her soul screamed to get her things and go home. Why was there something so soothing about Alec? After spending the last few hours out of her comfort zone, she felt like she craved that. It was an unsettling feeling, and she pushed it aside.

He was getting things out of the refrigerator, and she sat down at the table in the kitchen's nook. Accepting a glass of crisp Pinot Grigio, she watched him take out and uncover the meals the chef had left.

"So, does the chef prepare all your meals?"

He took a sip of wine. "*Si*. That makes me sound lazy, but honestly, I'm a terrible cook. If I didn't have him, Nia would starve. So would I, for that matter." He arranged some cheese, meat, and crackers on a plate.

Meara smiled. "Just so long as you don't ask me to cook, either. I'm terrible at it."

He grinned. "That's a promise." Pulling out a chair, he placed the plate on the table. "We'll have a little *aperitivo* while the lasagna heats," he said. He leaned back, staring at her, his face amused, despite his tired lines.

"What?"

"I can't get used to this new Meara." He pointed at the sweatshirt with "Italia" blazoned on it. "I take it these were some impulse buys."

Meara glanced down and grimaced. "I should have given Nicoletta more parameters. I look silly. I don't even know where she got these shoes," she said, looking down at the flat, unfashionable pair.

"You look charming," he said, his gaze locking with hers. She finally looked away, swallowing hard, feeling her heart thud.

"Be honest. Did Nia ruin another suit?"

Meara shrugged. "It's fine. It was an old one."

"I'll replace it," he said promptly.

Embarrassed, she shook her head. "Please, no, Alec. I probably wouldn't wear it that much longer anyway," she lied. "And by the way, how did you find the exact replica of my other suit? I know that designer no longer makes it."

He grinned. "I have ways."

"Well, never mind about this one," she rushed to reassure him. "It's a good excuse to go shopping."

"Speaking of shopping," he said, as he grabbed a cracker. "Where did all the organizational bins come from? I don't remember owning those."

She ignored his smirk and selected a piece of cheese. "I hope you don't mind. I saw a store on the way home. I asked Mario to stop. Valentina was asleep, so it seemed like a good opportunity."

"To teach her organizational skills?" he inquired and then laughed.

"I know. Don't say it. I'm ridiculous! I just didn't know what to do with her. And I saw the other night that...well, you could use some help."

He laid a hand over hers. "Meara, I'm not laughing *at* you. Her room looks very...tidy," he finished with a smile. "Who am I to complain? I am so grateful for what you did this afternoon. Truly. I wasn't expecting you to take care of her all afternoon. I really thought you would hand her off to Nicoletta and then to Alice."

"It just sort of unfolded the way it did. It wasn't that big of a deal," she muttered, trying to withdraw her hand.

He stubbornly kept his hand where it was. "It is to me," he said quietly. "Especially knowing that you don't do children."

She frowned. "It's not like I hate kids or am some kind of monster," she told him hesitantly. "I just don't know what to do with them. I'd rather face a boardroom full of angry shareholders than one small child. I'm completely out of my depth. Think *Bolognese*. That's me every single second with a kid."

He laughed. "You fed her a nourishing lunch. How about just thinking about that?"

She shook her head. "I've always felt this way. It always came so easily to Katie."

"Some people are more natural." He shrugged. "I am comfortable around kids, only because I grew up with what seemed like hundreds of small cousins." He looked off into the distance. "That doesn't mean I was prepared to take a child on now at this point in my life."

Meara felt a pang of empathy. She gave him a sympathetic smile. "I'm sorry, Alec. I never thought about what this means for you and your life. It must have been an adjustment."

He shrugged. "What do you Americans say? 'You have to play the cards you're dealt.' I guess I never understood that phrase until now. But I owed it to my sister and then to Valentina. And truth be told, as tough and frustrating as it's been, I've never regretted it."

Meara nibbled on a cracker now. She wasn't sure what to say. She picked up the resumes for something to do. "I'd love to go through these for you. I'm great at hiring."

He stared at her. "I imagine there isn't much you aren't great at."

"What does that mean?

He shrugged again. "I don't know. You seem able to take on most things. Look how you handled today. Meanwhile, I'm failing to get it all done. I'm leaving Valentina with this person and that person. It's not the ideal situation."

"Alec, your job is so important! Most people couldn't handle that and be a single parent as well."

He winced. "Single parent. I never thought of myself that way, but I guess I am." He leaned back and stared at her seriously. "Can I ask you something?"

She nodded, taking a sip of wine for bravery.

"Did you hear much about me before you met me?"

"About you being a doctor or your, er...private life?" she asked, trying to appear nonchalant.

"The latter," he said succinctly.

"Well, it's not like I was gossiping about you or anything. But yeah, Teresa or someone mentioned you were a..."

His lips twitched, watching her discomfort. "I don't think I've ever seen you struggle to finish a sentence. It's okay, you will not insult me."

"Player," she blurted.

He nodded, his gaze holding hers. "And there it is."

The oven timer beeped at that moment, and Meara tore her eyes away. "I guess the lasagna is done. Let me help you set the table." She moved the resumes over to the island and he directed her where to find utensils and napkins. He tossed a salad and dished up the lasagna. Soon, they were back at the table and began to eat.

She longed to continue their conversation. Abruptly, she put her fork down. "Were you?"

He swallowed his bite before answering. "I could ask you to clarify, but I won't. I figured we would end up back here." Twisting his wineglass, he stared at her. "No, I wasn't."

She looked at him speculatively but was unsure how to respond. Picking up her fork, she began eating again.

"I *am* being honest," he said emphatically. "Did I take various women out? Admittedly, I did. I imagine you must have dated a lot, too."

She narrowed her eyes. "Why would you think that? Well,

anyway, I don't even know why we're talking about this. We are business associates."

He smiled. "Business associates. Yes, that's right. Well, business associate, I have a proposal for you. Can we at least be friends, too? I'd like that, Meara." He held up his hand. "And before you say yes—which I hope you will—let me say those days are over. But they were over way before Valentina."

He pushed his plate away, his eyes intense. "I want to explain something to you."

She looked uncomfortable. "It's really none of my business."

"But it is," he said softly. "Especially if we are friends. I have heard over the years that there are rumors about my exploits, if you will. They have been greatly exaggerated. You see, I hardly dated at university or medical school. It was all-encompassing for me. A series of high-profile events with different women when I finally had the time to date probably started rumors. But player? Hardly. You see, most of my life I have been a nerd. Capital N."

"I can't believe that," she said, raising her eyebrows and smiling a little.

"I carried a briefcase in school," he admitted quietly.

The laughter bubbled up before she could stop it, and he joined her. She dabbed at the corners of her eyes. "Oh my God, Alec, sometimes I think we are so alike." Meara looked away. She hadn't meant to say that.

"Were you a nerd too?"

"Well, not quite. No capital N. I just studied all the time. Then when I wasn't studying, I was playing sports or volunteering for a club or doing God knows what I thought would look good on a college application."

"Why?"

She grimaced. "I had this foolish idea that I had to have as many extracurriculars as possible to get a scholarship. I had a list of very expensive universities, and I knew there was no way I could go without a scholarship. You're looking at the captain of the debate team, basketball player, student body treasurer. You name it, I did it."

"That sounds like you were very social," he said, shaking his head. "I didn't have many friends. My family moved from Rome down to the Amalfi Coast when I was young. My father got this sudden idea he wanted to live close to my uncle, and my mother agreed. You might remember, my uncle was the one who treated Kate when she broke her ankle." At Meara's nod, he continued. "That's how I met Marco. Then Stefano and I competed in a lot of academic events. But I was extremely shy, and all I knew how to do was study."

"It's interesting how your childhood influences you as an adult," Meara remarked thoughtfully. "But seems like that social part comes easily to you now."

His eyes widened. "Really? Half the time I feel like an imposter."

She rolled her eyes. "Women practically drop at your feet. Did you see my assistant today? She nearly swooned."

"To be honest, I didn't notice anyone but you," he said softly.

Meara's throat tightened, and her heart skipped a beat. He probably didn't mean it the way she was taking it. Changing the subject seemed to be her best choice. "Let's clean this up and go select a nanny," she suggested.

"Sure, but one thing first. You haven't answered my question." He stared at her, his eyes glinting. "Friends?"

"Friends," she agreed quietly, knowing deep in her heart she might want more.

ALEC SMILED as Meara sat on the floor, making piles. She had the pen in her mouth, and every so often, she would take it out and scribble something on a paper, mutter incoherently, and then shake her head.

He had been encouraged a little during and after dinner. He had opened up to her a little, hoping to hear more about her own life. Though she had talked about herself in high school, it was clear there was much more. His scientific mind wanted to figure her out, but his heart was really driving his interest. He had thrown out the promise of friendship, but he wanted more.

He ran his hand through his hair. He was being unfair. She had made it plain that kids were not part of who she was. He understood and accepted that. There had been many women he had seen over the years in his line of work who told him in no uncertain terms they did not want to become mothers.

However, the thought that he and Meara could only be business associates seemed ludicrous to him. He tried to ignore his internal warning bell. Pushing her to becoming involved wouldn't end well. Still, it was almost as if he couldn't help it. He smiled a little at his own musings. Something told him Meara Malone couldn't be pushed into anything unless she wanted to be.

She was staring inquiringly at him now. "*Mi dispiace.*" He inclined his head in apology. "What did you say?"

"I said you're going to have to interview these women," she said. "Who is going to care for Valentina until then?"

"My mother called me this afternoon. She regretted her decision not to pick her up today, and she has agreed to take her for a few days until I get things sorted out."

Meara frowned a little, looking uncomfortable. "Alec, I don't mean this to sound...well nosy, I guess. But is your mother capable of looking after Valentina? She takes a lot of energy."

He looked at her seriously, knowing she was asking sincerely. "Yes, I believe my mother is in a better place. And she has a good deal of help. Valentina will be fine. And if my housekeeper Rosalie was here, things would have been alright until I found a nanny. Rosalie is a sweetheart and loves Valentina dearly. Only she is also the primary caregiver for her own mother. Alice is a good back-up, but she's only a teenager. She has her studies."

Meara nodded absentmindedly, looking at the stacks before her. She picked up three sheets of paper. "So, here are the viable ones. The rest are clearly not qualified." She scoffed.

"Out of that entire stack? You came up with only three?" he asked, astonished.

"Yes. These three."

"But what about…?"

She interrupted. "Alec, you said you trusted me. I'm sorry, but you are not leaving Valentina with someone who…" She picked up a paper and waved it. "Lists one of her qualifications as humorous. Humorous? That's not even a qualification unless she's going to become a stand-up comedian."

Alec bit back his smile. He walked over and crouched down, casually putting a hand on her shoulder. He purposely picked up one on the stack that was clearly labeled *No*.

"What about her?"

"Puleeeze," she said, rolling her eyes. "She put her photo on the resume. Look at that cleavage! Is she taking care of a small child or is she going to take care of…"

"Me?" he filled in, his eyebrows raised.

His eyes were inches away from hers. In this light, her green eyes were dark, and they stared back at him determinedly. He could lean in and kiss her. They were so close. Remembering his pledge, he pulled back, took his hand away, and stood. Smiling down at her, he thanked her. "I trust your opinion. I can arrange for interviews."

"I think I should help with interviews. I've hired so many people over the years that I know all the tricks."

"If you have time," he responded, trying again not to smile. Meara may not want to be involved with him and Valentina, but she definitely cared. He could tell by the way she was still frowning at the resumes she had chosen.

"I'll make time," she said matter-of-factly. "This is too important. In fact, give me the agency's number, and I'll schedule them tomorrow afternoon."

"Tomorrow is an Italian holiday," he said. "It will have to be the day after."

Meara nodded, gathering the papers. "That's right. Okay, I'll do it then."

Alec helped her to her feet. He dropped his hands so he wouldn't be tempted to pull her close. It would feel so wonderful to hug her right now. Willing himself to not ruin this small truce they had, he smiled at her.

"Thank you," he said simply. "For everything." On impulse, he said, "How about I show you some more of Rome tomorrow as a small gesture of my appreciation?"

"I need to work," Meara said.

"No one will be working tomorrow. Why not go out and see a little more of our beautiful city?"

"Well..."

"I'll tell you what," he interrupted. "We'll compromise. My mother will be here in the morning. I will get them on their way, and then I will pick you up around eleven. We'll see some sights and have a late lunch. Wear some good walking shoes. Tomorrow the weather is supposed to be clear, but cold. We'll cover a lot of ground."

"Walking shoes?" Meara asked incredulously.

"Walking shoes. You must have some."

"We have been over this, Alec. I have running shoes, the shoes I work out in. But I'll not be seen all over Rome in them."

"We'll be on cobblestones most of the time. So wear something that is comfortable," he suggested firmly.

She rolled her eyes but shrugged into her coat, flipping her hair out. He watched her, longing to touch it. Thankfully, she stepped away before he did.

"My driver is here. I'll see you tomorrow," she said.

He bent and gave her a small kiss on each cheek and was amused at the darkening of her eyes. She clearly thought she was going to kiss her on the lips.

"*Domani,*" he said softly. "Tomorrow."

He opened the door, and she walked through, only to stop and glance behind her. "Alec, are you sure?"

It almost seemed as if the question held more meaning than his decision to spend the day with her.

"I am certain," he told her quietly. And he meant it.

twelve

Meara waited in the foyer of her apartment for Alec. She already told the concierge to let him come up. Rubbing her palms on her jeans, she tossed her long, wavy hair absent-mindedly. Straightening her black cashmere sweater, she tried to fend off her nerves. Alec had been right, and it was a gorgeous day. Spending the morning trying to work, she might as well have given up. Her thoughts constantly kept going back to him. Why in the world had she agreed to spend the day with him? Secretly, she knew why. He was fun and engaging, with a sense of solidness about him. She couldn't describe the calmness she felt when near him.

But spending more time around him was a bad idea. He was a package deal, and that couldn't change. She would never try to come between him and Valentina. Shaking away her doubts, she dismissed them. Why shouldn't she spend another fun day in Rome with him? There was still so much to see.

Opening the door to Alec's gentle knock, she was greeted by his bright white smile. His dimples were in full force, and his abundant hair was tousled. He wore dark jeans and an oatmeal-colored sweater covered by a chocolate brown leather jacket.

When he leaned in to give her a kiss on her cheeks, she automatically put her hand on his shoulder and immediately wanted to run her hands all over it. The leather was buttery soft.

"*Ciao*, Meara. You are ready?" he asked. Smiling, he glanced at her feet and back at her. She shrugged at her booties. "They are the lowest heels I have. I am not wearing those shoes Nicoletta bought me."

He took his arm from around his back. "Good thing I brought you these," he said, flashing a wide smile.

Backing up a step, she looked at the plain gold shoebox as if it contained a snake.

"Go ahead and open it," he prodded.

Swallowing hard, she took the lid off and pulled the tissue paper back. She had expected to see tennis shoes after all his teasing, but nestled in the box was an exquisite pair of low-heeled black leather shoes. Gently picking one up, she looked at him. "You bought these for me?"

He arched an eyebrow. "Are they hideous?"

Shaking her head, she smiled. "I'm just surprised. I thought it would be tennis shoes."

He laughed. "I pick my battles, Meara. These are made by an Italian designer, and they are supposed to be comfortable, yet fashionable. But I must tell you I am not an expert in women's fashion."

Meara ran her hands over the leather. "They're very soft and though the heel is lower than I usually wear, they are pretty," she admitted. Looking at him, she saw the sincerity and kindness in his eyes. She reached up and gave him a kiss on the cheek. "Thank you. Let me put these on."

Donning them, she walked a few steps, and it was like walking on air. Smiling, she shook her head at him. "How did you know my size?"

His answer was a knowing smile.

"I'M A LITTLE IN AWE," Meara said, walking out of St. Peter's Basilica. "I'm not even sure what I just saw. It's all so overwhelming." She gave him a slight smile, her eyes wide. "I guess this is where I tell you art history was not my best subject either."

They had started the day by walking through the vast Vatican Museum. Though they were technically supposed to be part of a tour, Alec described the art in her ear most of the time, including his usual graphic descriptions of the artists themselves. The artistry and gold was everywhere—on the walls, the ceiling, and even in the form of statues. Meara's head swiveled so much, her neck began to ache. Even though Alec was talking quietly, she wanted to laugh at the number of people who leaned in, wanting to hear what he had to say and not the tour guide.

Seeing the guide frown, she was relieved when eventually they were able to escape quietly from the group and run up the stairs to the Sistine Chapel. There, they walked the circumference of the room before going to sit on one of the benches on the side, staring up in silence for a long time. Absorbing it all was almost too much. By mutual agreement, they departed and went over to St. Peter's. As they walked in, they both stopped to stare at Michelangelo's *Madonna della Pietà*.

"I never tire of looking at this," Alec said softly, as they stared at the statue of the Virgin Mary holding Jesus' lifeless body. "Even if one isn't religious, Michelangelo captured a mother's love. I think about this all the time. Do you know he was only twenty-two when he made it? It's one of his first works and the only one he signed." Alec pointed out the signature Michelangelo Buonarroti on Mary's sash. "Reportedly, he snuck in one night and signed it."

His hand slipped into hers, and the familiar warmth traveled through her body. She couldn't resist squeezing his hand speechless at the beauty. They eventually began strolling slowly past altars and chapels until they approached the papal altar. Once again, Meara tried to absorb all the beauty from the statues, stained glass and artistry. Now outside, she felt a little drained.

"Lunch," Alec suggested, as always reading her mind.

She raised her eyebrows and pointed to the dome. "You aren't going to make me climb all the way up there in my new shoes?"

He laughed, linking an arm through hers. "I think you would agree with me that would definitely require trainers. There are a lot of stairs! But it is worth it."

She smiled. "Let me ease in today with these. I can't believe all we've already seen."

"There is so much more to explore. We didn't go down to the grottos. But there are other places I want to show you today, so let's continue."

As they walked, suddenly Alec pulled her over toward the colonnade, smiling at her. "Count how many rows of Bernini columns there are."

Meara walked through the massive columns and quizzically glanced at him. "I see four. Is this some kind of trick question?"

He grasped her hand and led her back toward the center of the square. Looking down, she saw a gray circle that said *Centro del Colonnato*.

He told her to stand on it and gently gripped her by the shoulders to face her back toward the columns. "Now, how many do you see?" he inquired.

Meara squinted and grinned. "One," she said. "An optical illusion, right?" From where she stood, there was one row of columns.

Alec nodded approvingly. "Bernini was said to create the colonnade to welcome the faithful and the non-faithful with open arms and reunite them to their faith. And while he did that, I think he wanted to have a little fun."

"There's just so much to see even in this square," she

commented, pointing to the ancient Egyptian obelisk at the center, the twin fountains on either side.

"The Basilica is said to be built on where St. Peter was killed and buried by Emperor Nero. I'll tell you about that and the obelisk over lunch. It was moved here and is the oldest thing in the *piazza*."

They walked to a nearby restaurant. "I hope you don't mind a casual lunch. This is my favorite pizza," he said excitedly, opening the door. Meara walked the length of the counter, admiring the various pizzas cut into squares. "It looks delicious," she agreed, and her stomach rumbled in anticipation.

Alec ordered three pieces, telling her Roman pizza was thicker and crispier than the Neapolitan pizza she probably had when visiting Kate. They shared a Pizza Bianca, a white pizza with rosemary, garlic and olive oil; a margherita with ripe tomatoes and mounds of buffalo mozzarella; and a *diavola* with spicy salami. Sitting outside at a small table, they slowly demolished all three, with Meara declaring she couldn't pick a winner.

"Always the Pizza Bianca for me," Alec said with a smile.

Meara took a sip of her lemonade, her face thoughtful. "Alec, why do you frequently go to see the Pietà?"

He looked off into the distance. "Pietà means pity or compassion. I guess it reminds me of the enormity of my job. The responsibility of helping a mother meet her baby. Sometimes it is easy to get caught up in the science of it, and I never want to be that kind of doctor." He turned back to meet her gaze, his brown eyes thoughtful. "I want to always remember why I'm here."

Meara's heart gave a somersault. There were no words she could possibly think of to respond properly. Desperately wanting to reach over and kiss him, she forced herself to physically push away from the table and stand. "Thank you for telling me," she finally managed to say.

She felt a strange disappointment that the poignant moment had passed. It should have been when she admitted to him that she thought he was one of the kindest, conscientious people she had ever come across. But she needed to keep this impersonal. He was her tour guide for the day.

He was looking at her with an unreadable expression, but finally gave her a half-hearted smile. "How about we grab a taxi and head over to the Pantheon?" Once there, their tour was short, but Alec entertained her with random stories and facts. Meara laughed and shook her head at some of the gorier stories. "You're making this up!'

"I am not!" he grinned. "I told you that Rome is filled with such stories." He glanced up at the oculus, with the sun coming in. "I'll have to bring you back in April," he murmured.

At Meara's confused look, he pointed to the arch. "For just a few days in April and September, the light coming through the oculus matches the arch above the door. It's a phenomenon."

Meara drew her eyebrows together. Once again he was making future plans that wouldn't be reality. Rather than point it out, she let it slide. They walked quietly through the cobblestone streets, taking in the bustle of the busy crowds. Every so often, Alec pulled her into yet another beautiful church to show her more exquisite artwork or Bernini statues. She laughed with him about the number of churches per square foot in Rome. Even if one lived there forever, it would be impossible to see them all.

After a time, they came to the Spanish Steps, where he insisted they take photos. Alec was intent on asking someone to take a photo of them together, rather than a selfie. He put his arm around her and whispered in her ear, "Once again, we will come back in the spring. The steps will be filled with flowers. It's amazing to see, and I want to see it with you, Meara." Meara was looking into the camera when he told her that, just in time for the photo to capture her regretful smile.

They wandered through the streets and more secret passageways until they finally agreed they were comfortably tired. Taking a taxi back to his car, they drove quickly to her apartment. Disappointment hit now that the day was over. It had been glorious. As he helped her out of his car, she turned to thank him for the day, but he waved her off. "We aren't done yet. I'll pick you up again tonight at eight. I owe you dinner from the last time we went on a Roman adventure."

Meara opened her mouth to refuse but closed it just as abruptly. Why not? All she would do was sit in her apartment alone. She might as well. The words were out before she could take them back. "I'll see you tonight, Alec."

thirteen

Meara shoved her laptop away from her and leaned back in her chair. Her one coping mechanism had always been working. No matter what was happening in her life, she would immerse herself in her job. Men problems, family issues and even grief over the loss of her mother somehow would fade away while she concentrated on work. Her safe world was always work, no matter where or who she worked for.

These days work wasn't fulfilling her the same way. She longed to go back out and explore more of the sights, sounds, smells and tastes of Rome. Definitely the tastes, remembering all she and Alec had consumed. After he picked her up for dinner, they went to the Monti neighborhood first for an aperitivo in a well-known craft brewpub. It was fun to see one. She had begun to think the country only consumed wine. Meara had told him more about her father's famous Irish pub. Of course, this Italian pub didn't resemble it in the slightest, but it was fun to sip a frothy unique beer and reminisce about her time bartending during summers in college.

They had wandered the streets after that, poking their heads into shops and art galleries that were still open before finally arriving at a restaurant where Alec had made a reservation. They had shared a variety of small plates, from steak tartare to fried eggplant and cod filets cooked with apricots and wine. Meara couldn't resist ordering some more *supplì*.

Trying now to focus on her laptop screen, she again became frustrated with herself for her lack of concentration. Part of her wanted to believe her trouble focusing was because she had veered her career away from all she had known. Leading a powerful high-tech company was immensely different from building a foundation that was going to impact people's lives.

She questioned if that was the true cause. Her new job came with the same responsibilities in a way: project management, financial stewardship, and accountability to a board. And it wasn't as if she hadn't been productive. In just a few weeks, she had a firm handle on the financial perspectives, hired a procurement director for medical equipment as well as a liaison with the Italian government who could help cut through red tape. Meara made a few calls and even poached someone from another nonprofit. She felt a little guilty, but she needed expertise in creating a solid structure that meant the foundation would live on. She had also contracted with financial and legal experts to work on bylaws and board structure. Smiling, she realized she had accomplished a great deal, even if her mind was elsewhere half the time.

Today, the agency was finally ready to have her interview the nannies for Valentina. Alec was on his way over, and they were to interview the three candidates who had passed Meara's preliminary approval.

She frowned when her building landlord's number appeared on her phone. A blast of Italian burst from the phone when she answered it.

"Carlo, *Inglese per favore*," Meara said, trying to remind him she was still learning his language.

"*Signorina*," he said, his voice frantic. "There is a water leak in your flat. We were fixing the plumbing in another flat, and the plumber did not know that it caused a pipe to burst in yours." He switched to Italian, and Meara winced, recognizing a few choice words of profanity.

"Carlo, Carlo, *Inglese, per favore*. Did it damage my apartment? Oh God, my clothes. Did it damage my clothes? Or worse, my shoes?"

"No *signorina*, no," he said. "It did not seep into the bedroom and closet area, but the living room and the kitchen are badly damaged. We will need to get in and make repairs as soon as possible. The carpets are soaking, the electrical needs to be addressed. There is a lot. You understand?"

Meara ran her hand through her hair. "Okay, what does that mean for me? Is there another place I can move while you do that?"

"No, *signorina*, I am sorry. There is nothing else currently in the building. We can put you up in a hotel."

"How long will it take to repair?"

She heard him chuckle. "Sometimes in Italy, we do not move too fast. *Sì*? You understand? It is hard to say. At least a month. Our contractors sometimes work on their own schedule. However, if you can give me a week to ten days, another apartment will be available. It isn't as large as yours," he hedged. "Once the tenant moves out, we will have it cleaned and ready if you are agreeable."

Meara's mind raced. She would try a hotel first before calling Kate. It was important to give her sister and Marco time alone.

"That would be just fine. I don't care about size. A week is fine. Let me make some calls, and I will let you know what I'm going to do," Meara told him firmly before hanging up.

An hour later, Meara sat back in frustration. An extensive search online found most hotels in Central Rome already booked. When she called a prominent hotel to inquire what was happening, they told her there was a large international tech conference in the city. The irony wasn't lost on her.

Now calling Kate, Meara bit her nail feeling guilty that she hadn't been in touch more with her sister lately. In reality, it was because she was worried Kate would ask about Alec. Her sister was great at reading people, and Kate would be able to detect even the slightest interest in Alec.

"Hey, stranger," Kate answered. "You never call, you never write."

"Oh, stuff it," Meara said. "Honestly, You're embracing this Italian mamma role too much. You're even starting with the guilt."

Kate laughed. "I'm trying! What's up? How are you? And what have you been doing?"

Meara smiled for a minute, thinking about her day in Rome with Alec. "Oh, having adventures," she said breezily.

"What? You mean adventures within your computer or phone?" Kate teased. "I didn't even know you knew that word."

"I know the word," Meara said defensively. "And yes, adventures. I am learning to...well, let's just say I'm learning to sometimes relax."

"Please put my real sister on the line!"

"Oh stop! People can change," Meara said defensively.

Kate's tone softened. "That's great news. I want to hear all about it."

Meara heard something catch in Kate's voice, and her eyebrows raised. "Katie, you don't sound like yourself. What's going on?"

Kate sighed. "I was going to come have lunch with you soon to talk. I don't know, Meara. It's been really hard for Marco and me to spend a lot of time together. He's like a madman running around trying to close deals and get things done before the baby comes. He's acting like he has to get everything out of the way so he can be with me and the baby for the first few months. But I need him now. I hate to complain, but I feel so needy. I don't know what's wrong with me! And then when his schedule does allow him to be around, it turns out I've got meetings of my own. Juggling the time change between here and the U.S. is difficult. I know I need to hire a social media team here, but I like the people I hired in San Francisco."

Meara felt guilty. She had been so wrapped up in her own world she had paid little attention to Kate. "I can help you find new staff, or you can get Marco to give them a bonus to relocate to Italy," Meara said and laughed.

"This is my company, not Marco's," Kate reminded her firmly. "But you're right. I need to figure that part out. Anyway, I was just having a few minutes of self-pity. I'm sorry. But the good news is I finally admitted to Marco how I was feeling. I didn't want to pressure him, but he understood, and we are compromising. He's bringing some work home, but we're going to spend all next week together. We're going to start choosing things for the nursery."

"You haven't done that yet?"

"Well, no. I wanted Marco to be a part of it, and we've just been two ships passing in the night. He's thrilled you're handling the foundation stuff. At least that's off his plate. But now I'm so excited to have him home for seven whole days. He's promised nothing will get in the way of us spending some quality time together."

Meara bit her lip indecisively. All she had to do was tell her sister about the apartment, and she would immediately invite Meara to stay with them. Certainly, the villa was big enough for all of them, but she would feel like an interloper. Marco was always so polite. There was no doubt he would insist she join them in the evening hours. Poor Kate, she would be happy to see her sister, but would also feel guilty about wishing Meara was anyplace *but* there. There was only so much time Marco and Kate had together before their life would change forever. The decision was made. She would find a hotel in the outskirts of the city center rather than disrupt them.

"Katie, I am sure you'll feel better after a few days with Marco. When you come up for air, let's have lunch or dinner or whatever, and I promise to catch you up."

"You don't mind?" Kate asked anxiously. "I want to see you, but I feel like my time with Marco is important right now."

"Sure, throw me over for your handsome, sexy husband!"

"Well, if you put it like that, then okay," Kate quipped. "Um, speaking of sexy, have you seen much of Dr. Amato?"

Meara rolled her eyes. "Katie, it's a little weird that you just called your doctor sexy. I can definitely tell Marco's not home."

Kate laughed. "Oh, it's nothing I haven't said to him. But believe me, Marco's feeling pretty secure these days. It must be the hormones. Every time he walks through the door, I practically..."

"Stop right there, please!" Meara cried. "Way too much information."

"Okay, okay. But back to Doctor..."

"You are tenacious. I swear you should have been some kind of reporter or something," Meara grumbled. "Okay, just between us, though. If you must know, we spent the day together yesterday. He showed me Rome. His Rome. It was amazing." Meara tried to keep her voice level, but by the silence, she knew Kate was already suspicious.

"Are you guys dating?"

"Katie, we're not in high school. No, we're not dating! We agreed friendship was the course for us right now."

"Because of Valentina?"

"She's..." Meara trailed off. She tried again. "Alec and I just decided friends were better right now."

"With benefits?"

"Oh my God, Katie, your mind today! I can tell you're missing Marco! No benefits. Just friends. I'm helping him find a nanny. He's helping me fall in love with Rome. Only Rome! And soon we're going to travel down south to evaluate some of the foundation work. Then I probably won't see that much of him because his role in that one project will be almost done."

"Uh huh," Kate said, clearly skeptical. "He's still on the board. And he has other ideas he's mentioned to Marco."

"Well, he hasn't told me those ideas. I'll ask him. But we are simply business acquaintances who have become friends," Meara said firmly.

"Sounds very safe," Kate remarked.

"What do you mean?"

"You always like things safe, Meara. You've put him in a box, and that's where he needs to stay so you won't have to deal with anything that might make you uncomfortable."

"In the last few weeks, did you get your doctorate or something? Are you through analyzing me?" Meara asked dryly.

"Oh no, I have lots of material," Kate said and laughed. "Okay, I'm sorry if I went too far. We can talk more in person. I just want to say one thing, and then I'll stop."

"One thing," Meara reluctantly agreed.

"Can you just this once go for it? He's a handsome, sexy, successful doctor, and I'm sure he's crazy about you."

"Do you know something? Did he say something to Marco?"

Kate giggled. "Talk about high school! No, he hasn't said a word. I just meant he'd be a fool not to be bowled over by you. So go for it. If nothing else, have some fun. Be with someone who's human and nice and not like those corporate robots you're used to."

"But Katie, he has a kid. She's technically his niece, but now, well, she's his. Which, by the way, you didn't answer my texts about that surprise. Why didn't you tell me? All this time and not a word from you!"

"I know," Kate acknowledged. "I should have. But then I figured you would pull back immediately if you knew. I wanted you to get to know him a little. And no, I'm not telling you to be someone you're not. But just live a little, Meara. If he makes you laugh and makes you happy—calculate the risk and return. Isn't that what you do in business?"

"I've taught you too well," Meara muttered.

"Promise me you'll think about it," Kate appealed. "But for once, just don't think too much."

"MEARA, you're being unreasonable. I agree, the first one won't do. But the other two were fine," Alec argued, looking at Meara's tight face.

She shook her head. "Are you kidding me? The second one was so distracted by you, she wouldn't even remember to take care of Valentina." Meara took an indignant breath. "And the last one? Two minutes into the interview, I was looking for the eject button."

"They all have great references," he reminded her, his lips twitching.

Meara shook her head. "You promised me that I could choose, and my vote is no."

He stood and took his suit jacket off, folding up the sleeves of his white shirt. He had purposely dressed up today. Feeling like he was a teenager, he wanted Meara to see a different side of him. It would be nice for her to see that he also fit into her corporate world. She only saw him in scrubs most of the time or wearing worn out jeans and baby-proof clothes. He almost winced at his old insecurities coming out. This woman twisted him up. He ran his hands through his thick hair.

Looking at her steadily, he tried to make her understand. "Meara, I *need* a nanny. I spoke to my mother last night and she's willing to have her for a week, but she has been invited to stay with a friend of hers in Paris. She would like to go, and I think it would be healthy for her. Mamma has not traveled at all these last few years."

"I'll find one, Alec. I promise. Just not these three. I'm going to call the agency. I don't know what they were thinking."

He stared at her seriously. "Is there something else bothering you? You seemed a little flustered when I walked in."

She gave him a cool look. "Most people say I do not fluster."

He laughed then and held up his hand. "*Mi dispiace*. It just looked like something else was on your mind."

She sighed. "It really isn't that big of a deal. My landlord called, and apparently there's been some plumbing nightmare in my apartment. I have to go pack some of my stuff and move to a hotel. It's fine. Only an inconvenience."

He stared at her intently. "Move in with me." The words were out before he could even think about them. But he knew why. He had thought of little else but Meara outside of work. If she asked, he planned to tell her that the dark circles under his eyes were from a late-night call. It would be a lie. He had lain awake most of the night, wondering what it would take to be with someone like Meara. Would she even fall in love with someone like him? Aside from the issue with Valentina, was he enough by himself? That's when all his insecurities came rushing back. The painful shyness, the awkwardness that stayed with him, and that he worked almost daily to push aside. He realized he had his own mask, just as Meara had hers.

Now she was looking at him, her eyes wide, her head shaking no.

He looked at her earnestly. "I have a whole villa sitting empty. I'm gone a lot. You can relax there and not have to even think about anything. Rosalie will be in and out. So will my chef. Unless you'd rather go to Marco and Kate's." He realized with a sinking heart he hadn't even thought that she'd rather be with her sister.

Meara was avoiding his steady gaze. "No, uh, they need time alone right now. I want to give them some space."

He approached her slowly, still gazing at her. "We are friends, remember? Friends help each other."

Meara turned, and her gaze finally met his. "I can't believe I'm saying this but okay. Thank you, Alec."

"I'll see you later, then," he said with a smile. "Rosalie will be there to let you in. I have appointments all afternoon, but I should be home by dinner. Don't cook anything, roomie!"

"As if that was an option!" She was looking at him, still uncertain. "I'll get my stuff, and I guess I'll be over later."

Nodding, he took a step forward, but didn't touch her. She looked tense, and with one wrong move on his part, she would change her mind. His heart was suddenly lighter, even hopeful now. More time together meant he had a chance with her. He praised whatever plumber it was that had caused damage in her apartment. Pasting what he hoped was a polite smile on his face, he walked to the door. "*Ciao*," he said and left quickly before she could change her mind.

fourteen

W hat in the world was she thinking?

"Stupid, stupid, stupid," Meara muttered, zippering her second suitcase. Why did she accept his offer? Rolling her eyes, she went to gather the last of her cosmetics and stuff them in her large toiletries bag. In addition to her poor decision-making, moving for a week was a major pain. There was no way she could take all her clothes, so she had to carefully select what she wanted to wear for the next week. Carlo was so relieved when she told him she had other plans, but he cautioned her it would be difficult for her to come back to the apartment to retrieve anything for several days. They would need to seal off her bedroom because of the expected dust and fans they had to use to absorb the water.

She still was shocked at her sudden loss of willpower, which had led her to accept his suggestion. He almost looked surprised when he had made the offer. She smiled a little at the memory of his expression.

Thinking back to Kate's words, she finished packing and decided to let her fears go. She muscled her suitcases downstairs herself rather than call for a porter. Cosmo was already in the lobby and frowned at her. She received his admonishment as he took her suitcases from her and let him settle her in the luxurious auto.

As he drove, Cosmo was looking at her in the rearview mirror. He had asked no questions about her re-locating to Alec's. She had only told him her apartment was damaged. Since then, the older gentleman had kept a discreet smile on his face. She absentmindedly answered his comments about the beauty of the local sights as the evening sky pinkened. She smiled at the golden hue of the Colosseum, thinking back to her time with Alec there. Her heart raced a little. He said he'd be home for dinner. Suddenly, she had inspiration.

"Cosmo, is there a place we can stop on the way for some food? I'd like to bring something with me for Doctor Amato."

"I know just the place," he said with a grin in the rearview mirror.

Sometime later, Cosmo unloaded her suitcases while she carried a shopping bag of fantastic smelling cuisine. Cosmo had driven her to a family-run restaurant close to Alec's. Cosmo told her his cousin was the owner and chef, and they had the best food in Rome. Meara smiled, as it seemed as if everyone had a cousin who did something in Italy.

The door was flung open, but it was not Alec who greeted her, but a petite middle-aged woman with short blond hair. She wore a simple floral dress.

"*Buonasera*," she called cheerfully. She spoke in rapid Italian, which Cosmo answered.

Meara stepped into the vast entry hall. "Rosalie?" she asked, sticking out her hand.

Rosalie apparently had other ideas. Grabbing on to her hand, she yanked her forward, so Meara felt compelled to lean down for the small woman to kiss her on both cheeks. Despite her size, this petite woman was strong.

She addressed Meara in English. "*Signorina*! The *Signore* said you were coming to stay," she said carefully. "Follow me to the bedroom."

Meara and Cosmo trailed after her into the house and through the hallways until they arrived at a corner room. Rosalie swept her arm proudly. "I hope you like it," she said grandly.

Meara walked into the enormous bedroom, her heels sinking into the deep carpet. Exquisitely furnished, it featured a large mahogany bed and a sitting area with comfortable gray chairs and a couch. Walking over to the window, she admired the view of the gardens and pool. The well-appointed adjacent bathroom featured exquisite white-and-gray Italian marble and a large shower with multiple shower heads. A separate immense tub was in an alcove, designed to also have a view. The suspended vanity had a sink on either side. This was more than a guest bedroom. It appeared to be the primary bedroom.

Walking into the adjacent room, she realized it was a massive closet. Closets lined both sides of the room and were separated by sleek white dressers. Glancing over her shoulder, she saw Rosalie chatting comfortably with Cosmo in the bedroom. Meara drew back a heavy white lacquer closet door to see Alec's numerous tailored Italian suits hanging in a perfect row. Behind another door was an array of pressed shirts. Meara glided a dresser drawer out to see pressed and folded T-shirts.

Her heart beat faster. She had agreed to move in with him, but that didn't mean sharing a room with him! Her mind was whirling. How in the world did she get herself into this mess? Hearing her name, she tried to compose her face and walk back to where Rosalie and Cosmo stood. The older man was asking her if she needed him for the rest of the evening. They were both watching her closely. How could she tell him to take her to a hotel after all this? No, she would wait for Alec, say a few choice words, and then take a taxi to anywhere but there.

Excusing Cosmo with a sincere thank you, she smiled at Rosalie, who interspersed her Italian and English. From what

Meara could determine, the housekeeper was telling her she was leaving for the day and to make herself at home until the *Signore* returned. In the meantime, Rosalie offered to take the bag containing their scrumptious dinner into the kitchen for her and the *Signore* to enjoy later. Meara forced a smile. Oh, she'd take care of the *Signore* all right. Wrinkling her nose, she wondered if it could wait until after dinner, though. She had been so looking forward to trying Cosmo's cousin's delectable Italian dishes.

Unpacking was unnecessary since she would be leaving. Meara brushed her hair quickly and grabbed her laptop. She might as well get some work done. Walking into the kitchen, she registered the silence that meant she was now alone in the house. Resisting an urge to snoop, she poured herself a glass of water and settled in at the kitchen table. It wasn't long before her stomach rumbled. Maybe she could eat before Alec got home, and then she would be ready to exit promptly after she questioned his integrity. It would be one thing if they were at that point. Friends? Really? Did he share bedrooms with his friends? Her eyebrows raised.

"Nerd? Give me a break, Alec," she muttered, staring at her laptop screen. Shoot, she didn't have the wi-fi code. She let out an unladylike expletive, slamming her laptop shut.

"I really must teach you some Italian. Those words sound so much better in my language."

Meara glanced up to see Alec leaning on the doorjamb. He was still in his suit, but he had lost his jacket and his tie was askew. His hair was tousled, and tired lines surrounded his eyes. His mocking smile did nothing to cool her temper.

"I don't need any improvement in that area of my Italian vocabulary," Meara said coolly. "I was able to pick up those words quickly."

He strode in and looked like he was going to approach her, but stopped, his questioned gaze searching her face. "What's the matter?"

"Why do you think anything is the matter?"

He smiled gently. "I can tell. Your eyebrows always tell me the story."

She stared at him, expressionless. "I have always been told my face is virtually unreadable in the boardroom."

"Well, it's readable in the kitchen," he quipped. "What's the matter?"

Feeling uncomfortable at his penetrating stare, she willed herself to pull herself together. "I believe you got the wrong idea. I'm not here to add to your long list of women, Alec. You offered your place. I didn't know that meant your *bed.* I was just going to look for a hotel."

He looked at her quizzically. "I did not realize I had offered you that intimacy," he said silkily.

She looked at him suspiciously. His expression was grim, and a muscle twitched in his jaw. When had the power dynamic changed? She should be the one outraged.

Standing, she kept her expression stern. "Oh, really? Then why did Rosalie move me into the primary bedroom? You know, the luxurious one down the hall that has all your clothes in it?" Meara felt embarrassment seep in, realizing she had just admitted that she must have opened the closet and wardrobe.

His astonished chuckle almost made her jump. "So you think I invited you over with the covert goal of getting you into my bed?" Walking over to her, he put his hands on her shoulders and hauled her closer to him. Her eyes widened as his lips descended. He stopped just inches from her, and she looked at his heated gaze. "When I invite you into my bed, you will know it, Meara," he said quietly.

Taking his hands off her and walking away, he turned his head to stare. "You are correct. That room is mine. But I use a bedroom next to Nia in case she needs me during the night. It's easier to keep most of my clothes in the bigger wardrobe. I haven't slept in the room Rosalie showed you to since Nia came to live with me."

He looked at her solemnly. "It surprises me how little you think of me that you believe I would try to somehow trick you into sleeping with me. What was my secret plan? Make you so uncomfortable you would say yes?" He shook his head in disgust. "Please excuse me while I get changed."

Meara watched him retreat from the kitchen. Reaching for the chair, she sagged into it. This time, her expletives were in Italian, and they were about her own stupidity.

MEARA SPOONED PASTA ONTO PLATES. She had bought too much food, but it all looked so good. She opened the container of Caprese salad with its buffalo mozzarella cheese, ripe tomatoes, and fragrant basil. Since she couldn't decide on the pasta, she had chosen two: *cacio e pepe*, fresh spaghetti with *parmesano reggiano* and pepper; and *penne al sugo di carne*, penne smothered with shredded beef, simmered in wine and espresso.

After Alec had walked out, she helped herself to a glass of Chianti and started to unpack dinner. She practiced her apology in her head. He must think she was very vain to assume he immediately wanted to jump her as soon as he convinced her to stay in his home. Feeling ashamed of not giving him the benefit of the doubt, she wanted to make amends. Well, they said a way to a man's heart was through his stomach. But did she want to get to his heart? A shiver ran up her spine. One thing she knew was she never wanted him to look at her again like he had. It had made her feel two inches high rather than almost six feet tall.

"Something smells good."

Her head whipped up, and she couldn't keep from smiling.

"What now?" he asked, clearly exasperated.

She shook her head, her lips twitching. "I'm sorry, I've...I've just never seen you wear glasses."

He was in his usual worn jeans and T-shirt, and she tried not to stare at his broad shoulders and defined chest. He was wearing thick framed black glasses that caught her by surprise. But the last thing she needed to do was insult him again.

He pushed the glasses up self-consciously. "I have to wear them when my eyes get tired," he said. "Today my contacts felt like they were cemented to my eyes."

She grinned, spooning more food onto plates. "It's okay, you look like Clark Kent."

"Clark Kent?"

Meara glanced up to see his startled expression. "Sorry, sometimes you almost seem American. I forget you might not know fictional characters. Um, he's..."

"Superman," Alec finished, grabbing a glass, and pouring himself some wine from the same bottle she had used.

"So you know who he is?"

He took a sip, still looking serious. "I am a comic fan. I was just confused why you think I have anything in common with that bumbling, dorky character."

She was embarrassed now. "It's just the glasses. That's all I meant," she muttered. She needed to distract him. Stepping back, she waved her arms. "Dinner is served!"

"Who else is coming?"

Looking at him cautiously, she saw the gleam that was back in his eyes. "You're kind of sassy tonight," she informed him with a smile. His grin deepened, and he carried their plates over to the table.

He looked around for a minute. "You know we can eat in the dining room or even in the family room."

"This is cozier," said Meara, instantly regretting it. He might think she was now trying to have an intimate dining experience with him. Almost rolling her eyes, she sat down in the chair he was holding, glad he didn't respond. So far, this roommate thing was awkward.

Eyeing the food appreciatively, he looked up at her. "How did you know Marchellino's was my favorite *ristorante*?"

She laughed. "I didn't! Cosmo's cousin is Marchellino. We stopped on the way. I just re-heated it. I hope it's okay."

He took a bite and sighed in appreciation. Tipping his head back, his face was rapturous. He looked tired, though. He opened his eyes and noticed her stare. "It could be cold and still be fantastic."

Meara took a bite and almost moaned. He was right. While she wanted to keep eating, she put her fork down to stare at him. She couldn't relax until she got this over with. Suddenly, her carefully rehearsed apology had completely left her brain.

"Alec, I'm an idiot."

He glanced up, putting another forkful in his mouth.

She swallowed and tried again. "Thank you for inviting me to your home. I am sorry I... got the wrong impression. I should have known you wouldn't be like that. I apologize for acting like some distressed Victorian maiden. It's not as if I haven't..."

Oh God, she was making things worse. Taking a gulp of her wine, she quickly ate a bite. Glancing up, she saw him smirking a little before continuing to eat. It seemed an eternity before he spoke.

"While I am all ears if you want to tell me more, I accept your apology," he said with a small smile. "And I apologize for my anger. It caught me by surprise. It was natural you should be confused when Rosalie showed you into that bedroom. I just get tired of that whole player reputation, though. It comes with certain expectations."

Meara returned his steady gaze. "Maybe I shouldn't ask, but what expectations?"

"In my line of work, it's critical that people understand I am a professional. And in my personal life, it is tedious when women believe that I'm going to make some kind of play for them. Sometimes it's awkward to explain that I am not interested."

"But why don't you start dating again, Alec? You're an amazing guy."

His face clouded for a moment before he resumed eating. Meara did the same, feeling uncertain. Had she just overstepped her boundaries?

He finally sat back and sipped his wine, looking thoughtful. "To be honest, until recently, there was no one who has interested me."

"Oh, so you found someone?" she asked softly, her heart tumbling. She wondered if this woman was a nurse or a doctor at the hospital. Someone gorgeous who he saw every day.

"Yes, Meara, I did. You."

MEARA SAT BACK, swallowing hard. "Alec, I thought we've been through this. I can't... Your life isn't..." Oh God, how could she continue? It was like she couldn't formulate a coherent thought. It was so unlike her.

He nodded and refilled their glasses. "I understand," he said gently. Shrugging, he looked at her, sincerity in his eyes. "I just wanted you to know."

Emotion stirred in her. While there was still a deep attraction, they had also developed an easy friendship. She longed to get up and give him a hug. It had been wrong to come here for the week. He seemed to sense her discomfort and stood abruptly. "Let's clean up and go outside. I have something to show you."

They worked together to put the dishes in the dishwasher and wrap up the food. "You know you have a housekeeper," Meara teased.

He shrugged. "My mother always taught me to clean up after

myself. It's a habit. Go get a coat or jacket and meet me on the verandah," he said, heading off toward the other end of the house.

Meara went to do as he suggested. Grabbing her coat, she stepped into the bathroom to take a long look at herself. Her face appeared calm, even though her heart was thumping. The atmosphere over dinner had been positively electric. Washing her hands and making sure she had nothing in her teeth, she fluffed her hair.

Closing the verandah doors behind her, something scraped, and Alec, clad in a sweatshirt, pulled an elongated object out from underneath a vinyl cover.

Her eyes widened. "Oh my God, Alec, that's a gorgeous telescope!"

He smiled almost shyly at her, dialing the levers on top of it a certain way. "There is a planetary alignment tonight. Five planets will be visible," he told her excitedly as he maneuvered the telescope.

"How do you know that?"

Glancing back at her, he grinned wider. "I pay attention to that sort of thing. In school, I was a member of the Astronomy Club."

She returned his grin. He really was a nerd.

fifteen

Meara closed the door behind her, walking into the foyer. "Alec?" Nothing. "Rosalie?" she tried again. Not a sound. Shrugging, she walked through the house, past the expensive artwork and Italian pottery to her corner bedroom. Automatically kicking off her shoes, she entered the closet to decide what to change into. It had felt weird, but Alec had encouraged her to hang her clothes in the closet on the other side of the room from his. There was plenty of space, and it was virtually empty. He had come in on her first night there and taken some more of his clothes out. She had protested it was fine and that he could use his own closet. But he shook his head and continued until he had an armful of Italian menswear and casual clothes.

They had settled into a routine of sorts. It had been almost a week. Each night, they relaxed over a glass of wine or lemonade and rummaged through the refrigerator, before agreeing on a dinner selection. Often, they went into the family room, and sometimes they talked for hours or debated certain topics. Other evenings, Alec would apologize and pull out his laptop to make notes on his patients. At first, Meara was a little peeved for some unidentifiable reason. But soon it became apparent that he had work to do, so she took out her own laptop. Two nights in a row, he had insisted she watch some of the *Star Wars* series, astounded beyond belief that she had never seen it. He recited entire monologues verbatim, especially anything Yoda said. She rolled her eyes but giggled at his nerdiness. Last night, they played chess. The competitiveness had come out and each was desperate to win, until Alec finally prevailed. Laughing, she told him she played the game most days in the boardroom, not on a physical board.

They concluded every night on the verandah, taking turns looking through the giant telescope. Fortunately, most nights had been clear. Alec had taught her so much. She had never found astronomy that exciting, but when he talked about it, he became so animated, she wanted to know more. Just to hear that calm voice become enthused as he maneuvered the dials and took his glasses off to peer in. She resisted the urge to lean down and ruffle his hair as it bent over the viewfinder.

When it was time to go to bed, he always casually said good-night. He had been careful not to touch her since their talk that first night. It was almost as if he feared any slight movement would be misinterpreted.

She was excited to tell him that today she finally found the nanny. The agency had sent over more hopefuls the last two days, but the last one was perfect. Not only was she qualified, she just happened to be a fifty-year-old widow. Meara didn't care if Alec read something into that or not. The woman was highly skilled, and they were fortunate the family she had worked for moved to Australia and she didn't want to go with them.

Sighing now, she was reaching for jeans when she heard her phone ping. Picking it up, she smiled when she saw it was a text from Alec. The smile disappeared when she read it, for he was informing her he needed to stay at the hospital. The day had not gone well, and he was suspecting he would need to operate before the night was over.

Tossing her phone on her bed, she sat down. In the old days —as in before she moved in with Alec—she wouldn't have thought twice about spending the evening by herself. Now it seemed like it would stretch on endlessly. Changing into jeans and a top, she grabbed her laptop and headed down the hall.

After sorting through some meals in the refrigerator, she found she didn't have much of an appetite. She found a salad and ate that, while checking her email. Of course, there was work she could do, but that didn't have its usual appeal. Checking her watch, she thought better about phoning Katie. She had texted with her earlier, but now Kate would be dining with Marco.

Picking up the phone, she did the next best thing. "Hi, Dad."

"Hey, honey. How are you?"

She smiled at her dad's cheerful voice. He always made her feel better. "I'm doing well, Dad. I just called to check on you and the bar."

He laughed. "Meara, I know you've checked all the books this month. You know how we are doing."

It was her turn to chuckle. "You're right, and I am so happy for you, Dad. It sounds like business has been great."

"It is, but it's because of you and Katie." Meara smiled a little, thinking back to all she and Katie had done to renovate the bar and find a good business manager. They had worked together to make changes while he was in the hospital following his heart attack. Finn Malone was good at a lot of things, but finances were not his strength. His skill was keeping customers happy. Still, she had his pride to protect.

"No, Dad. You're the one who built Malone's and kept it going all these years. We just helped you revamp it a little."

"I'll never be able to pay you all the money back," he said quietly.

She sighed. "Dad, honestly, do we have to go through this every time I call?" Her tone was sharper than usual, and she took a calming breath. "I know you appreciate it. That's all you need to say."

"Then that's all I'll say," he responded immediately. After a minute of silence, he added, "Hey, are you okay? You aren't firing off the usual questions about my health."

"Oh, I'm fine, Dad. I know you're taking care of yourself," she said distractedly.

"You like living in Rome, honey, or are you thinking of looking for something else? Maybe coming back home?"

She smiled, knowing how much he was missing both of his daughters. "Yes, I'm liking it, Daddy," she said softly. "I miss you, though."

"Something else is not right. You sound funny."

Meara cleared her voice. Suddenly, she was filled with emotion. She missed him. She missed her mom. And most of all, she missed being part of something so solid and whole, like her family had been. "I'm okay. Really. It's just good to hear your voice. Can we please talk about you coming over earlier in the spring?"

"I told you, sweetie, I'll come in April. I can see the baby then, and it will be after St. Patrick's Day."

"I can't wait."

"Honey, Jimmy is waving at me. I have to go. We have a big meeting with our beer distributor today. Are you sure you're alright?"

Meara bit her lip. "Just fine. I love you," she added before hanging up. Setting her phone down on the table, she realized why she had called. When she was younger, her dad was the one she confided in. Katie was closer to their mom, but Meara had a kinship of sorts with her father. They used to joke it was their shared red hair and green eyes. Meara inherited his Irish genes while Kate favored their mom.

What would she have said if she could be honest? "Hey, Dad, so I'm sort of here living with this hot man that makes my heart race whenever I think about him. Oh, and guess what? He has put me in the friend zone now because I insisted that's what I wanted because he's got a kid. Only now I'm not sure what I want."

She rolled her eyes at her imaginary conversation and got up to go into the family room. She liked it in there, and it reminded her of the closeness she shared with Alec each night. Tonight, she spent some time looking over his books and the frames on the shelves. She smiled, running a finger over a photo of him. Replacing the frame, she went to the sofa and nestled in. To her left was a frame containing a photo of a frowning Italian woman with steel black hair and black eyebrows. Her beady eyes penetrated displeasure toward her. Meara made a face back and turned away, opening her computer to watch a movie. She glanced back. The woman was still staring. Standing, she went over and took the frame and turned it over on the table. She would put it back upright before Alec got home, but that glare was unnerving her.

Two hours later, Meara sat up for a second, disoriented when there was a noise. Alec walked into the room quietly, setting his bag down. Wearing scrubs and his glasses, he looked utterly exhausted.

She stretched, glancing at him. "Alec! What time is it?"

"After midnight. You didn't have to wait up for me," he told her quietly.

"Um, I didn't. I wanted to, but then I fell asleep."

He glanced over at the side table. "What happened to *Zia* Seena?" He went over and picked up the ornate frame.

"That's your aunt? Honestly, Alec, she was creeping me out. She looked at me so disapprovingly."

He chuckled. "She does have an air of haughtiness about her, doesn't she? She was my great-aunt, my *nonna*'s sister. She was like a *nonna* to me, and I assure you she was actually very kind, though she could be a little judgmental. I keep a photo of her up because my mamma told me she'd probably haunt me if I didn't."

Meara smiled. "I get that. I wouldn't put it past her after seeing that face. But what about a nice room in the back of the house?"

He laughed now before setting the photo down. Walking over to her, he pulled her to her feet. "Thank you for making me laugh for the first time today."

Her hands seemed to have a mind of their own. Reaching up, she smoothed his hair. "It really was a rough day, wasn't it?"

He nodded but stayed silent. She avoided asking more questions because it didn't seem to be the right time. "Have you eaten?"

"I had a *panino* at the hospital a few hours ago."

"Then it's time, my friend, to have something to make your day a little better."

He leaned in, and his breath fanned her face. "What?" he asked expectantly.

She smiled. It was the first time he had flirted with her for several days. She leaned up and gently kissed his cheek. "Gelato."

"YOU'RE LIVING WITH MY DOCTOR?" Kate asked incredulously. "You and Dr. Amato are like..."

Meara laughed, sitting back in her chair. Marco had stopped by the office for a few minutes to sign some papers, and Kate had come with him. Meara had been knee-deep in appraisals and procurement lists, getting ready to authorize the first shipment of medical equipment to the hospital and clinics on the Amalfi Coast when Kate burst into her office.

"I love that you can't finish that sentence," Meara said dryly. "I'm not living—okay, yes, I'm living with him but not in the way you think. Believe me, not in that way at all." She thought wryly back to the last couple of nights. In the past, she had guy friends who touched her more than Alec. Other than the mild flirting when he came home so tired, he had been extremely careful to avoid any physical touch. Since she had told him she wasn't interested in pursuing anything, she only had herself to blame.

Kate sunk into a chair. "What's wrong with you?"

At Meara's shrug, Kate rolled her eyes. "Most women with any type of pulse would have jumped that guy. I thought we talked about this."

Meara looked down at her spreadsheets guiltily. "We did, and then I don't know, we kind of had this talk and it freaked me out. He said...well, he was interested in me. That I was the first woman he wanted in a long time."

Kate put her hand over her mouth, making a small squeak. Meara winced. "Please don't say anything to Marco."

Kate nodded, her eyes wide. "What did you say?"

"I said I wasn't the one for him. Listen, Katie, he needs someone more like you. Someone who can be a mom to Valentina and be there for him when he gets home late."

Smiling a little to herself, she remembered the other night when he had come home late. They sat up eating gelato out of the containers. Eventually, he had told her about his patient's delivery. It had gone well, but the tiny baby was in the Neonatal Intensive Care Unit, and he was concerned about her. Meara had listened, and since she knew nothing about obstetrics, she asked a lot of questions. He seemed to enjoy talking to her, but occasionally he moved his neck around like he was stiff. Impulsively, she had gone around to rub his neck and shoulders. "Where did you learn to massage like that?" he'd asked, clearly enjoying it. She hadn't answered him because her heart was thudding so loudly. He felt so warm and wonderful, and all she could think about was rubbing her hands over his bare skin.

As if he read her mind, abruptly, he had stood and put the gelato away, suggesting it was time to go to bed. She lay awake for a long time, thinking about him down the hall. How could a person be so lonely, yet be just yards away from someone they wanted to be with?

"Meara, you haven't heard a word I said," Kate protested.

"I'm sorry, Katie. I'm just tired."

"Dad said you sounded weird when you called the other night," Kate said, looking at her closely. "And you're acting even weirder now. Are you regretting your decision?"

Meara stared at her sister, feeling her emotions bubbling up. "I wish I could be the right person for him. But I'm not."

"You're sure?"

Meara nodded because the lump in her throat was too big to answer.

sixteen

"This was a great idea," Meara said. It was Friday night, and Alec didn't have to work the next day and wasn't on call all weekend. He had suggested they do a little exploring. Meara left work early to the amazement of her staff. She even told them to go home early as well, and they rushed out almost as if they were concerned she would change her mind.

"Remember, I promised you a sunset?" Alec asked as he parked the car. "This is one of my favorite places, though, sometime I will take you to Janiculum Hill, which also has breathtaking views. Tonight, since it's so nice, I thought we'd visit the Villa Borghese Gardens."

"Which hill are we on now?" Meara inquired, knowing from Alec that there were seven of them in Rome.

"Pincian Hill," he responded, nodding approvingly at her newly acquired knowledge. "We're quite close to the Spanish Steps, right down there."

He led her around the garden, admiring statues, lush green grass, and formal gardens. "There are temples, a lake, a secret garden, and a Galleria. We can't see it all tonight because there's close to eighty acres. Some other time, we'll visit the museum. I believe it to be the best in Rome," he told her.

They walked onto a busy walkway where vendors were selling gelato and other snacks. He led her to a nearby bench and pointed at the view. "This is what I brought you up here for."

Meara sat down and took in the captivating, panoramic view of Rome. "I could never get tired of looking at this," she said with a sigh. He turned and assessed her, as if he was deciding something. Slowly, he put an arm around her and drew her close, and her heart beat faster. To distract herself, she asked questions of what she was seeing, and he answered them patiently.

"I love seeing St. Peter's Basilica from here," she remarked.

"Did you ever wonder why Rome isn't filled with high-rises like other major cities or capitals?" he asked.

She turned to look at him and fought the desire to reach up and kiss him. He was so close. She shook her head. "You're right. I hadn't realized it until now."

He smiled down at her. "Rome is laid out more horizontally than vertically because legend has it there is an unwritten rule about not making any buildings higher than St. Peter's."

"That's a good rule. I would hate for this view to be ruined," Meara said quietly as their gazes locked. It seemed the intensity had suddenly been turned up, and the world melted away except for Alec. His lips slowly descended, and what started as a soft caress became a burning kiss that went on and on. Finally, he drew away and looked at her intently before sliding his arm around her shoulders tighter. Meara was stunned by the intensity of his kiss. This feeling of everything being in its place and being just right shook her. It seemed only natural for her to lay her head down on his shoulder. They sat there for a long time until the sky deepened into colors of pink and orange, lighting up all of Rome in its glory.

It was only after they soaked in the magnificent scene that

Alec finally cleared his throat. He dropped a quick kiss on top of her head before straightening up and standing. Holding a hand out to her, he smiled. "Come on, I have another surprise."

"I hope it contains something to eat," Meara said, trying to lighten the mood. "I'm starving."

He laughed and led her back to the car and told her they were going back to the Travestere neighborhood. "I have reservations at a *ristorante* there, so I promise you that you will not go hungry."

Once parked and out of the car, they strolled through the quaint streets. Yellow, orange, and pink buildings with greenery overflowing down the sides, dotted the landscape. They walked past numerous restaurants and bars, burgeoning with crowds, eating outside on the surprisingly warm night, surrounded by light twinkly lights. Stopping at a corner restaurant, Alec led her to the hostess, who greeted him with a kiss on each cheek cheerfully and seated them at a corner table.

The waiter instantly appeared, slapping Alec on the back, and speaking to him in rapid Italian. He came back with a bottle of wine without even asking, quickly filling their glasses. Following him was the chef, who wrapped Alec in a long embrace. Alec politely introduced Meara to Maurizio, who instantly provided her with an enthusiastic hug as well. Her surprised gaze met Alec's amused one over Maurizio's shoulder. Finally disengaging herself, she listened to the two men catch up for a few minutes. Maurizio then begged Alec to let him cook for them.

When he finally departed back to the kitchen, Alec picked up his Pinot Grigio and clinked glasses with her. "*Cin Cin,*" he said with a smile. At her confused glance back toward the beaming waiter and departing chef, he laughed. "I come here a lot."

Meara smiled, but deep down there was a part of her who wondered just how many dates he had brought there. Alec's smiled deepened as if he could read her thoughts. But before she could ask, he launched into a few details about Travestere. "We'll come back during the day so you can see more of it," he promised.

As the waiter set several dishes down, Alec looked at her, his brown eyes reflecting off the candlelight. "I hope you don't mind that Maurizio is just cooking what he wants for us."

Her eyes widened. "I don't mind in the least if it's as delicious as it looks."

They ate their way through appetizers of cured meats, cheeses, and bruschetta. Then came pastas from carbonara to tagliatelle with a tomato sauce and freshly made meatballs. The second courses contained a tasting menu of *Saltimbocca*, which was chicken rolled in herbs and parma ham, Alec explained to her. There was also *Straccetti*, sliced beef cooked in wine with roasted potatoes.

They talked quietly over dinner, as they ate slowly, sampling everything. Alec told her how he had tried to learn to cook when he went to college and medical school. He failed, for the most part, he told her ruefully.

"You were educated a lot in the States, weren't you?" Meara asked. "You barely have an accent sometimes, and you're so fluent."

He smiled. "I learned English in school growing up. But yes, I studied at Harvard and later Johns Hopkins. Then I came back and studied here, in both Milan and Bologna."

They talked about their days in college, reminiscing about what subjects they most enjoyed. Meara was surprised how similar they were in their competitiveness. They both relished in absorbing knowledge, and Alec's eyes shone as he talked about his academic success once he found his calling and the professors who had made such a difference in his life.

Meara sat back. "I am stuffed. I can't believe we ate all that. Was this my surprise? Because you can surprise me with this anytime."

He laughed. "No, it is not. Let's depart, and I'll show you."

Their exit took some time, extricating themselves from Maurizio. They finally strolled hand-in-hand down the cobblestone streets. Arriving at the Botanical Gardens, Meara looked at Alec, confused. What could they possibly see at night? He paid for the tickets and grabbed her hand excitedly. He grinned at her gasp as they walked under a tunnel of twinkling blue lights. The pathways glittered alongside trees lit up in pinks, greens, oranges, and blues. They eventually came to a halo of white lights over a pond, and later to the planet earth suspended and lit up. Music played from hidden speakers, perfectly timed with the light show.

He stopped in front of a display. "It's a light festival that's not always here. I just read about it and thought you would enjoy it."

"It's enchanting," Meara whispered, unusually touched by it all. She turned to him sincerely. "Thank you for bringing me, Alec. In fact, thank you for everything."

He looked at her steadily. Bending, he kissed her softly, but quickly, just like the last time, it became intense, burning with heat. Just as suddenly, he stepped back, as if he was fighting for control. "You are enchanting, Meara," he said, still breathing heavily and staring at her intently. "Let's go home."

On the drive back to his villa, Meara knew with all her heart she didn't want tonight to end. The closeness she had felt tonight had reminded her of their first adventure in Rome together. That feeling, combined with all they had been through, seemed to launch a desire to throw all caution to the wind. Her heart raced remembering his kisses in public. What would they be like in private?

Alec pulled up in front of his *casa* quickly, as if he, too, was eager to get inside. As they walked in, she felt a tug on her arm and turned as he yanked her against the wall. His lips were on hers, and she wound her arms around his neck. She ran her hands through his hair, something she had been dying to do. He deepened the kiss, and his hands ran down her sides and moved inside her coat. As he pulled away, she tugged on him to keep him there, and the kissing continued. His lips traveled down her cheek and back to her ear and then to her lips. She wanted it to go on and on.

"Meara," he said hoarsely. "We can't."

She reached for him, but he stepped back. She blinked, not wanting to face reality. "Why not?"

He took big, deep gulping breaths. "Because I want all of you, that's why." He ran his hands through his hair before looking at her solemnly. "I want your heart. I want your soul. I want your body. I can't have one without the other."

Meara put a trembling hand over her mouth, staring at him wide-eyed. Finally, she withdrew her hand to speak. "I'm not sure what I can give you, Alec. I'm trying. I really am."

"Tell me how you feel," he commanded quietly.

"Like I can't breathe," she answered honestly.

He smiled tenderly at her and smoothed some strands of hair away from her face. "*Mi dispiace.* I'm not trying to give you an ultimatum. Let's go sit down and talk."

He helped her out of her coat, tossing it and his on a leather bench nearby. Holding her hand, he led her to the family room. Sitting down on the sectional, he stretched his arm around her shoulders and put his feet on the coffee table. She snuggled into his warmth.

"Let's start the negotiations," he said quietly, dropping a kiss on her head. "I haven't touched you for a week because I knew once we got started, the intensity would be too great." He turned to smile at her. "I hope I was not wrong in feeling you are attracted to me, despite everything." At her uncertain smile, he continued. "So, we take this slow. Baby steps, if you will. And, yes, I recognize the irony of what I just said, *cuore mio.*"

"What does that mean?" She whispered.

His gaze held hers. "My heart."

Her own heart skipped a beat. Impulsively, she reached up and kissed her way down his jaw.

"Oh, no you don't. That is not an approved negotiation tactic," he protested, glancing down at her with glinting eyes.

Meara stopped and then turned so she was laying across his lap facing him.

"This move is definitely not a permitted tactic," he said with laughter in his eyes. His arms went tightly around her, and he began stroking her hair.

"Do you know how much I think about touching this hair? Constantly. Since the first time I saw you," he murmured. "It feels as silky as I imagined."

He leaned forward and kissed her neck, swiping her hair out of the way. She craned her neck so he could have better access. "Now who's not playing fair?" She asked hoarsely.

He pulled back, his eyes glinted with passion. "Let's just end the negotiations then. Are you in?"

Looking at him, she remembered what he had said in the foyer. It gave her pause, and yet she couldn't resist his expression. "I'm in," she whispered and let him capture her lips in a searing kiss. She broke away for a minute to stare at him, putting a hand against his cheek. He turned to kiss her palm, and a shiver ran up her spine.

"There's just one thing," she said quietly.

"Anything," he answered quickly.

She nodded toward the table. "*Zia* Seena has to go."

His laughter rang out before he swooped back in to devour her lips.

seventeen

Meara sat on the counter, swinging her legs, munching on a piece of toast. "I'm no expert, but I think the pan is too hot," she joked.

A string of Italian expletives followed as Alec stirred the eggs.

Nonplused, she continued. "I've heard of green eggs like in a kid's book, but not gray," she remarked, covering her mouth before she laughed out loud. It was mean to tease him since he had been so sweet trying to make breakfast.

Last night had been the most romantic night of her life, and now this morning, the sun was shining despite it still being on the edge of winter. Meara had just gotten out of the shower when Alec yelled that breakfast was almost ready. Donning his big white robe, she fluffed her hair and decided to let it dry naturally. It would be a mess later to deal with, but she couldn't wait to join him for what she thought was going to be a delicious breakfast.

He took the pan off the heat and looked at it in disgust. "*Mi dispiace*," he said. "I wanted to make you a beautiful breakfast."

"Alec, it's fine. I don't eat a lot for breakfast anyway. Usually just toast or maybe a *cornetto*. I'm kind of addicted to those."

"That's just technically a croissant. We can do better than that. How about we have an early start to our day? We'll go find a *maritozzo.*"

"What's that?"

"It's an Italian pastry filled with cream. You'll love it."

Meara stared at him, loving his ruffled hair. He was wearing his faded jeans and T-shirt and now, knowing what was under it, he was beyond sexy to her. As if reading her thoughts, he pulled her toward him on the counter. "Or we could stay in."

"After you just told me about that pastry?" she teased. His lips came down on hers, and she melted into his embrace, kissing him with a growing passion. The thought of exploring Rome now held little appeal. She sunk into his kiss, wanting more.

"Mamma!"

They separated as if they were on fire, and Meara grabbed the edges of her robe. She ran a hand through her hair, completely disoriented.

Alec was breathing hard, but he was the first to recover. "Nia!" he exclaimed, picking up the giggling child. And then it was his turn to greet the woman who stood in the doorway, her mouth open in shock. "*Buongiorno, Mamma.*"

Those two words made Meara want the floor to swallow her up. Jumping off the counter as quickly as she could, she turned to face Alec's mother. The petite woman she had seen in the photos was now looking at her speculatively.

Meara had never blushed in her life, but she felt like her face must be turning as red as her hair. She immediately switched into professional mode, sticking her hand out. "*Buongiorno, Signora Amato.* I am Meara Malone." The older woman accepted her hand and shook it loosely, her eyes wide. "Jacquetta Amato," she acknowledged softly.

Meara smiled politely. "If you don't mind, I think I'll go get dressed." After a quick glance at Alec, she walked out of the kitchen with as much poise as she could muster. She only sagged when she got to her room and shut the door. Suddenly, reality was right in front of them in the shape of one small child and a protective mother.

~

ALEC RAN his hand up and down Valentina's back, glad for once to use her as a shield. His mother was rooted to the entrance of the kitchen, one eyebrow raised and looking at him as if he just got caught stealing a *biscotti* before dinner. He could see a hint of amusement in her eyes, but he knew she was bursting with questions.

The timing couldn't have been worse. He had been soaking in the luxury of having Meara all to himself. Last night had been amazing, and he had finally broken down barriers. They still had things to overcome, and he worried that in the end, Valentina might be the deal breaker. If only he could first ensure that her heart was his, she might be able to explore at least the idea of being around a child. He wanted her to realize that he was not just looking for a ready-made mother for Valentina. Everything first was about the two of them. Meara had captured his heart from the moment she looked at him with those piercing green eyes in Marco and Kate's living room. That seemed so long ago.

Spending all week trying hard to keep his hands to himself was difficult. He sensed the more they got to know each other, the more the attraction grew. But he had purposely stayed friendly and physically distant to honor her wishes. Last night he had meant it when he said he wanted everything. However, when he had looked into her eyes, he could see unintentionally giving her that ultimatum was a mistake. Bringing her into the family room was his way of cooling things down. Smiling, he remembered their negotiations. She had made it clear she was

165

jumping in—at least physically. That memory made his smile grow.

"Alessandro, are you just going to stand there grinning, or are you going to tell me what we just walked in on?"

Glancing at his mother, it was his turn to raise an eyebrow. "Mamma, I don't think I want to..."

She held up a hand. "I'm not asking for details." She shuddered. "Who is that? And why did Nia call her Mamma?"

"*Italiano, per favore*," he reminded her quietly, glancing out into the hall. There was no sign of Meara.

"I thought you wanted us to speak English around Nia to expose her." At his speaking look, she quickly switched to Italian, asking again who Meara was. He filled her in about how they met and that she was leading the foundation.

"Is it serious?"

He nodded. "At least for me."

"It looked like it is from her, too," his mother remarked dryly. "She was certainly, uh, kissing you enthusiastically."

Valentina fortunately spared him from answering. "Mamma!" she shrieked again, holding her arms out, twisting in his arms. Meara appeared behind his mother, now wearing a casual sage green top and jeans. Meara stepped around his mother and came to stand near him, almost as if she was seeking his closeness. Meara automatically accepted the child and held on to her.

"Hi, sweetie," Meara said uncertainly. Nia was giggling and running her face against Meara's chest. "Yes, I wore Valentina-proof clothes today."

Alec winced at the memory of Meara's suits and turned to give her a questioning look to ensure she was okay holding Nia. There was something about her eyes that told him to just leave the child as is. He cleared his throat. "Mamma, I clearly wasn't expecting you."

"Well, you would have if you had checked your phone this morning, Alessandro," she said, looking amused. "I texted you I was bringing Valentina back a day early." She turned to address Meara. "My friends have invited me to Paris, and they have decided to depart earlier than I expected. I must return home and pack."

Meara nodded. "Alec...Alessandro told me you were going. I love Paris. I hope you have an enjoyable trip."

"Thank you, Meara," she said with a genuine smile. Staring at them, she raised her eyebrows. "I just have two questions before I leave. I hope they aren't intrusive."

At Meara's nervous nod, she continued. "Why does Nia call you Mamma?"

Alec put an arm protectively around Meara and answered for her. "I think it's one of her picture books. There is a woman in it with long red hair."

Valentina was staring up at Meara, her eyes big. She reached up and grabbed a handful of hair and tugged. Alec did his best to disengage the tiny hand. "Sorry about that," he muttered.

Meara exchanged a smile with him. "That's okay, I have plenty."

She shifted Valentina a little on her hip and grabbed her hair and pulled it to the other side so that it was out of Valentina's reach.

Alec turned back to his mother. "What was your second question, Mamma?"

This time, her eyes were dancing. "Why are those eggs gray?"

<h1 style="text-align:center">eighteen</h1>

Meara sat quietly as Alec parked the car deftly and then turned to smile at her. After his mother left, Meara casually remarked that their plans of spending the day exploring would now change. He told her firmly that they were only slightly altered. "We'll still go into the city center, but maybe we'll find a few things that will entertain Nia as well."

The child had fallen asleep on their drive, and Meara looked behind her to see Valentina blinking awake in her car seat. She smiled brightly with the exact same smile as Alec, dimples and all. How had she not noticed that?

Alec extracted her from her car seat easily and popped her into a stroller, grabbing a backpack filled with snacks and her cup. Meara commented before they left how efficiently and quickly he packed the child up. He only shrugged and said it was from practice. She strolled next to him now while he pushed the stroller. Valentina jabbered as they walked, and occasionally she shrieked in delight when a pigeon took off flying near her. Meara glanced around as they entered the *Piazza Navona*.

She smiled at Alec. "I know where I am. We have come back to the scene of the crime."

At his quizzical look, she pointed up at the white mask, remembering the gory story he had told her their first night when they stuffed themselves with gelato. He chuckled at the memory and then stopped the stroller near one of the fountains. Bending to undo Valentina's seatbelt, he said, "We'll let her run for a minute after the car ride."

They stood a little apart from each other so they could both see Valentina run around the fountain. When she stopped, Alec lunged for her, and she screamed and ran the other way. Meara laughed at Alec's theatrics.

A vendor was selling stuffed animals and balloons nearby. "Alec, I'll be right back," Meara called. He nodded absentmindedly as he swooped in to pick up the child and swing her around.

Purchasing a giant purple balloon, Meara returned to them and presented it to the little girl. Valentina's eyes grew wide, watching Meara tie it around her wrist. Meara looked up at Alec, and an expression crossed his face that she couldn't quite read. It was gone just as quickly.

Meara shrugged. "This way we can spot her more easily."

He laughed. "That's a great idea. It's either that or a microchip!"

Valentina was now obsessed with lowering the balloon and batting at it, and she sat in her stroller, admiring it. Grateful for the reprieve, Alec and Meara sat near the stone fountain, watching her with amusement.

"This is a busy *piazza*," Meara remarked, watching the crowds.

Alec agreed. "And the most beautiful one, I think. Did you know it was built on a stadium?"

"Really?"

"It's the reason it's oval-shaped. It was called the Domitian Stadium and was built by an emperor who wanted to bring Greek-style games to Rome. It wasn't that popular because the Romans wanted to go to the Colosseum to see their regular familiar gory shows. Eventually, it was covered," he explained. "There's a way to go see some of it, but that will be for another time."

Standing, he held out a hand. "Let's go explore the market over there."

They walked around a small farmer's market that featured produce and flowers. "When the season starts, this market is a lot bigger," Alec told her. "It's bursting with fruit and vegetables. That's my favorite time here."

They walked through the *piazza,* and Alec seemed to have a destination in mind as he led her through several streets. Meara didn't even bother asking where they were going. Based on her experience, Alec would show her once they got there. They entered a courtyard, and Alec turned to smile at her. "Want to play a game?"

Meara glanced around and burst out laughing. There were several tables with groups of two people at each table playing a competitive game of chess. Shaking her head, she rolled her eyes. "Did you bring me here to remind me how terrible I am at this game?"

He shook his head, smiling. "This is how I improved. It's a chess club that meets every Saturday. I used to come and play matches."

Several people looked up and nodded his way and smiled. His name was shouted a few times, but it was obvious everyone was intent on their game.

Meara smiled and put her arm through his. "You really are a nerd."

He grinned. "And proud of it."

They turned and began walking down another side street until they reached a stunning, immense basilica. Alec stopped wheeling the stroller so they could look at it from a distance.

"Shocker, there's another church," Meara commented dryly.

"It's the *Basilica di Sant'Andrea della Valle,*" he told her.

Putting an arm around her shoulders, he stood behind her and leaned his face near to hers. "See that angel on that corner on the left?" At Meara's nod, he continued. "Now look to the right."

On the right of the church, there was nothing. "I don't get it. Did someone steal it? It looks lopsided."

"It is, but no one stole anything. The legend goes that the sculptor made the first angel, and the public criticized him for it. The pope at the time even made nasty remarks. So, the sculptor told everyone he was done, and if the pope wanted the other angel, he could make one himself!"

Meara laughed, turning around. "At least no one died this time in your story."

He was watching her intently and leaned in to give her a brief kiss. Pulling back, his gaze met hers before taking her lips again, this time for a longer, deeper kiss. It was only Valentina's loud voice complaining that she was hungry and that snapped them out of it.

Still dazed, Meara heard Alec telling the child they would go in search of pizza. Valentina was proclaiming her love for pizza as they wheeled away.

It wasn't long before they saw a small, casual restaurant that Alec liked. Meara sat at a table with Valentina in a highchair while Alec went to order a few slices. Over lunch, they talked about anything and everything. She answered his gentle questions, unaware of how much she was revealing. Distracted, she watched him casually wiping Valentina's mouth and hands, tending to her needs.

"How do you do all that so easily?" Meara asked guardedly. At his questioning look, she continued. "You just make taking care of her look so automatic."

He smiled at her. "My mother reminds me every day that this is the easiest part. When kids get older, you can't always solve everything with a piece of pizza or a toss in the air. As Mamma loves to tell me, when Angelina and I were teenagers, we nearly killed her. And she said the worry is never-ending. In fact, she worries about me still. Parenthood never ends."

Meara nodded, swallowing the lump in her throat.

"Obviously, I am not a good salesman," Alec remarked wryly, his eyes searching her face. "It's important to be honest with you, though. It's not all sweetness and light. I'm sure when she is a teenager she will slam her door and tell me she hates me or something similar. I'm preparing myself already."

Meara covered his hand with hers. "She's never going to say that. You're too wonderful to her."

He turned her hand over, rubbing her palm slowly and sending tingles down her spine. "Oh, she'll say it. But deep down, she'll always know she is loved."

His gaze met hers, and suddenly the air vibrated between them. Meara wondered what it would be like to wake up every day knowing that she was loved by this man. He would cherish whoever he was with. Suddenly, a little overwhelmed, she broke the spell.

"Come on, there's a lot more of Rome to see," she said as she stood, gathering her jacket. He sat for a minute and blinked as if he wasn't ready to change the subject. Eventually, he stood and disengaged Valentina from the highchair, transferring her back to the stroller.

Walking through a passageway with a ceiling covered with a fresco, Meara glanced up, admiring the artistry. "It's almost like I'm just getting used to all this beauty," she told him as they exited and continued walking.

"You never get used to it," he told her. "There's parts of *Roma* I have never seen. And if you grow tired of it, all you have to do is travel to another city in Italy. There's a lot of the country I don't even know well."

They strolled through the streets, stopping by mutual consent every so often to look at something. Alec told her funny tidbits or serious facts about so many places that Meara's brain was tired.

She would have to read about some of these places later. The history was so awe-inspiring.

They came upon a church, and Alec's eyes lit up. "This is the *Santa Maria in Cosmedin Church*."

Meara walked toward the front door, and Alec put out an arm. "Oh, we aren't going in this time. We are going to the side." His eyes glinted with humor.

People were queued up, and Meara stood next to Alec, trying to peer ahead to see what they were in line for. He was bent down talking to Valentina, who had started to fuss. Alec unbuckled her and held her to his shoulder.

"She's tired," Meara observed. "Maybe we should go home."

He shook his head. "Once we finish here, she can take a small nap while we walk. She will undoubtedly fall asleep on our way home in the car as well. I don't want her to sleep too much."

"What are we lined up for?"

"You'll see," Alec teased, as he rubbed Valentina's back soothingly.

Meara bit her lip and looked away from him. Was it silly that she was jealous of a toddler? It would be lovely if he was rubbing her back that way. Breaking out of her musings, she realized they were in the front of the line and she saw a round stone with a carved face. Its eyes stared back at her, its mouth open.

"Did you ever see that movie with Audrey Hepburn? *Roman Holiday*?"

She shook her head. "It was one of Katie's favorite movies, but I never saw it."

He grinned at her. "This makes it even better. It's called the *Bocca della Verità*. Mouth of truth," he explained. "Legend has it that it will bite the hand of those who lie." His eyes twinkled. "Go ahead. Stick your hand in."

"I'm not sticking my hand in there!"

"Come on. What do you have to fear? Have you lied?"

Meara wrestled with a small feeling of uncertainty. This was ridiculous. She hadn't lied to him, but she also hadn't been too honest about how much she already cared for him, despite knowing that they would not have a future.

"Do it," he commanded softly.

"There could be a spider in there!"

He laughed and stuck his hand in. Bringing it out, he showed it to her. "See, all in one piece! In the movie, Gregory Peck pretends his hand is gone. It's a great scene. You should watch it sometime."

Meara chuckled and patted the statue's head. "That's the closest I'm getting."

Walking through the cobblestone streets, Alec told her there was one more place he wanted to end the day. On Capitoline Hill, they wove around until they came to the *Church of the Gesu.*

"I guess it's church day," he told her with amusement in his eyes. "But this is something to see."

Entering the cool church, Meara walked across the pink marble, taking in the Roman Baroque architecture. The simple wood pews were filled with people craning their necks toward the left.

"What are they looking at?" she whispered, clutching Alec's arm.

He didn't answer her but led her to a pew. "It will happen in just a few minutes," he told her, glancing at his watch. As they sat waiting, Meara looked down at Valentina. She was fast asleep. "We should get her home," she whispered to Alec.

He shook his head. "No, let's wait for it. We've come this far," he whispered.

Turning his body toward her, he draped an arm loosely around her shoulders, and his eyes searched her face. "Did you have a good time today?"

Meara nodded at the memories. It had differed from when it was just the two of them, but still just as fun. Glancing at

Valentina, she felt an odd sense of protectiveness. Alec's lips twitched earlier when she had described Anna, the new nanny. He hadn't said a word but solemnly agreed that her qualifications sounded excellent. Now Meara felt a sense of alarm. What if the agency hadn't vetted her properly? What if she had made a mistake? Frowning, she decided to call all Anna's references herself again tomorrow before she started.

"Hey, where are you?" he asked softly, his gaze steady.

Shaking her head, she shrugged. "I was just...thinking," she finished lamely.

"Regrets?"

Turning, she saw the look of anxiety on his face. "No!" she assured him, laying her hand over his. "Of course not!"

He looked relieved but still unsure. "I just thought with Nia coming home, things might have changed."

Meara glanced again at the sleeping child. "Remarkably, no." She took a deep breath and blew it out. "Alec, I'm willing to try this—whatever this is. But I don't want Valentina to get too attached to me. Does that make sense? I know she's still small, but I don't want her to have another loss."

Staring at her, he nodded silently. He appeared as if he was trying to speak but cleared his throat. "Thank you," he finally said simply. "That is something I didn't even think about."

She looked down at their clasped hands. "I have to tell you something, but I don't want you to read too much into it."

"Okaaaaay," he drew out the word.

"I'm moving back tomorrow. Carlo texted me the new apartment is empty and cleaned. He went to a lot of extra trouble to get it ready for me so I feel like I need to return. I just didn't want you to think I was moving out because of..."

"Nia," he finished quietly. "I'll be sorry to see you go. It's been..."

Suddenly, they heard murmurs around them. He pointed

over to the painting. "Saint Ignatius appears every day at 5:30," he whispered.

Meara gasped as triumphant music rang through the quiet church. Suddenly, the painting lowered, and a statue of St. Ignatius was visible. "This has been happening since the 1600s," he whispered. The music soared, and then the lights turned on throughout the ceiling, highlighting the frescos that almost looked three dimensional in their glorious colors, and the golden arches shone above them. Music played as a voice narrated the story of St. Ignatius. Finally, it was over, and there was stillness. She was aware Alec had been watching her face the whole time.

"Well, that's kind of amazing," Meara breathed. Once again, she felt that calmness around Alec, that she felt nowhere else.

"That's the word I was looking for," he said. He picked up her hand and kissed it. "Let's go home. One more night, *cuore mio.*"

nineteen

Meara finished packing her suitcase and picked up her purse. She and Alec were on their way to Naples and the Amalfi Coast and the surrounding area to finish the first phase of the foundation's work. Alec had shown excitement about the arrival of the modern equipment they had procured for the hospital. She was also eager to see it firsthand and show Alec the site for a new clinic and visit one that was to be renovated. One would be dedicated to women's primary health care, and the other would be for children. It was mind-boggling how much she learned and still needed to absorb. Meara was thankful she had made some excellent decisions in hiring and appreciated being surrounded by knowledge. She hired a multimedia specialist as well to take photos of their progress for a presentation she was working on for the board's introductory gala.

The importance of this work was not lost on her. It was critical that she see everything in person. Even though Marco was distracted with Kate and the arrival of their baby, she knew he was still feeling wary of things not under his control. She needed to reassure him everything was under control.

Sitting down on her bed, Meara stared off into space, remembering the last few weeks. Anna was working out, and based on a recommendation, they hired a friend of hers as an alternative nanny. Rosalie was back full-time as well and agreed on staying with Valentina if Alec was called out in the middle of the night. She lived close and could be there quickly. It seemed as if the childcare issue had gotten resolved, and Alec repeatedly thanked Meara for her help.

After moving back to her apartment, she and Alec continued to spend as much time together as possible. True to his word, he had not pressed Valentina on her, but Meara still spent time with them both occasionally. They went to the zoo and to a nearby park so Valentina could play with other children. Meara watched the other moms ogling Alec while glancing at her ringless finger with speculative glances. She still felt like a fish out of water and awkward when it came to any maternal actions.

Deferring to Alec, he was the one to feed, bathe, and put Valentina to bed when Meara was around. There was only once that he had gotten tied up on the phone talking to another physician that she found Valentina staring at her, her fingers in her mouth. Meara could sense the tension in the child, and she had tried to distract her with a few toys, but to no avail. It was ridiculous that the only time she was uncertain was when she was left alone with a tiny human. In a brief epiphany, Meara grabbed her phone and turned on music, and they had a dance party. Apparently, "dance party" was understandable in any language. Alec walked in to see Meara and Valentina jumping around, their arms over their heads, oblivious to anything. Meara was mortified when she finally realized he was watching them from the doorjamb. Shrugging, she told him later it was her one release, but she had never had an audience. He seemed happy about that, kissing her with increasing passion until they both realized the dance party was not over.

"Papa!" Valentina shrieked and did a few uncoordinated

dance moves that made him laugh and pick her up to dance even more.

They also spent some time alone, roaming through the streets of Rome to find more cherished spaces of his. It was getting increasingly difficult for her to separate herself from him, and she tried her best to dampen the tiny misgiving that was deep inside her. No man had ever meant so much to her. That was all she could admit to for now. In the meantime, she kept telling herself to relax and enjoy it. The future might work itself out. For someone who had spent her whole life planning every step of her life, even she was puzzled by her behavior.

Meara's phone buzzed, and it was Alec. She rolled her suitcases toward the front door. She answered his quiet knock and found herself quickly in his arms. Sinking into his kiss, her arms automatically went around him.

He finally broke the kiss to hug her even tighter. This was usual for him. "I'm a hugger," he once told her, and she was almost alarmed. Classifying herself as not a hugger, she wasn't sure they were compatible on that level. Now she understood that all these years, she just had never been with a man she wanted to hug. Sure, she was used to hugging members of her family. But wow, this man loved to wrap his strong arms around her. She sunk willingly into his long, deep embrace and it was as if his body chased away any of her problems. Finally, he released her, almost looking refreshed. "Ready to go?"

They had agreed to drive south together, though Alec was worried he might have to leave early if one of his partners needed him. They had agreed to take his patients for a few days, but Alec was conscientious and wanted to return to Rome if he was needed. Marco told Meara if that happened, he would send his helicopter for her. She watched Alec put her cases in his car, and then he came around to help her into a Ferrari.

"How many cars do you have?"

He shrugged and smiled. "I told you I like cars."

Meara shook her head in wonderment. She had seen the extensive garage on the property. One of these days, she was going to ask him for a peek.

The drive down went quickly, and Alec seemed excited to see the results of their work. After parking at the hospital, Alec came around to help her out of the car and automatically reached for her hand. Meara gave him a speaking look.

"Oh, I forgot, we are business acquaintances again," he teased. She turned to roll her eyes at his tone when she was practically knocked over.

"Meara! Alec! I've been waiting for you!" Teresa hugged each of them, craning her neck to smile up at them. Petite and full of energy, Teresa was excitedly beaming. Meara was pleased to see her, knowing how much work she and Alec had done before Meara had even come on board. In fact, Marco gave Teresa a lot of credit for the initial idea to start the foundation. It was only after Teresa told him stories of inequity at the hospital where she had worked as a nurse, that he realized a foundation could make an impact on their own health care system.

"Teresa, I'm so glad you joined us. I didn't know if you got my message or not," Alec said with a smile. Meara bit her lip. She hadn't even thought of that, but of course, Alec would.

"I'm so sorry I didn't return your call. I wasn't sure I'd be able to come or not," Teresa answered earnestly. "I have been traveling with Stefano while he's building his new pasta company. But you know the Angelo Foundation is deep in my heart, too. I hope I'm not in the way, Meara. I know you're in charge now."

Meara reached over and put a hand on her shoulder. "Teresa, we are glad you're here with us," she reassured her. Glancing at Alec, she didn't allow her gaze to meet his. She was embarrassed that she wasn't as thoughtful as he was. "And I'm glad Alec invited you."

Two members of the foundation's staff also approached them. They both had clear assignments, and Meara greeted them cheerfully. That was a big change for her, too. In the past, she always felt the need to lead, almost with a sense of intimidation or fear. Somehow, she thought it made her more powerful. It was only after taking the time to watch Marco in action and have some soul-searching talks with Alec that she realized for years she overcompensated to prove she was tough enough for the corporate world. It was still a work in progress, but now her staff didn't scurry away or whisper when she entered the office.

Their first stop was the Neonatal Intensive Care Unit. Meara was out of her depth. It was as if Alec and Teresa were almost speaking a different language. Alec was so excited to see some of the complex equipment that he was at a loss for words. At one point, he turned his handsome head to give her a look filled with emotion. It was as though it were all-consuming for him, and a muscle twitched in his jaw as he tried to get control of his feelings. They stared at one another and shared a poignant moment. Suddenly, it seemed they both realized how big of an impact the foundation would have on people's lives.

"Are those grandmothers?" she asked, breaking the moment nervously. She pointed to several older women, rocking and cooing the tiniest infants she had ever seen. All the babies had an alarming number of tubes and machines hooked up to them.

Alec smiled gently at them. "They are volunteers. Many Neonatal Units have found that as the babies get stronger, they need a human touch. The nurses don't have enough time, and so if the baby is healthy enough and their parents can't be present, a volunteer steps in to...well, rock.

Meara opened her mouth. She was about to say that would be the last job she would volunteer for. Babies were scary enough, but tiny and sick babies? No, thank you.

"I volunteer occasionally myself," Alec whispered quietly, with a small smile. "It's one of my most favorite things to do. It brings me back to when Nia was so little. There's a serenity and peace. Watching a small baby's face is better than any movie or television."

Meara kept her expression neutral. Alec had just proven in a few words how different they were. "Alec," she said softly. Before she could say anything else, the hospital director appeared. Speaking in Italian, she seemed to be admonishing them for not having someone alert her they had arrived. Alec smiled, cajoling the woman, pouring on the charm. Meara almost rolled her eyes at the director's complete change in character. Now she was all smiles, laughing and batting her eyelashes. False eyelashes, if Meara wasn't mistaken.

Meara silently seethed as they heard about all the updates and new equipment. The renovations to the Neonatal Unit had all been completed without a hitch. Now they were speaking English, and Alec told the director they owed a lot of the success of the project to Meara and her attention to detail. The other staff members present nodded and murmured their praise. Meara was embarrassed about receiving the appreciation of the medical professionals. She wished Marco could be there to feel it instead. All she had done was simple project management. Watching her staff taking photos and video, she realized this would be the most satisfying presentation to a board she had ever done.

The staff was also thanking Alec. Meara frowned darkly for a minute as they strolled down the hallway in a group. Of course, he deserved their gratitude for even suggesting the upgrades for the hospital, but the appreciation from some of the women present had gone to almost adoration. In fact, she had seen more than one of them place a hand on his arm or back, looking into his eyes and whispering what appeared to be humorous observations. He smiled and nodded, seemingly oblivious to their flirting. Meara reminded herself they all worked with him, but their clear fandom was over the top. There was a part of her who now wished he would grab her hand or put a casual arm around her.

That would be so inappropriate, but at least it would place some of these women on notice.

As they left the hospital, Alec made no attempt to grab her hand as he did before. Helping her into the car, he ran around to his seat.

"That was quite the little fan club you have there," Meara remarked dryly.

He looked at her confused, and she rolled her eyes. "Oh, please. Those women were all over you. And the director of the hospital? She was holding nothing back!"

He smiled a little. "I think you're exaggerating. They were all appreciative of our work. In fact, they were very grateful for everything you have done. You should be proud of yourself."

She looked away, avoiding his gaze, but he placed a hand on her jaw, turning her face back toward him. "You should be proud rather than jealous," he pointed out softly.

"I'm not..." Before she could finish, Meara was startled as Teresa quickly opened the door and got into the backseat. "Thanks for waiting. I just had a few people to catch up with."

Teresa smiled at Meara's obvious confusion. "Didn't Alec tell you? You're giving me a ride to the lemon grove."

"We were discussing other matters," Alec said with a smirk, pulling the car out of the parking lot.

"Oh, I see," Teresa said hesitantly, clearly not understanding by the tone of her voice. "I'm meeting Stefano there. In fact, he's making us dinner right now," she promised cheerfully.

Meara glanced over at Alec, but his face was expressionless. He had told her at one point that he knew Stefano didn't like him. She wondered how they would act toward each other. As Alec navigated the evening traffic, he was unusually quiet. Meara stared out the window silently, and Teresa chattered from the back seat, seemingly unaware of the moods of the occupants in the front seat. Images of the day flashed in Meara's mind: the women fawning all over Alec, the tiny babies, and the volunteers rocking them. She could almost picture Alec in scrubs and a mask, cradling a tiny baby. She and Alec were too different. He must have seen it as well. He was grimly staring straight ahead, occasionally murmuring a suitable reply to Teresa.

Meara was looking forward to staying the night at the family's estate at the lemon grove. The family dynasty had started there, and it was still a small part of their operation. Tours, events and spectacular celebrations were held on the working farm. Most importantly, it contained the family home.

At first when Marco and Kate suggested it, she had demurred. They could get a hotel somewhere. Kate explained that the family would find it rude, and besides, Margherita would love to see her. Meara acquiesced, as she loved the lemon grove. It now felt like home since she had visited several times.

Driving through the gates and eventually pulling up to a circular drive, Meara smiled at the picturesque fountain that stood in the middle, ringed by flower beds. The nearby expansive cream-colored house with its wide terrace, arched windows, all rimmed in black, and wrought-iron balcony in the center stood welcoming them. Despite its size, its warmth demonstrated it was a family's home. Alec barely stopped the car when Margherita was strolling out the front door.

Teresa jumped out, not waiting for Alec. "I'm going to find my husband," she called excitedly.

Margherita strode down the stairs, her hands outstretched. "*Buonasera*," she called. Kissing them each, she greeted them warmly.

"We feel honored you are staying with us tonight," she told them. "Stefano has been cooking for over an hour now, and I'm sure he is creating something spectacular."

Meara glanced over, and Alec was running his hands through his hair and rubbing his neck before popping the trunk and retrieving their suitcases. Margherita was directing them inside when Nico emerged, wearing his usual wide smile.

"*Mia sorella*," he greeted her with a big hug.

"I'm not your sister, too," Meara teased.

He hugged her again. "Yes, we are all part of the same *famiglia* now! We have gone over this!"

Meara laughed. It was their usual greeting. Nico was always warm and friendly. Looking at him closely, she raised her eyebrows. "You look older."

"Ha! I'm maturing," he said with a wink before shaking his head. "Or is that aging? This company takes its toll. But I am hopeful I can take on a different role soon."

Meara opened her mouth to ask what that would mean, but Nico turned to greet Alec with his usual friendliness. Nico helped Alec with the bags, and they all entered the house.

"They can take the luggage upstairs, Meara," Margherita said. "Come into the kitchen and let's see what Stefano is making for dinner." Meara glanced at Alec, but his face still was impassive. Resolutely, she followed the older woman and entered the expansive kitchen. Stefano was standing at the island rapidly chopping vegetables, and Teresa was sitting in a chair at the island, talking. "Oh my God, that ride was a little intense. I don't know what was going on between them..."

"Hey, you," Meara interrupted purposefully and saw Teresa flush a little. It appeared Teresa hadn't been as oblivious as she had acted. Stefano carefully put the knife down and came over to greet Meara, kissing her on each cheek. "*Buonasera*, Meara." His big smile transformed his face. Meara noticed the change in him once Teresa came into his life. This new relaxed Stefano seemed almost cheerful.

His grin faded abruptly, and she glanced behind her to see Alec and Nico entering the kitchen. A dark look came over Alec's face for a moment before he masked it with a neutral expression. Stefano nodded in acknowledgement. "Alessandro." He made no move toward him. In fact, he walked back around the island and resumed his chopping. Tension filled the air.

Meara saw Margherita frown as she asked her guests what she could get them to drink. Alec walked over to Meara and slipped a casual arm around her waist. Stefano glanced up and saw, not hiding his displeasure.

"I'll have some wine," Meara answered brightly and glanced over at Teresa to see what her reaction was. She was looking at both men with frustration.

Margherita handed them both a glass absentmindedly. Then a look of determination came across her face, and Meara braced herself. She had seen that expression before on the older woman's face.

"Teresa and Meara, you will join me outside. Nico, you, too. Alec and Stefano are going to stay in the house. I believe they have some talking to do," she said carefully. At Stefano's dark look, she spoke in Italian for a few minutes. Meara's comprehension was improving, and she understood a few words, including "must" and "no choice." There was also a reminder about Alec being a guest.

Stefano accepted his mother's admonishment as if he was a small boy. Margherita smiled and went over to kiss his cheek and whisper something in his ear that made him finally grin a little. Margherita walked out of the room with Teresa and Nico following her. Meara slowly disengaged herself from Alec. He moved toward the island but didn't glance at her.

"It's safe to leave your boyfriend here," Stefano said roughly. "I'm not going to use a knife on him."

Meara stared at him coolly. "I didn't think you were," she replied and then sniffed. "But if you do, please manage to save the dinner. Something smells fantastic."

That comment at least drew a reluctant smile from both men. Leaning up, she gave Alec a kiss on the cheek. Something in her made her want to show Stefano that Alec meant something to her. Picking up her wine, she walked out, wishing she could be a fly on the wall.

<h1 style="text-align:center">twenty</h1>

Alec leaned on the back of the chair at the island, deciding against sitting. Stefano was standing and that would give him a physical advantage in this conversation. Alec had been expecting it ever since he had found out that Stefano would be present this evening. A confrontation between them was long overdue.

For a few minutes, Stefano continued to focus his attention on dinner. He checked the oven and stirred something on the stove, adding the chopped vegetables. Alec waited him out. Stefano couldn't avoid him forever.

Finally, Stefano turned around to stare hard at him. "I hate that you're with Meara."

Alec arched an eyebrow, not surprised at Stefano's desire to get to the bottom line. Alec stayed silent, as it was clear Stefano needed to air his feelings.

"Meara is special," he said roughly, slamming down the dishcloth that had been lying over his shoulder. "Our family owes her greatly for helping us uncover what Sal did. We could have lost the company to his fraud. Even though she was still uncertain about Marco and Katie's relationship, she came and helped us. *A lot*," he emphasized.

Alec willed his expression to stay impassive. It seemed to him Stefano was challenging him to declare his feelings. Running his hand through his hair, he rubbed his neck tiredly. Finally, he pulled a chair out and sat down at the island. He would concede the physical advantage to Stefano. It was only then he spoke firmly. "Stefano, we finally agree on something. Meara *is* special. I knew that before I met her. I know what you think of me, and all I can do is tell you that I have feelings for Meara and they are real."

"Feelings," scoffed Stefano. "What does that mean? Are you in love with her?"

Alec gave him a piercing stare. "Excuse me if I would rather tell the woman I have a relationship with how I'm feeling about her before I tell *you*."

"You haven't even talked about it yet?" exploded Stefano.

Alec took a deep breath. "No, we haven't. We initially discussed our relationship, but Meara has some concerns about being involved with someone who has children."

Stefano looked confused and then comprehension slowly dawned. "*Mi dispiace*, I didn't realize how much you are caring for your niece. I assumed she was living with your mother."

Alec shook his head, his eyes downcast, his hand playing with his wineglass. "Mamma has not been in a good place. She is improving, but Nia is my responsibility. And Meara...well I understand her feelings. It's a lot for a person to want to take on."

Stefano's shoulders now slumped, and he seemed to have lost his will to fight. "I never told you I was sorry for the loss of your sister...and your father."

Alec nodded. "Your family sent their condolences and flowers for both funerals. *Grazie.*"

Stefano's expression softened. "I just assumed you were

dating Meara casually, and I jumped to conclusions. I just want more for her."

Alec gazed at him steadily. "I know I'm not good enough for her, Stefano. But that doesn't mean I can't help wanting her."

Stefano looked confused. "I'm not saying you're not good enough. If you have true feelings for her, then fine. I just didn't want her to be another one to add to your long list."

Alec burst out laughing, and Stefano frowned. "Where is this list? Are you kidding me? An occasional date with a woman does not make me a player."

"I heard the rumors."

Alec grew serious. "And they were just that. Did I take various women out to social functions? Yes. Was I a player? Not really. Not in the true sense of the word. And for the last two-and-a-half years, the only female in my life has been a baby girl who needed me."

Stefano stared at him as if he was trying to decide to accept what Alec was telling him.

Alec returned his stare. Finally decided to unload what had always bothered him. "You never liked me, Stefano," he said bitterly. "Admit it. I remember being the new kid, trying to befriend you, and you wanted nothing to do with me in school."

"Because you were smarter than me," Stefano acknowledged quietly. "No one had ever been smarter than me. It was my one trait—my intelligence. Marco has charm, Nico has a quick wit and sense of humor. My gift was my intelligence. Then you came along, and that all ended." He shook his head ruefully. "It all sounds so ridiculous now. Even as I say it. But there it is. I couldn't beat you despite having an eidetic memory. And it all came so easily to you."

"Easily?" Alec asked, astounded. "I had no life. I studied all the time. I was so scared I wouldn't be able to keep up. I was terrified when my parents decided to move down here. I had skipped ahead in school. Did you know that? I am younger than you. All I wanted to do was fit in and I couldn't socially, so that meant being the smartest. You were always there on my heels. I don't remember always winning either. I am sure there were times you beat me academically."

Stefano grinned. "There were a few tests now that I think about it."

Alec smiled slightly. "Can we call a truce, Stefano? We are both on the board of the Angelo Foundation, and we will be seeing more of each other. I would like it if we can put the past behind us."

Stefano shrugged, his own expression serious "I think for the sake of everyone around us, we can try. I know Mamma will box my ears if I do not treat you as a guest in our home."

He stared thoughtfully at Alec for a minute. "Just promise me one thing. Don't hurt Meara. I know she acts tough, but so did Teresa and it wasn't true. Deep down, Meara isn't as tough as she portrays. I'd hate to see her hurt like I hurt Teresa. I'm still trying to make that up to her. Meara deserves more, so this is your notice. I'll be watching you, Alec," he stated seriously.

"My intention is to never hurt her," Alec said defensively. "Frankly, I worry more about my own heart. She has made it clear she has restrictions for our future, yet here we are." He spread his hands wide. "And I'm going to enjoy it until I can't."

Stefano picked up his own glass and held it up in a toast. "I wish you all the best." He grinned suddenly. "And now, let's talk about that time you cheated."

"AND THEN THERE was the time he opened his briefcase and took out his calculator," Stefano said, wiping his eyes with laughter. "None of us had ever seen one. Of course, the teacher made him put it right back inside his briefcase."

Alec shook his head, rolling his eyes. He sat back, putting a well-shod foot over one of his jean-clad knees. He had changed before dinner into a dark-washed pair of jeans and a blue and white-striped button-down shirt, with the sleeves rolled up. Now he draped an arm across Meara's chair.

Dinner had been over for some time, but the family remained relaxing in the dining room. Meara leaned forward eagerly. "Tell us some more, Stefano. I find this fascinating." She glanced at Alec, her eyes lit up with humor.

"I think I've been humiliated enough tonight," Alec interrupted with a laugh. "We've talked about every single embarrassing moment I had until the age of eighteen."

Margherita smiled at the table. "It's nice to hear the laughter and have you here. I am pleased no blood was shed prior to dinner."

Everyone laughed, but Meara glanced uneasily over at Alec. Despite her worries, he now seemed very relaxed. She had gone upstairs to find him after his talk with Stefano. Despite her tenuous prodding, he hadn't revealed anything. "There is nothing to be concerned about," he whispered, snatching a few kisses before dinner. "Let's just say we cleared the air."

Now, after an exquisite dinner of *Pasta e Fagioli*, a salad with fresh *burrata* and tomatoes, and a pillowy focaccia with herbs, the family was sated and wanting to share stories. Meara turned to Nico, who was quieter than usual, almost letting Stefano command the attention. "Nico, you mentioned earlier some changes. What are you up to?"

Nico looked uncomfortable, twisting his glass. "Nothing is set yet, but I want to study agricultural science." At her confused expression, he continued. "Soil cultivation, crop cultivation. How things like climate change or weather patterns affect our crops."

"Nico lives in the soil," said Margherita with a laugh. "He always has." Her eyes lost a bit of their twinkle. "Just like his father," she finished softly.

"I've applied a few places, but I'm just waiting to hear," Nico said. "I would still play a role in the company, but not as much as I have been."

Meara smiled encouragingly. "I think it's great, Nico. You're challenging yourself, and that can be scary. Trust me. I didn't know anything about building a foundation or even health care. Thank God I have the right people around me."

"Yep, they're right here," Alec remarked proudly.

Meara groaned, elbowing him. "I meant the people I've hired." At the family's laughter, she acknowledged, "It is true, though. Alec and Teresa paved the way for all of this. Tomorrow we are going to tour a building that we can renovate and a new construction site."

"I wanted to go with you guys, but Stefano and I want to get back to Capri for a few days," Teresa said wistfully. "We haven't been there hardly at all since we married."

Stefano reached down to give her a small kiss. "Yes, sorry, my new bride is unavailable for a few days," he said meaningfully.

"Stop right there," Nico told him, putting up a hand. "We don't need any more information."

Meara smiled at him. "What about you, Nico? Dating anyone?" she asked in a singsongy voice, teasing him like an older sister.

"No."

"Nico is a confirmed bachelor," said Stefano with a laugh. "In fact, the last woman he was crazy about…"

"Stop talking right now, big brother, or there will be the bloodshed Mamma was trying to avoid," Nico said sharply. His usual laughter was gone.

Stefano's eyes widened at his brother's tone, and he held up a hand. "Settle down, Niccolo," he admonished. Shifting in his chair, he seemed to want to change the subject. He raised his glass, "Let's have one last toast to the Angelo Foundation. And to our guests, here's to your good health and to your future," he remarked with a smile.

Meara raised her glass with the others, but inside she could only think about one word: future.

~

"THIS IS IT?" Meara asked incredulously. "It's one step up from a shack."

Alec took his sunglasses off and stared at the dilapidated building. "It's not hard to imagine the importance of the foundation on these small clinics." He came around to Meara's side and opened the door. "The staff has a heart of gold, though. It is not their fault they do not have the means to have a better facility and up-to-date equipment."

Meara followed him in, trying to keep her expression from showing her disgust. It wouldn't be professional if she appeared to be judgmental. Alec was immediately embraced by the woman at the front desk. She shouted to the others, and a doctor and nurse appeared, all speaking rapidly in Italian.

Alec turned to introduce Meara. "They are already very excited about the prospect of improvements," he translated. "They said your staff was here yesterday to take before photos, and the contractors have visited many times.

Meara nodded and greeted each person. Managing a project was familiar territory for her, and she immediately launched into specifics. Most of the reports she already committed to memory. They discussed the architectural drawings and she confirmed with all of them that they had given their unfiltered input.

Sitting down at a small table, she accepted weak tea and homemade biscotti from them since it would be rude to refuse. Alec was talking animatedly, and she tried not to feel jealous when the female doctor repeatedly touched him. Meara almost rolled her eyes. She wasn't only touching him, she was stroking him. They appeared on very good terms.

"Would you like a tour?" one of the nurses asked, who had introduced herself as Anita.

Meara nodded politely but was torn between leaving Alec with Dr. Handsy or seeing the small clinic. Alec smiled encouragingly at her, so she followed Anita through the small rooms. There wasn't much to look at. It might have been better if they had just leveled the place and started over, but Anita's eyes glimmered with pride with what they currently had. It was important to recognize and support them for their current efforts. Meara tried to comment positively and nod approvingly, especially at the shelves of supplies.

"We owe Dr. Amato for all this," Anita told her wide-eyed. "He is very good to us, you understand? He sends boxes of supplies each month. Though sometimes he brings them himself."

"You mean he visits here?" Meara asked, looking around.

Anita looked confused. "He did not tell you? He works here often when he can get away. When he is here, we have a long line of patients waiting. He stays late to make sure he sees everyone. Sometimes he brings other doctors as well."

"He must have forgotten to tell me that," Meara mumbled.

There wasn't much else to show her, and Meara walked back to watch the doctor's hands in motion. "We should go," she said a little louder than she intended.

Alec looked up and grinned, standing and disentangling himself at the same time. After a lengthy goodbye, they drove away silently. Finally, Meara couldn't resist. "You're on awfully good terms with them all, especially the doctor."

He glanced at her and smiled. "Yes, I told you they are all good people."

Meara narrowed her eyes at him, but he didn't expound. "That doctor seems very hands on," she finally said.

"Jealous again, Meara?" he asked with a small smirk.

"Not in the least."

"That's too bad. I was hoping you were," he said, his eyes glinting.

Her only answer was to glare at him before turning to watch the beautiful scenery go by as they drove to the second clinic. It had been torn down, and the new building was just starting construction. Marco told her this project was a priority and building it quickly was critical. Work to cut through the red tape was already started before Meara came on board. All she did was review the final architectural renderings and project's plans.

As they drove, Alec's mood seemed to darken. He was no longer smiling, but seemed tense. His hands gripped the steering wheel tighter. Meara wished she could see his eyes, but they were hidden behind his sunglasses. She made a few attempts at conversation, but he clearly was not interested in talking.

Driving down a gravel road, he abruptly swung into an area near the road and parked. Dump trucks were at the site, and a foundation stood before them. Apparently, the workers had already left for the day.

Alec stared straight ahead. "It looks like they have made good progress," he remarked, his voice sounding hoarse. He made no attempt to get out, and Meara looked at him thoughtfully. "The report said the building was torn down recently. It saved us a lot of money. We didn't have to pay for the demo work."

He continued to stare straight ahead. "Yes, I know. I had it torn down."

"But why?" Meara asked, turning to look at him. He was silent, the muscle clenching in his jaw. Finally, comprehension dawned on her.

"Oh, Alec, is this where..."

"My sister died here," he interrupted roughly. "I wanted to tear it down myself, piece by piece, right after it happened. But if I had, it would have left nothing for the people who live here. No medical care at all. So, I left it here, and I tried to at least improve it with supplies and equipment."

"I heard you volunteer at the clinic we just visited," Meara said softly.

"I volunteer there because I couldn't bear to walk into the building that was here. I was a coward."

She leaned over and covered one of his hands, still gripping the steering wheel. "Alec, no. You're not a coward. You were just grieving. I think you still are."

"Every time I look at Nia, I see her," he said, finally turning to Meara. He took off his sunglasses, and tears shone in his eyes.

Meara smiled gently at him. "That's good, Alec. Don't you see? That's a piece of your sister! She would be so proud of you, taking such great care of her daughter."

He gave her a watery smile. "*Grazie.*" Leaning over, he gave her a small kiss. "That means everything to me."

They were silent for a minute. He turned to her suddenly. "Meara, about Nia. Do you think..."

She flashed him a wide smile. "We better get going if we're going to get back to the lemon grove tonight," she blurted. "I promised Margherita we would take her out for dinner."

His eyes searched her face, and then he finally nodded before starting the car and driving away in a spurt of gravel.

twenty-one

Meara sat back at her expansive desk. She was having a difficult time focusing again. Twirling her chair, she stared at the view and the street below where people moved about. Too bad she couldn't be out there as well.

Frowning, she remembered how work used to satisfy her and be everything to her. Now she distracted easily, wanting to explore Rome. No, not really. She wanted to explore *with Alec*. She had found out there was a difference.

The last few days he had been in Milan, where he was asked to consult on a few cases. After reading a few guides online, Meara ventured out. She didn't need Alec to have an adventure. Joining a tour, she found the guide dry as dust. There were no fascinating tidbits or gruesome stories like Alec loved to share. She had visited the *Basilica of Santa Maria Maggiore* because Alec had told her it was one of four papal basilicas and, more importantly, his favorite. There was no denying it was stunning, and Meara sat in the church for what seemed like hours. But rather than leaving it uplifted, her heart felt heavy. Even Rome's cuisine didn't taste as delicious, but maybe she didn't know the really good places to go. She found herself sinking back into her old habits of staying home and getting takeout.

Her heart screamed Alec, her brain screamed run. That was the only explanation she had for panicking in the car when he asked about Nia. She assumed he was going to ask her if she had a change of heart. They were growing closer, and it was frightening and exhilarating all at the same time. Last night, she had gone to dine with Marco and Kate and tried carefully to sidestep all Kate's questions. There had been a lot.

Growing more uncomfortable in her pregnancy, Kate was looking for any topic to take her interest off herself. Meara had deftly fended the questions off, as if she were playing in Wimbledon. So much so that Marco had smiled gently at Kate after a while and tried to take control of the conversation, asking more questions about the foundation's work at the hospital and clinics. Meara had launched into extensive detail about the project's timeline. Finally, Kate stood to walk around, apparently giving up.

Meara came home uneasy, though. Kate hadn't looked well. She was far larger than the last time Meara saw her and was very uncomfortable. When Marco was out of the room, Kate had confided that her nausea had returned, and she was getting frequent headaches. Meara casually asked when her next doctor's appointment was, and she said it was in just a few days.

Meara understood there was patient confidentiality, but she would ask Alec to move up the appointment. With that decision made, Meara turned back to her computer and forced herself to look over the inspections and reports regarding the clinics.

Hours later, Meara sat up and rubbed her neck. Satisfied that she had finally gotten some critical work completed, she glanced at the clock and was surprised how late it was. Alec said he would return before dinner. In fact, she had told him she would order something, and they could dine at her place for once. Valentina was visiting her great aunt, Jacquetta's sister.

Standing, Meara gathered her laptop and papers and put them in her bag. She would start for home, and by then, Alec would certainly call her or might even be waiting for her. The concierge knew him by now and would just allow him to go up. She admitted to herself she couldn't wait to see him. Planning their evening, she decided to stop at that cute *ristorante* on the next block. Alec said they had reasonable *cacio e pepe*. That sounded fantastic.

Her staff had long left for the day, and Meara walked out of the darkened building, nodding to the security that Marco employed. Her apartment was just a few blocks away, but Cosmo insisted on driving her. He opened the door with a flourish, and she smiled at him as she slid in. It was then she heard her phone. Alec, finally. Taking her phone out of her coat pocket, she saw it was Marco instead.

"*Mio fratello,*" she greeted him cheerfully.

"Meara, it's Katie," came Marco's hoarse reply. "Come quickly." He gave her the name of the hospital, and she quickly relayed it to Cosmo.

Mcara's heart plummeted. "Marco, what's wrong? Is it bad?"

"No...I don't know. Her blood pressure is really high. They took her into a special unit, and I can't go in right now. Alec said they are running tests."

"Alec is there?"

Marco cleared his throat as if he could barely get out the words. "*Si. Per favore Sbrigati!...Hurry!*"

"I am on my way," Meara said as reassuringly as she could, shutting off her phone. She had noticed a long time ago Marco lapsed into Italian when he was really excited or worried. It was definitely the latter. Thank God Alec was there. Kate would be fine!

~

"WHY IS IT TAKING SO LONG?" Meara repeated, pacing the waiting room. Still in her charcoal-colored suit and high heels, she stood out against the hospital's white walls and floor.

Marco was sitting on the couch in the waiting room, his head in his hands. He had been that way for the last hour. The first hour after she arrived, he joined her in the pacing. Her heart melted for him. "Marco, everything is okay. You must know that."

He nodded, still not looking at her. She knew he was trying to be brave.

"Where is she?" Teresa demanded as she burst into the room, Stefano trailing behind her. "I need to see her!"

Meara almost smiled at Teresa's dynamic energy. Petite yet powerful, she almost came in swinging. Meara took a step back, just as Stefano put a steady arm around her.

"*Mi dispiace*, we came as fast as we could," Stefano said quietly. "We took the helicopter, but we should have taken a supersonic jet. It wasn't fast enough for Teresa, and she's a bit anxious."

"We all are," Meara acknowledged. "The last we heard was that she was stabilized, and they are running tests."

"Does she have preeclampsia?" Teresa asked, staring at Meara.

"Yes, she does," said a voice. Meara's head snapped up. Alec had emerged from the locked double doors. Wearing doctor's lab coat over his street clothes, his expression was unreadable.

Marco jumped up, "Alec!"

Alec glanced at all of them, but his attention was on Marco. "Marco, she's okay. I have to ask, is it okay if I speak in front of the group?"

Meara stepped forward. "Alec, come on!"

It was Teresa who put a calming hand on Meara's arm. "He has to ask that, Meara. Katie is his patient, and Marco is her husband."

"Well, I'm her sister, and I was here first," muttered Meara.

"*Per favore*, Alec. Tell me how she is. How is the baby?" Marco asked frantically.

"They are both fine. She is sleeping right now. But Kate's blood pressure was dangerously high when you brought her in. Has she been complaining of headaches recently?"

At Marco's confused head shake no, Meara softly interrupted. "Yes."

Startled, Marco turned to her, and she shrugged. "Last night she told me she's been getting frequent headaches. She was looking forward to seeing Alec in a couple of days to ask if that was normal."

"And you didn't think to tell me?" Marco exploded.

"I am sorry! She just mentioned it at the end of the evening. I assumed she told you. I was going to talk to Alec about it tonight when..." Meara trailed off. Swallowing her guilt, she looked at Alec. "Is weight gain part of it? Because last night she just looked, I don't know...swollen."

Alec nodded. "Yes, actually, but it's not true weight gain. It's edema. Her ankles and her hands were badly swollen. It was affecting her breathing as well. Marco, you did the right thing in getting her to the hospital."

Despite his Mediterranean skin, Marco's face was pale. "She said she was nauseous and dizzy. As a precaution, I told her we were going to the hospital. But as I drove, she got worse and said she was having problems breathing and then she fainted. It was the worst moment of my life, but by that time I was closer to the hospital than pulling over to call an ambulance."

Alec put a steady hand on him. "I'm sure that was frightening for you, but those symptoms are all part of her condition. You did the right thing," he repeated.

Meara frowned. "I don't understand, Alec. Why didn't you know about this sooner?"

He blinked at her, almost taken aback. "I can't know about something unless my patient tells me," he responded firmly.

"Katie said she had an appointment with you in a few days. Maybe you should have been seeing her more!" Meara burst out.

Now she felt everyone's startled gaze on her. She took a deep breath, and knew she was being unreasonable. It was just that her heart had not stopped racing since the moment Marco had called. The queasiness took over now. She couldn't lose Katie!

Marco gave her a look of quiet reprimand and spoke with authority, obviously pulling himself together. "Alec, we appreciate your response tonight. Let's focus on the next step. What now?"

"We treat her with medication. We put her on bedrest, and we monitor her," Alec answered calmly. "She's stable and feeling more like herself. Of course, she's asking for you, Marco."

Marco turned quickly, striding toward the locked doors.

"You need me to get through those doors, Marco. I'll take you back!" Alec said, before glancing at them all, his gaze not meeting Meara's. "I know you'd like to see Katie, but I think we'll keep it pretty quiet tonight."

Turning, he walked away, using a keycard to open the doors. Putting a gentle hand on Marco's back, he led him through. Still reeling, Meara turned to Teresa. "What's the real story? How bad can this be?"

Teresa was wiping away tears. She sniffed. "My professional opinion or my personal one?"

"Both."

"Very bad."

～

MEARA WALKED into her apartment overcome with fatigue. Sitting down on the sofa, she laid her head back on the sofa. Teresa had rushed to explain that what she meant to say

204

was it *could* be bad. They had gone to the cafeteria to eat, only to just push it around their plates. Over the next hour, Teresa explained every detail of the medical issue. Meara felt like she could diagnose it herself now.

Meara's phone rang, and she saw it was Alec. Alarmed, she answered right away. "Alec! Is it Katie? Did something happen?"

"No, she's fine," he said reassuringly. "You left before I could come back and talk with you."

"Oh, sorry. I thought after you left with Marco, you weren't coming back. I figured you were mad at me," she admitted sadly. "I am sorry I lashed out at you. Of course, it wasn't your fault."

"I came right back, Meara," he said quietly. "Thank you for your apology. I hope you know I am a conscientious doctor, no matter who my patient is. I always want to provide the best medical care."

"I know that," she answered softly. Taking a deep breath, she said, "Alec, Teresa said this could be bad."

"It can be, but we are keeping a close eye on her."

"What does that mean?" Meara asked hoarsely. Swallowing hard, she tried again. "Can you just tell me more about what's going on? Teresa tried, but I want to hear from you. And talk to me like I'm a ten-year-old. Plain language."

Alec chuckled softly. "Meara, you are the most intelligent woman I know. I think you can handle some medical terminology."

"Not when it's my sister."

"I understand," he said calmly. Clearing his voice, he continued, sounding very official. "In general, preeclampsia is something that can occur in pregnancies. Sometimes there's another condition that sparks it, such as gestational diabetes. But in Kate's case, she is just one of those unfortunate women who got it for whatever reason, and we must manage it. I am not going to lie to you. It's something I wouldn't wish on her, and it can be dangerous if it's not monitored but we are doing that now."

She was silent, her thoughts tumultuous. "It's nothing I haven't dealt with before, Meara," he said softly. "I will take care of her."

"I know you will," she acknowledged.

"That's why I'm calling. I don't think I can come over at all tonight. I was looking forward to it. I missed you," he whispered.

Meara chose not to acknowledge the last part. "Of course you can't, and I understand. I would rather you stayed and looked after Katie."

"I actually have two other patients tonight. One is in labor and one is probably in false labor, so I would have ended up here anyway. But, yes. I'll be checking on Katie between things."

"Alec, do I have to worry?"

She could almost see his gentle smile. "Let me be the one to do so. You try to get some sleep."

twenty-two

"You look like hell," Meara commented, as she walked into her sister's room, holding a bouquet of daffodils.

Kate, sitting up in bed with an IV tube in her and two monitors attached to her, made a face at her.

"I was going to say the same about you," Kate said, arching an eyebrow. "I know why I do, but why do you look like you haven't slept in weeks?"

"Probably because I haven't," Meara muttered. She glanced around at the number of bouquets. "I guess I should have brought you something else."

Kate winced. "I know. It's a bit much, but thank you, sis." She put her hand out to take the bouquet. "Mom's favorite." She smiled tremulously at Meara.

Reluctantly, Kate handed them back to Meara. "Will you put them in a vase? There's an extra one over there by the sink. I'm going to have Marco go sprinkle the rest of these around the ward before I have an asthma attack. I'll keep yours and his," she said, indicating the large crystal vase holding dozens of red roses.

Meara finished putting the flowers in a vase, filled it with water, and put them where Kate could see them. She perched on the bed. "Where is my esteemed brother-in-law?"

"I finally talked him into going home to at least take a shower and eat some real food. He'll be back soon."

"I am sure he will be! Have you eaten anything?"

"I ate some toast they sent up. That was the only thing I could recognize," Kate grumbled.

Meara smiled. "I was actually going to bring you a cappuccino, but I wasn't sure that was allowed."

Kate sighs. "No, it's not. Just like a lot of other things."

"I was only kidding about how you looked," Meara said, eyeing her. "You actually seem better. Less puffy."

Kate glanced warily up at the monitor. "I guess I am, though when I look at those numbers, they freak me out."

Meara smiled. "Well, there's one way to take care of that!" She stood and rolled the monitor, so it was facing the doorway.

"Meara! I need to watch it!"

"No, you don't, Katie! It's not a television set. Let the medical professionals evaluate it. I just walked by outside, and they can see it from the nurses' station. You concentrate on other stuff."

"That's just it. I'm tired of thinking about myself. Please, for the love of God, talk to me about anything!"

Meara walked over to the window to look at the view. "It's sunny outside today. It's almost springlike." Glancing around the expansive room, she arched her eyebrows. "Pretty sweet digs," she commented.

"Yes, it's an excellent hospital," Kate said and rolled her eyes. "Marco made sure I got a nice room, too. He probably donated the wing. He was out of his mind last night."

Meara's face grew serious at the memory. "We all were, Katie."

"I know. I'm sorry I worried everyone. I should have spoken up sooner. But let's talk about something else. Tell me about your trip! How did it go down south?"

Meara sat down in the chair near the window and told her sister about touring the hospital and clinic. She didn't mention the part about the women flirting with Alec and her own jealousy.

"Was the Neonatal Unit fascinating? Marco showed me some pictures you sent. I just don't want to think about those tiny babies," Kate said, shuddering. "You need to stay in there," she whispered and patted her belly.

"He or she will! Though are you going to tell me what you're having?"

"Nope!" Kate said, smiling. "It's a surprise. For us, too!"

"I'll ask Alec," Meara said smugly.

"He can't tell you! Patient confidentiality and all that," Kate insisted. "But since you brought him up, how did things go with him on your trip?"

Meara frowned a little. "They went fine, but I don't want to talk about it."

"Oh, no you don't," Kate insisted. "It's your job as my sister. It's my time of need. You have to distract me, and if that means finally discussing Alec with me, then that's your duty."

"I don't remember those rules written anywhere," Meara stalled.

"Talk to me, Meara," Katie commanded softly.

Meara sighed. "He's just so…"

"Wonderful?" Kate finished.

Meara laughed. "Well, yes, but that's not what I was going to say. I don't know Katie…he and I are sometimes so alike and then other times, there are too many differences."

"Because of Valentina?"

"That's not the only reason. I'm getting a little more comfortable around her. It's just that I realized how much babies are his life. He's delivering them every day, and when he's not, he's thinking about them. He should have ten kids."

Kate's eyes widened in horror. "Did he tell you that's what he wants?"

"Well, no," Meara admitted. "But I can tell. He just loves babies! You should hear the way he talks about them. His face just radiates happiness. Then sometimes he's so self-assured and suave, and the next minute, he's this big nerd. I just can't figure him out."

"Figure what out?"

Meara glanced quickly over to the door. Alec had entered the room. He wore green scrubs, a lab coat, and a stethoscope was slung around his neck. His big, thick black glasses were perched high on his nose. He looked every inch the doctor, but he also looked exhausted.

"Alec, I didn't see you."

"Are you here disturbing my patient?" he asked with a small smile. Walking over to the monitor, he took a glance at it.

"What's this doing over here?"

"I moved it because Katie kept staring at it. Frankly, I thought it was making her blood pressure go higher," Meara explained.

He laughed, coming over to stand near Kate, assessing her.

"How do her numbers look? Is she okay?" Meara asked anxiously, standing quickly.

Alec glanced at her and back at Kate. "Is it okay if we talk in front of Meara?"

"What do you mean, is it okay to talk in front of me? Are you kidding me? She's my sister!" Meara reminded him roughly.

"Meara, sit down," Kate said, and then laughed. "He has to ask that! He's being ethical. Calm the heck down, or you're going to get me all riled up."

Meara sat obediently and took a deep breath. Alec didn't glance her way but was staring at Kate. "How are you feeling, Kate?"

"Better than last night," she said, looking up at him with a smile.

"Anymore headaches?"

She shook her head.

He indicated the monitor around Kate's stomach. "The baby's heartbeat looks good. Let me take a look at the ultrasound images." He went over to the laptop that was on a stand. Logging in, he read over the notes silently, and then took a little notebook from his pocket and wrote in it. Pushing the computer away, he turned to face them, his calm expression showing nothing. "The baby's heartbeat looks good. I don't see any signs of distress."

Meara felt her own heart beating faster. "What do you mean distress? Is that a possibility?"

Alec glanced at her. "It's just part of all this monitoring. We are here for a reason, and we're being careful," he explained patiently.

"But her blood pressure still seems high to me," Meara said. "I'm not a doctor, but I can look online at what a good blood pressure is. And Katie and I learned a lot when our dad was in the hospital."

Alec sent her a speaking look. "Her blood pressure is still in an acceptable range. If it goes any higher, there are several medications we can use safely."

"What number is dangerous?"

He smirked a little. "You can't find that online?"

Meara frowned. "Of course I can, but I'm asking you."

"There's no need to discuss what-ifs at this point." He turned to smile at Kate. "I heard you didn't think much of your breakfast," he teased.

"It was pretty bland."

"I know. I'm sure you're missing your sodium. But it's important you stay away from that now. I'll ask the nurses to find a snack for you."

Meara was staring at him. "Alec, how long does she have to stay here? Can she go home?"

"Not right now," he hedged.

"Do you think she's going to have the baby sooner than later?"

He turned again to look at her, his eyebrows narrowed. "I explained the situation and various scenarios to Kate and Marco last night. Why don't we go into the hall and discuss this?"

Meara opened her mouth to argue, just as Marco swept in. "Sorry I took so long. There was a lot of traffic on the way back." Kate held her arms out, and Marco strode quickly to her.

"Meara, let's give them some privacy," Alec said quietly. "Come into the hall with me."

She nodded, glancing at the couple before following him.

"Just a moment," he told her. Kate's room was right across from the nurses' station, and he walked over and took out his notebook. The nurse nodded and went to the computer, typing in something. Alec and the nurse talked for a minute before he appeared to thank her. Turning around, he glanced at Meara with a thoughtful stare. "Let's go down the hall. There's a quiet room where we can talk."

He led her into a door that had two small sofas with some tables and chairs. Glancing around, she asked, "Is this a waiting room?"

He shook his head.

"Then what is it?"

He looked uncomfortable. "This is a room where we take family members when we need to talk."

She narrowed her gaze. "You mean when things go bad?"

He stared at her before nodding.

"Are things going badly?" she asked, her voice cracking.

"No, Meara, they aren't. But your questions in there were not helping Kate feel better. If you kept going, you were going to create distress!"

She rolled her eyes. "Katie is used to me. She watched me drill the doctor when our dad was sick. In fact, she thanked me! I asked questions she didn't even think of."

Alec sat down and took his glasses off, rubbing his eyes. Meara sat down on the sofa next to him, and her heart softened. "You look tired," she said softly.

"I am. It was a long night."

"Did you deliver a new baby?"

"Yes, but it was a little dicey."

She smiled a little. "Dicey? Is that a medical term?"

He put his glasses back on and smiled at her. "Today it is." Putting a hand on her jean-clad knee, he grew serious. "Meara, I'll answer any questions you have right now because Kate gave me permission. I know you're worried, and I understand. But I had to get you out of there before you sounded any more alarms."

"I just want to make sure you've thought of everything! At this point, why don't you just deliver the baby and be done with it?"

He shook his head. "I know that sounds like a good option, but it's not. Katie is only 35 weeks. Gestation is 40 weeks. Babies' organs mature throughout each stage of the pregnancy, and though that seems like only five weeks, this time is important, especially for the lungs. That baby is getting stronger every day he stays inside Katie."

"He?" Meara asked, raising her eyebrows.

"That was a figure of speech," Alec murmured. "He or she."

"Uh, huh. You just blew it, Dr. Amato."

He gave her a small scowl. "I will not confirm or deny anything. Our plan is to keep Kate right here under our nose. Some women can go home and stay on bed rest. In this case, even with a fleet of nurses that Marco would hire, that's probably not the best course."

"There's something bothering you, isn't there?" Meara asked, feeling the hairs on her neck stand up.

He stared at her thoughtfully, blinking through his thick lenses. "No, I wouldn't say that. I think it's just a feeling I have. I believe in science, but occasionally I need to trust my instinct."

"And what does your instinct say?" Meara asked, hoping he would share more.

"To keep her here," he said firmly.

"But, Alec, what if…"

He held up a hand and interrupted. "Meara, I have to ask that you respect boundaries. I know we have a personal relationship, but this is my profession and Kate is my patient. I'm going to keep a careful watch on her." He stared at her for a minute. "Do you trust me?"

She nodded slowly. "Of course I do. It's just I like to…"

"Be in control?" he asked softly. "Just this one you are going to have to concede. I'm the one who went to medical school."

Before she could answer, he stood, giving her a small smile. "Want to go see what the special is in the cafeteria?"

Meara bit her lip. "Alec, she's my sister."

"I am well aware of that."

Meara stood, finding her legs finally steady again. He leaned in and gave her a small kiss. "Maybe it's tacos," he said hopefully.

"They have tacos?"

"Sure! What Italian hospital doesn't?" As they got to the door, he gave her one long kiss before opening the door for her. "I've never had a cafeteria date before."

She laughed. "And I've never been asked on one!" Glancing down, she arched her eyebrows at his hospital clogs. "Or dated anyone wearing those shoes."

~

ALEC TRIED to get comfortable on the cot in the physician's quiet room. Though he was exhausted, his mind wouldn't settle. His lunch with Meara had become strained. Every time he tried to talk about something else, she brought the conversation back to Kate. He understood Meara was scared and he tried to do his best to answer her questions, but he also felt a sense of distrust from her. Her skeptical looks at his explanations made him wonder if she was going to look up his answers online.

It was his ego, and he knew it. He was used to people taking his word for it. Meara kept pushing, and though he tried to be understanding, he grew impatient with her. Part of it was exhaustion. Last night had been a tough one. He didn't want to tell Meara how close he had come to losing his patient. She didn't need to hear that right now with all her current fears. Most people assumed his life was all rainbows and happiness. Most often it was joyous, but there were times it wasn't. Pregnancy was a complex medical condition. Two patients for one, he often joked.

Yawning, he punched his pillow and willed himself to sleep. He wished he could have talked to Meara the way he really wanted to. Pouring out his thoughts and feelings to someone else would feel wonderful. But he couldn't. The truth was, he was concerned about Kate. He was confident in his own abilities, but that didn't always guarantee everything would turn out perfectly. He had seen complications before even with excellent medical care.

After Kate had the baby, he could talk a little more to Meara. It would be amazing to share not only the bad, but the good. Someone to celebrate and commiserate with. Closing his eyes, he drifted off. His last thoughts were of Meara before he fell into a deep sleep.

<h1 style="text-align:center">twenty-three</h1>

The next few days had a rhythm to them. Meara arrived at the office early, went through the pretense of getting work done and then left early to visit Kate. She knew her staff was confused by her behavior. She couldn't explain it either, except that Kate was more important than work. Meara also acknowledged Alec was right, and she did want control. And though she couldn't control this, she felt a twisted belief that if she was around, she somehow could. Kate was her little sister, and though they hadn't always been close, Meara was there to protect her.

She had seen little of Alec, except a couple more cafeteria dates and a few stolen kisses in the quiet room. He had warned her when they had their cafeteria date he had an influx of patients. Meara understood, and it was fine with her. When they were together, she couldn't resist plying him with questions, and things had been a little strained. He had assured her he understood how worried she was and was patient. But he always sidestepped her what-if questions.

She looked out the window at the *Piazza Venezia* from the

car. She was on her way back to the hospital now. It seemed like ages since Alec had shown her the hidden walks and passageways near there. The thought of him made her glance guiltily at her phone. Earlier that day, she had given in to impulse and contacted a former colleague, Michael, who had once professed an attraction to her. They had never dated, and she hadn't seen him in years. But she remembered his boasting about his father, an esteemed OB/GYN physician at Cedars Sinai in Los Angeles. Looking up Michael's father online, she saw all the honors and accolades and had been impressed. Getting in touch with him was easier than she thought. Michael was happy to hear from her and offered to call his father immediately. Before he hung up, she had ignored his hint that they could get together when she returned to the States. Within minutes, she was talking to the doctor. Speaking with him had been comforting. He was reassuring about preeclampsia and the ways to treat it. He had patiently answered the dozens of questions she had. It was true, Alec had answered the same questions, but it felt great hearing it from this doctor. And in addition, he had provided information about preventative actions Kate's doctor should be taking.

At the end of the call, he had casually asked her the name of the hospital. When he asked her who Kate's physician was, Meara hesitated, suddenly feeling nervous. How small of a world could it be? She felt compelled to tell him, given that she kept him on the phone for so long. She sensed surprise in his tone, but he simply told her that her sister was undoubtedly in good hands. He had been called away before she could ask if he heard of Alec.

Glancing at her phone, she saw the numerous notes she had made. If she saw Alec today, she wanted to ask more questions to verify he was doing what this doctor had told her about. Knowledge was power, and Meara was determined to get it.

Striding toward Kate's room, her heart began to thud at the amount of activity near it. A nurse was busy wheeling a machine into the room. "What's going on?" she demanded to one of the nurses. He looked up from his computer quizzically, and Meara pointed to Kate's door, now closed.

"*Il Dottore* ordered an ultrasound," he said nonchalantly. "It will only take about fifteen minutes. You can go down the hall to the waiting room. Or if you want, I can go ask if you can go in."

Meara shook her head and thanked him, feeling a little deflated. As much medical knowledge as she had gained, it didn't mean she wanted to actually see anything. Marco would be with Kate, and it was their time. Besides, she would end up asking the ultrasound technician questions, and Kate would become annoyed with her. Her sister had been so positive over the last few days, and Meara tried to pretend she was as well. She couldn't forget the wary expression Alec had so carefully tried to hide from her.

Walking toward the large waiting room she had visited a few times, she passed the quiet room. The door was propped open, and she stopped abruptly at his voice. Was he giving a patient bad news? No, the door wouldn't be open if he were. She peeked in to see him on the phone. He was by the window, sitting on a ledge, holding his phone out in a video call. She heard Valentina's sweet voice and smiled. It had been a while since she saw the little girl.

Excited to say hello, Meara walked in when she heard her name. Stopping in her tracks, she backed up a little. She knew it was wrong to eavesdrop, but she was curious about what was being said.

Alec was talking to his mother, and Meara frowned, focusing on her growing knowledge of Italian. He was telling his mother he hadn't been able to see Meara because of his workload. She was telling him he needed to work less. Or was that more? Meara always got that word mixed up. His mother said something about love. She definitely knew that word— *amore.*

"Mamma, let's speak in English. I don't want small ears to hear. But this is the wrong time for this discussion," he hedged.

"When is the right time?" his mother asked. "I have barely seen you in the last few weeks. You are always so busy. This child needs a proper home. She needs a mamma and a papa. An aging *nonna* can only do so much. I saw how happy she was that morning with Meara. She talks about her all the time."

"Mamma, *per favore*. Meara is not in my future. It is short-term. She is not a ready-made mother for Valentina."

"But, Alec, I know you have feelings for her."

"Any feelings I have for Meara are irrelevant," he answered.

Meara put a shaking hand to her mouth. He sounded so cold. So clinical. *Any feelings.* He had not said he loved her. She scrunched up her face. Come to think of it, he never once said anything about how he was feeling about her since they had gotten together. She realized now how much of her heart she had given to him. What a fool she was.

Alec switched abruptly back to Italian, and she heard him stand. He was getting ready to end the call. Trying not to make a sound in her high heels, she hurried to the large waiting room at the end of the hallway. There were several people there, reading, working on jigsaw puzzles, and talking softly. She found a corner spot, and stared blankly out the window.

Meara took a deep breath. She had lost control of this part of her life. How ridiculous she had been. Suddenly, she needed a plan. Her mind whirled. How would she act when she saw Alec? Nothing had really changed, but suddenly, everything seemed like it had.

She wasn't sure how long she sat there. Long enough for her racing heart to slow its beat. Now she had a pit in her stomach. This was why she never wanted a relationship. She never wanted to feel like this.

"Meara."

She turned her head to see Alec standing before her. Wearing his scrubs and lab coat, he looked so handsome. There was something about his eyes, though. They usually glinted with kindness and humor. Now they were hard. "Why are you in here?"

She twisted her purse in her lap, avoiding his gaze. Did he see her eavesdropping on him? Was that why he looked so angry?

"They were doing an ultrasound. The nurse told me to wait here."

"Come with me," he ordered.

She noticed he didn't put his hand on her back to guide her like he usually did. In fact, he started walking ahead, apparently assuming she would just follow him. They would have to talk later, after she saw Kate. It was time for her to take her own control back and tell him they were over. It should have never started. While they had foundation work to do still, she could easily hand off some of it to the new project manager she just hired. He could work with Alec, and she would minimize contact with him. Occasional board meetings would be the only time she would have to see him.

Assuming they were going to Kate's room, she was surprised when he led her into a crowded elevator and then through the lobby. Suddenly, she found herself in a small courtyard to the side of the front doors.

"What are we doing out here?" she asked anxiously. She felt her heart thud, then the dawning realization that he was going to break up with her. She knew he liked to be outside when he was upset. Well, she would do it first!

"Alec, I need to talk to you," she said forcibly, before he could answer her. Straightening her shoulders, she was ready for a confrontation. She was Meara Malone, for God's sake. It was time to act like her true self and not some cowering little girlfriend who was about to be dumped.

He was turned away from her, breathing deeply, running his hand through his thick wavy hair. "And I want to talk to you," he said in clipped tones. Turning his head toward her she saw his steel-eyed gaze. She tried not to flinch. "How could you?" he exploded.

Looking at him, her eyes wide, she was stunned and could only squeak out one word. "What?"

"You called Dr. Davis to check on me? To consult on Kate's case?"

Willing her face to remain neutral, she asked, "How did you know?"

"I got off the phone with him thirty minutes ago. He told me all about your call. How uncertain you were about the care your sister was getting from her physician!"

"No, I didn't say that!" Meara burst out.

"Well, that was the impression he got! He said you asked him numerous questions and seemed very uneasy about everything. Apparently, I hadn't answered your questions sufficiently."

"You've been busy. I didn't want to bother you..." she fibbed.

"You expect me to believe that? You were double checking me. You purposely reached out to a prominent physician in the States. Someone apparently you thought you could *trust*," he said angrily.

She took a deep breath. His anger stung her, and she realized how much he had become a steady, calm force in her life. The last week had been awful, and she missed his solid comfort. Walking forward, she put her hand on his arm. He was so upset. "Alec, I'm sorry. I...how did he know how to contact you?"

He shook off her hand, and she blinked at the depth of his fury. He seemed to be focusing on his breathing, and when he spoke, his voice was calmer. He would not look at her. "Dr. Davis and I have consulted on several high-profile cases before. He's called me in as a specialist to some celebrities he's treated."

"But you are..."

"Are what, Meara?" he said flatly. "Not smart enough? Not skilled enough?"

"Of course you are!"

"Yet you don't trust me," he said sadly.

"It's not that! It's just I had a lot of questions, and it seemed like you weren't being completely honest with me."

"I *was* being honest with you! But I will not play Internet Doctor with you!" he said roughly. His anger was back. "And I will not entertain every conceivable problem that might surface. I am a scientist, and I deal with facts, not what-ifs or rare things that could occur."

She tried to speak, but no words would come. He continued talking as if he couldn't stop. "I understand she's your sister, and you always want to feel in control. But I am her doctor. At the very least, I would think you would have some faith in me." He now looked at her, his eyes still hard.

"I do, Alec! People get second opinions all the time," she said defiantly. Now she was getting angry. All she had done was ask another doctor to confirm the information he had told her. "I just wanted to double check..."

"Me," he interrupted. "Double check me. I'm used to patients or their families wanting a second opinion. I just didn't think it would be you, Meara."

She saw the defeat in his expression, and she knew what was coming. "While we have no future, I thought at the very least you believed in me. But it's over, isn't it? Aside from Kate and this situation, you have made your decision, haven't you?" he asked quietly.

Meara's mind raced. Hadn't he already decided? She heard what he had said to his mother about *any feelings.*

Suddenly, she wanted to tell him she *did* have feelings. She hadn't meant to hurt him. And now she wanted him in her life. She *needed* him in her life. Swallowing hard, she realized it was time to have this talk.

"Alec," she choked out. "Actually, I have been thinking..."

His phone suddenly rang, and he glanced at it. "*Pronto!*" His eyes widened, and he spoke rapidly in Italian, already starting toward the front door. Turning toward her, he hung up his phone, his expression grave. "It's Kate. We have to go."

<h1 style="text-align:center">twenty-four</h1>

"Why is it taking so long?" Meara asked yet again, looking at Teresa and Stefano. She paced the same path, muttering the same mantra. "She'll be fine. The baby will be fine."

Teresa came over and put her hand on her arm, looking at her kindly. "Meara, sit down for a minute. You're making us dizzy," she teased with a small smile.

Meara stared at Teresa, almost as if she wasn't seeing her. "Come on, you're hurting my neck," Teresa joked, as she looked up at Meara. Grabbing Meara's arm, she pulled her to sit down.

"It's going to take as long as it takes. C-sections are done every day," Teresa said reassuringly. "Honestly, part of the delay is just getting the patient in there and all the prep. The surgery itself isn't that long."

Meara nodded. Teresa had told her this now about five times, but it still seemed to take forever. "It's just scary that they had to rush her in to do it," Meara said, staring at her hands in her lap. It was hard to imagine that Alec was in there now, operating on her sister.

"I know, but Alec wasn't going to take any chances," Teresa

explained patiently. "I was in there when the monitors started beeping, and even though they gave her the additional drugs, her blood pressure was hovering too high. He could have waited and been more conservative, but he has to go with his instinct."

"There's that word again," Meara grumbled. "Instinct. Alec said something about his instincts to me one time. I thought you all believed in science."

"We do," responded Teresa matter-of-factly. "But an eminent physician like Alec has learned through his experience that he also has to trust his gut. That's what makes him so sought after."

"What do you mean, eminent?" Meara asked numbly. She had been so worried about Kate that her fight with Alec had been shoved away for her to deal with later.

"You haven't reviewed his qualifications?" Teresa asked, wide eyed.

"No, I never thought to," Meara said. "He was already Kate's doctor and then he was on the foundation, and you worked with him."

"I can't believe this. You of all people, Meara," Teresa shook her head. "Look him up," she challenged.

Meara shot Teresa a dark look but pulled out her phone. She entered Alec's name and dozens of hits lit up her screen. Scanning them, she finally began to click to read. It only took two articles for the shock to set in. She looked at Teresa, her expression one of dread.

"He's like a…"

"God," Teresa finished. "He's one of the best, most talented specialists in the world."

Meara looked back at her phone and then at Teresa. "But I thought he was just your everyday OB/GYN. I know he's always busy, but this says he lectures and consults all over the world. He's so young for that."

Teresa laughed. "He is young, but he is brilliant and has the skills to match. Do you think for one minute, Marco would let

Kate go to some average doctor? No, he chose the best. You should hear some of the information I learned from the medical staff when I was working with him. They just revere him."

"But how can he do all this and still practice?" Meara asked. "He sees patients all the time."

Teresa shrugged. "That's why he's so respected. He knows people might question his youth. He's heard jokes about being 'the boy wonder.' It was by paying his dues that he gained the trust of older doctors. I also heard he does a lot of volunteer work."

"Trust," Meara whispered.

Teresa looked confused, and Meara shook her head. "Just something we were talking about."

As the door opened, they all jumped to their feet. Marco came out, taking the mask off, grinning. "Everyone is fine," he said.

"Katie?" Meara asked frantically.

"She's amazing. Superwoman. Calm and so very brave," he said with a smile.

Teresa grabbed on to Stefano in relief. "The baby?"

"We have a son," Marco said proudly.

Teresa flung herself at Marco, and he embraced her. Meara turned away to take a deep breath for the first time since Alec's phone rang.

"Unfortunately, he's pretty little. They took him to the Neonatal Intensive Care Unit. A neonatologist is checking him out right now. Alec is finishing up, and Kate will be in recovery for a bit."

"Is she still hypertensive?" Teresa asked, going into nurse mode.

"It's still higher than normal, but in an acceptable range. Alec said it might take a few days to go down. She wants me to go be with the baby. I'll try to come out when I can," Marco said anxiously, already retreating. He turned around again and looked dazed. "We have a son!"

Stefano and Teresa were hugging, and Meara stood there awkwardly. Finally, she sat, staring straight ahead. The last several hours had been the most chaotic of her life. It had been a roller coaster of emotions. Glancing up, she realized Teresa and Stefano were staring at her.

Meara smiled for the first time in several hours. "I'm an aunt."

ALEC TORE his operating gown off and shoved it in the bin. Washing his hands, he relayed some notes to his operating room nurse and then left the room to go get changed. In the physician's locker room, he sat down on the bench and blinked his dry eyes. He needed to take his contacts out and put his glasses on. It had already been a long day.

As he changed into his street clothes, he reviewed the rest of his evening. He would chart his last notes, check in on Kate, and then go have a few words with the neonatologist. Kate and Marco's baby was now under her care. He had followed all the best protocols to take care of Kate and the baby. Alec had only briefly glanced at the baby. His focus was on Kate, while his physician's assistant, Martie, evaluated the baby and accompanied him to the Neonatal Unit. By all accounts, the infant was doing reasonably well. Alec would go find out what he could before seeing Kate.

Sitting back down on the bench, he felt his exhaustion take over. When was the last time he ate anything? After he finished, he would go home and find something to eat. He had hardly slept in his own bed, and he was looking forward to it.

Could he sleep, though? He had pushed all his thoughts aside during surgery. He was used to compartmentalizing, and it was imperative that he focused only on his patient. Now he began to mentally retrace the argument with Meara. It was unfortunate that he had lost his temper. Any patient of his was free to seek a second opinion. In fact, many times he encouraged it. It was just that this was Meara. He had spent the last several weeks feeling insecure, knowing that she was out of his league. He was in awe of her. She always had an answer for everything and commanded a room.

Meanwhile, his old insecurities surfaced, and he felt like a part of him was still the dorky kid with the glasses and a brief-case. Their intellects were well-matched, but that was about all. She was sophisticated, socially proficient, and used to a high-profile corporate lifestyle. Meanwhile, he lived off cafeteria food, would rather wear his old, faded jeans most of the time, and probably bored her with his exhaustive tours and love of sci-fi. She sparkled, and he...well, he did not.

It was for the best. The conversation with his mother had made him admit what he had been feeling for days. While his work had been the most important thing in his life, now it was Valentina. It would mean restructuring some of his traveling and work, but he was willing to do it. It was time he took control of his life. In the next couple of days, he would drive up and retrieve her and start a new routine with her. He missed her.

He didn't blame Meara for not wanting to step in and be an instant mother. A lot of women wouldn't want to take on someone else's child. It was senseless that he even entertained the idea that she would change her mind. It had become clear Meara wasn't even going to stay in Italy. She had already done more work for the foundation than most people would have completed in double the amount of time. Once she steered it toward a steady place, she would move on to her next challenge. It was too bad that they had to end that way. What did he expect, though?

Standing, he straightened his shoulders. He needed to get a second wind and do what he did best: be a doctor.

twenty-five

Meara hauled the giant giraffe into Kate's room. "Ta da," she said, setting him down with a flourish.

"What is that?" Kate asked, pausing her spoon in mid-air, a bowl of gelato in her hand.

"Did giving birth ruin your eyesight? It's a giraffe!"

Kate took another bite but made a face. "I guess I should have asked *why* is there is a giraffe in my room?"

"Because my nephew needs it," Meara explained with a smile.

"The giraffe has kind of a creepy face," Kate observed.

"Oh my God, Katie, you're killing me!" Meara said. She peered closely at the stuffed animal and then back at her sister. Grimacing, her eyes widened. "Oh, you are right. He is a little scary."

Picking him up, she turned him toward the wall. "I'll take him back later!"

Kate laughed, scraping the bowl. "Dang, that went down too fast," she complained.

Meara grinned. "Back to your old ways, I see."

"Yeah, but now I don't have the baby as an excuse, so I better slow down." Her smile grew. "Have you seen him? Isn't he gorgeous?"

Meara looked uneasy, and Kate narrowed her gaze. "Meara Malone, you haven't seen your nephew yet? I gave birth yesterday! He's already a day old and changing by the minute!"

"I don't think he's ready for his first car yet," Meara said dryly. "Look, you are my priority. It was late last night by the time they let me see you. I wasn't going to go demand to see the baby then. I figured I'd go see him today. That is, if they'll even let me."

"You probably can't go in, but if you ask the nurse, they can wheel him over to the window so you can see. Oh, Meara, he's so handsome. Just like his daddy."

"No bias there." Meara smiled wryly. "He's okay though?"

Kate nodded. "Perfectly. They said that Alec did a great job ensuring I was given steroids and magnesium to help the baby's lungs. I guess they are one of the last things to develop. They are just monitoring him because he is a little small, but they are having me feed him, and he definitely knows me," she said and smiled. "Marco is with him now."

Meara didn't say anything, but she remembered Dr. Davis mentioning a drug that he explained was a steroid. It had been on her list to ask Alec about.

"Does this magical child have a name?"

Kate grinned. "Francesco Giacamo Fintan Rinaldi."

"That's quite a mouthful for someone so tiny," Meara observed with a smirk.

"I wanted to name him after Grandpa Francesco. He was such a wonderful man, and he'd be so happy we are living in his homeland! Marco was kind enough to agree. Giacomo is Marco's father. He was a little uncertain about that idea, but I think he's happy now. And I think Margherita will like that, too. She is on her way back from a trip with Sergio, so we'll see her in a couple days. And of course, Fintan in honor of Dad."

"That's perfect," Meara said softly.

"I thought so, too. We are going to call him Frankie for now. But go see him! Please. I want him to bond with you."

"He's not going to bond with me through a window," Meara grumbled.

"I know, but I still want you to visit him. Come back and tell me how wonderful he looks." Kate leaned back and yawned. "Meanwhile, I'll just take a tiny nap."

"Okay, Mamma," Meara whispered. She sat looking at her sister for a moment. Thank God she was okay. Last night Meara had gone home after seeing her, still worrying. What if they were wrong? What if her blood pressure shot up again? What if Alec wasn't there to help?

Marco had mentioned to her Alec had left the hospital after verifying that Frankie was doing well. Meara had wanted so badly to call him last night. So many nights when he was at the hospital, he called her just to check in. She had gotten used to hearing his voice before she went to sleep. It always soothed her. Longing for that feeling, she held her phone for a while, tempted to reach out. Finally, she had plugged her phone into the charger and had fallen into a dreamless, exhausted sleep.

Now, as she stared at her sleeping sister, she swallowed hard, wondering what he was thinking. Was he still angry with her? Did he miss her at all? He'd looked disgusted and then just defeated. If he hadn't gotten the phone call from Kate, she would have finished her sentence. The thought of losing him suddenly made her see everything with such clarity. Possibly she was wrong and could mother a small child. She had grown very fond of Valentina. Motherhood was never something she had sought, but now she was more confident that she could learn. If he would just let her try. From his conversation yesterday with his mother and now his anger toward her, it appeared she wouldn't get the chance.

A gentle snore came from Kate, and Meara smiled. It was time to go meet her new nephew.

MARCO GRINNED THROUGH THE GLASS. He was masked and gowned, and he pointed to the isolette proudly. He said something to the nurse, who nodded. Gently, they wheeled the isolette closer to the window, along with a monitor that was attached.

Meara's eyes widened in alarm. Even all bundled up, he looked much tinier than she expected. She gazed down at the little infant with his little blue hat on. He looked so very frail and so innocent. How could Kate have thought he resembled anyone with that scrunched up little face?

Marco reached into the armhole of the isolette. With his gloved hand, he picked up the tiniest of hands Meara had ever seen and waved it at her. She put a shaking hand to her mouth, feeling the rush of emotion. This baby was half of Kate. He was part of her family now. She was oblivious of the tears that finally dropped from her eyes.

LATER THAT DAY as dusk was settling in, Meara walked into the hospital. Rome was glowing as it did this time of day, and her heart tugged, thinking about the sunsets she had watched with Alec. He had shown her a side of Rome she would never have known without him.

Riding the elevator to the fourth floor, she automatically headed to the Neonatal Unit. Her routine now was to check on Frankie and then go to see Kate and update her on how wonderful he looked. Kate was scheduled to be discharged the next day, and she wasn't very happy about going home without their son. The neonatologist had promised that the baby would follow them soon. Kate grudgingly agreed, knowing that she wanted him to be as healthy as possible.

Meara arrived at the window and searched for her nephew's name on the isolette. There were only five babies in the unit, and she prided herself that she could easily identify him. Her eyes found his name, but the isolette was empty. Her heart thudded. Where was he? Had something happened?

A movement caught her eye, and she glanced over to see the nurses tending to a baby in a different incubator, their movements practiced and sure. Suddenly, one of them moved and Meara saw Alec. Sitting in a rocking chair, gowned and masked, he was holding a tiny infant with a blue hat. It had to be her nephew. As if he felt her stare, he suddenly looked up, and his gaze met hers. Even from a distance, she felt its intensity. She couldn't see much of his face because of his mask, but his eyes told the story. He appeared to stare right through her. The enormity of everything in the last few days hit her with a stunning force, almost making her dizzy. Standing there for what seemed like forever, she finally did something she had never done before: Meara turned and walked away rather than face her opponent.

twenty-six

Meara sat down in the plush nursery rocking chair and wiped her hands again on her black jeans.

"Katie, are you sure you want me to do this?"

Katie was holding Frankie, standing and softly rocking. She chuckled. "I have been waiting for this moment! He's almost two weeks old, and you have refused to touch him."

"You've been waiting for me to drop and dent your baby?

"You're not going to drop him," Kate insisted. "I've been waiting for you to bond with Frankie."

"I can bond with him just fine from across the room," Meara argued, pursing her lips. "Look, Katie, you worked hard for this baby. You don't want to turn him over to an amateur."

Kate only shook her head ruefully. With one hand, she draped a baby blanket over Meara's blouse. "I told you not to wear silk today. He likes to spit up a lot."

"Can't you train him not to do that?"

Kate's muffled laughter was the answer. Gently, she placed him in Meara's arms. Meara held him stiffly, scared to move. She had never been so terrified by anything. Facing off with the most formidable high-powered people on the planet, she had never felt the swooshing she was hearing in her brain.

"Just make sure you support his neck. That's really the only thing you have to remember," Kate told her.

"And don't drop him."

Kate smiled. "Yes, ideally, you don't want to do that."

Meara took a deep breath. Fortunately, Frankie was sound asleep and therefore, not squirming as she had seen him do. Watching his mouth move into small Os, his face crinkled as if he was dreaming. His mouth moved, almost into a smile.

"He's smiling! He likes me," Meara whispered.

Kate laughed. "Babies don't really smile this young. He's probably pooping."

"Ewww."

"He has a diaper on, Meara. It will be fine. That will be lesson two."

Meara glanced up at Kate and frowned. "That's not happening."

Kate was busy loading toys and books onto shelves in his room. She turned and laughed. "Okay, okay, I thought it was worth a try."

"I should be doing that organizing, and you can sit here with your baby," Meara pleaded.

Kate shook her head. "Since I didn't have time to have a shower, people have been visiting nonstop and sending gifts. Things have gotten out of control here! Just keep holding him while I sort stuff out. You can rock a little, too."

Meara toed the carpet with her foot and rocked gently. Frankie was definitely dreaming about something. She watched the tiny movements of his face, utterly transfixed. It was actually kind of therapeutic until he squirmed. She automatically tightened her hold. He fell back into a restful sleep, and the Os began again. Meara sighed without knowing it.

"He's beautiful, isn't he?" Marco asked proudly. She had been so mesmerized, she didn't see him standing in the doorway.

"He is," Meara agreed. "You should come and take him. He needs his papa."

Kate turned around sharply. "No, you don't, Meara. Rock. Bond. I'll be right back."

Meara's eyes widened in horror. "Katie, you're not leaving me with him?"

She laughed, grabbing Marco's hand. "We'll be right down the hall. I just want to talk to my husband."

"Katie, I don't know what I'm doing!"

"I'm not flying to Tahiti," Kate teased. "I'll be right back."

Meara watched them depart and took a deep breath. "Well, you're stuck with me, little guy. I'm your aunt. Aunt Newbie."

He continued making his O's, his face full of expression. She searched for his tiny hand inside the blanket. His fingers were long, and she watched captivated as he quickly wrapped them around her finger. And that's when Meara realized her nephew had just wrapped himself around her heart.

"I HEARD you held your nephew today."

Meara smiled at her phone, seeing her father's astounded face on the video call. "I did, Daddy. He's pretty cute. You know how some babies kind of aren't?" Her father laughed, and she continued. "I can't wait for you to get here to see him."

"Just a few weeks, honey. He came a little ahead of schedule. But I'll be there," he promised. "Honey, you look kind of tired. I hope you're not worried about Katie and the baby. Everything is fine, isn't it?"

"Yes, Dad. I would have told you if it wasn't. I know it was hard being so far away when it was all happening, but it all worked out so we can relax."

He nodded. "Thank God she had such a great doctor. I want to meet this guy and thank him. I'll give him a bottle of Irish Whiskey."

Meara blinked the sudden tears in her eyes. It should be her introducing Alec to her father. Just the thought of them meeting without her tore at her heart.

"You're working too much," Finn observed.

"Not really. It's just that the foundation's first gala is coming up. Everything has to be perfect. Marco is counting on me, and I don't want to let him down."

"I am sure you can handle it, honey. You always do everything so well," he said confidently.

"Not everything," Meara muttered.

"What's that, sweetie?"

"Oh, nothing, Dad. I just can't wait for you to get here."

"I'll be there for that fancy event of yours," he said. "Katie told me to bring that expensive Italian suit she had made for me. You know, the one I wore to her wedding."

"You look great in that suit, Dad!"

"Stuffy affairs. You know I hate that kind of thing," he grumbled.

Meara smiled. "It's only for one night. Then you can relax and get to know your grandson."

They talked for a few more minutes before Meara finally said goodbye and put her phone down. Twirling in her chair, she looked out at the streets of Rome. Closing her eyes, images of her and Alec swirled in her mind. Walking in Monti, sitting in silence overwhelmed by the beauty in so many churches, eating gelato in the piazza. It seemed a lifetime ago.

The gala was in two weeks in a ballroom of one of Rome's most prestigious hotels. Just walking in and seeing the black-and-white marble floors and striking chandeliers took her breath away. It was to be a formal affair, and Meara was making a small presentation before Marco would take the microphone for a small appeal. It was important to him that others were also involved in the foundation. He had told Meara he could fund it personally, but it would mean more if it was a combined effort involving others. Marco had told her that his uncle's finest trait was bringing people together for a common goal, and that's what he hoped the foundation would do.

Meara had recognized that her dad was right. She was exhausted but not from work. During the day working at the foundation was where she felt at peace. It was when she went back to her lonely apartment, ate a solitary dinner, and sat on the sofa to watch the lights turn on in the city that she thought only of Alec. What was he doing? Was he playing with Valentina? Was he planning adventures with her?

She picked up her phone more than once to text him. They couldn't leave it where it was. Yet, by the same token, how could they move forward? She'd thought their relationship was leading somewhere. Then he'd coldly stated to his mother that they had no future, and she would not be a ready-made mother to Valentina. What did that even mean? He had talked about her lack of trust in him. But what about his complete dismissal of her? While she had told him she didn't do kids, they hadn't discussed it further. Of course, she realized guiltily he had brought it up in the car. But she had felt humiliated, listening to him make light of their entire relationship with his mother. Nothing made sense anymore.

She grabbed her laptop to work for a while. At least she would be productive with her insomnia. If nothing else, it kept her mind off her own troubles and fortunately, off of Alec.

"DAD SAID you are working too hard," Kate told her with a frown. She was sitting on the window seat in the nursery, folding tiny clothes and putting them in a dresser. Meara was rocking

Frankie, feeling proud of her newly acquired technique. Kate had shown her step two, which was actually moving him to nestle into her shoulder, holding on to his neck and head with one hand. It did feel good to have that baby breath on her neck as he nuzzled into her skin, trying to get comfortable.

"Am I doing this right, Katie?"

She nodded. "Yes, you are for the tenth time. And stop deflecting. You look awful, Meara. Good thing you have all that glorious hair because the rest of you doesn't look so hot."

"Thanks," Meara said sarcastically. "I guess I can count on you to tell me the truth."

"Always," Kate said firmly. "So now it's your turn to tell me the truth. What happened with Alec? And please don't tell me nothing." She rolled her eyes. "He was over here the other night, and he was as tight-lipped as they come."

"He was here?" Meara asked quickly. She regretted it as soon as she saw the look pass on Kate's face.

"Yes, he only stopped by for a minute to see the baby and make sure we liked the pediatrician he referred us to. He's so good with Frankie and so knowledgeable. Sometimes I think he should have been a neonatologist or a pediatrician himself." She glanced at Meara quizzically. "What? What did I say?"

Meara looked down at her nephew and continued to rock gently. "He just loves babies," she said softly. "And though I am less terrified than I was, I don't think I ever really want this."

"You don't have to," Kate said. "But is that why you guys broke up? Did you finally have that talk?"

"It's complicated," Meara muttered.

"That's what he said."

Meara startled, and Frankie gave a whimper before nestling back into her neck. "What did he say? Oh my God, Katie, you didn't ask him anything, did you?"

"Shh, you're going to wake the baby. No sudden movements, remember?" She looked guilty. "I didn't say a thing, but Marco did as he was leaving. It was just something casual about maybe the two of you could come over some night or something and Alec just told him things were complicated."

"They are."

Kate stopped folding clothes to eye her sister closely. "Good thing I'm a smart person. No matter how complicated this thing is, I think I can follow along. Tell me what happened."

Taking a deep breath, Meara began to talk. For the next hour, she told her sister the entire story from beginning to end. From the closeness they had shared to the call with his mother.

Kate's face went dark. "He said that? *Any* feelings he had? And you weren't going to be a ready-made mother? How arrogant! I take back every nice thing I said about him. If he walked in here right now, I'd..."

Meara shook her head sadly. "You would what, Katie? Defend my honor? He's right, you know. I'm not good at this, and you know it."

Kate rolled her eyes. "Somewhere you got this thing in your head you're not nurturing. Look at what you did for me? For Dad. You advocate and fight for people. Okay, maybe you should have talked to Alec more, but you made that call to that LA doctor because you wanted only the best for me."

"Alec was the best," Meara said quietly. "He was right. I didn't trust him."

"He needs to put his ego away," Kate responded dutifully. "You would second-guess anyone because you want to protect me. You always have, even when we weren't getting along."

Meara only smiled and continued to rock.

"You are really in love with him, aren't you?"

Meara stopped rocking abruptly. Finally, she nodded.

Kate smiled. "I've never seen you at a loss for words before. What about Valentina?"

"I was getting more comfortable around her. She's not so

fragile like this guy, and even though I'm not sure I will ever truly understand a kid, she seemed to like me."

"I'm sure she loved you," said Kate confidently.

Kate was thoughtful for a minute. "I just wonder about one thing."

At Meara's quizzical look, Kate smiled a little. "How many coins did Alec tell you to throw in the fountain?"

"Three."

"That's interesting," Kate said, her eyes dancing. "Why would he do that when that means the person will find the love of their life and marry?"

Meara rolled her eyes. "I don't believe in that kind of nonsense."

Kate smiled tremulously. "Yeah, but why did he give you three coins?"

"I don't know. Maybe he had three in his pocket."

Kate shook her head knowingly. "It was for a reason, Meara."

Meara looked at her sister speculatively for a minute before she suddenly wrinkled her nose. "Katie, something smells over here."

Kate grinned. "Want to learn how to change a diaper?"

Meara returned the grin. "Nope."

twenty-seven

Meara walked into the ballroom and glanced around. She knew she looked her best. It wasn't often that she got this glammed up, but it had been fun to go with Kate and get spoiled. Her hair was curled in even more waves. It was the perfect foil for her icy blue gown with its strapless, fitted bodice that showed off just enough cleavage. A sheer blue overlay was embellished with silver and blue sequins. Its long slit showed off her legs. The diamond earrings she had bought herself years ago as a reward looked lovely with it. On her feet, she had bought new silver Italian strappy sandals.

"This tie is choking me," Finn Malone complained, grabbing at his tie yet again.

Meara turned to him and smoothed it down comfortingly. "I promise this will be the only time you have to wear it on this trip."

"I could have stayed home with the baby," he grumbled. "I hope you're sure that nanny you helped Katie get is qualified to take care of my grandson."

Meara smiled indulgently at him. "Daddy, I promise you she was thoroughly vetted by Marco's security people. Worse, she had to pass Katie's scrutiny. And I need you here. This is my big night! I want you to meet some people."

"Do I get to meet that doctor friend of yours? The one who saved my Katie and the baby?"

Meara tried not to visibly choke. "I'm not sure he'll be here, and if he is, Katie can introduce you," she hedged.

"Bull crackers."

Meara laughed out loud. "I haven't heard you say that in years."

"You know what it means. I'm not buying it. Katie shouldn't be introducing me to him, you should. He was your boyfriend, after all."

She glanced around anxiously. "Shhh, dad, keep your voice down. He's not my boyfriend. We aren't in high school."

"But you were dating."

"Do we have to label it? Yes, I had a relationship with him, but it's over."

"I hear it's complicated."

Meara frowned. "I'm going to kill my little sister."

"She's just telling me what you should have a few months ago when you were with him."

At her father's expression, Meara grabbed his arm. "Dad, I didn't talk to you about it because I didn't really think it was going anywhere."

"They never do," he said matter-of-factly.

"What is this, some kind of tough love session? You mean my relationships? Can we talk about this later, please?"

He sighed. "All I'm saying is one of these days you need to pull your head out of that computer and phone of yours and glance around at life. It goes too fast, honey. And when you find someone that you share something special with, snag it while you can. I had that kind of love with your mother."

She nodded, swallowing the lump in her throat. Finally, she choked out, "He didn't love me, Dad."

"I think you're wrong."

She brushed the invisible lint off the shoulder of his jacket. "Why do you think that?"

"Because he's been staring at you ever since we walked into this room. And if that's not a besotted man, I don't know what is.

ALARMED, Meara's gaze abruptly met her father's solemn one. Emerald green eyes that mirrored her own stared back at her. It took every fiber of her willpower not to spin around to find Alec. "Dad, how did you know who he was?"

"Pretty obvious, honey. And that's why he's headed over here now like a man on a mission. I'm going to take my cue and go talk to your sister. While I can't wait to meet him, something tells me I should let you two talk first."

Meara frantically watched him stride away before feeling the familiar warmth of a gentle hand on her shoulder.

"*Buonasera*, Meara,"

She turned quickly, not realizing how close he was. His face was inches from hers, and, thanks to her new shoe purchase, she was looking at him directly in the eyes. Trying not to focus on how handsome he looked in his black suit and royal blue tie, she willed her heart to slow down its racing beat.

"Alec, hi. Good evening to you, too. Thank you for coming," she said mechanically, shifting into hostess mode. "Isn't it great so many people came? I know Marco will be excited. And I'm glad it's not raining so people can go out to the balcony if they want and look at the view." She knew she was babbling but couldn't stop herself.

"Meara, I don't want to talk about the weather."

Glancing around to avoid his intense gaze, she tried again. "Marco is so excited to formally launch the foundation and showcase all the success so far."

"I don't want to talk about the foundation either."

"What do you want to talk about?" she snapped, exasperated.

"Us."

That one word tore her heart out. Her head whipped back to meet his hard stare. Now she noticed the dark smudges under his eyes, the fine lines next to them that always appeared when he was tired. Her heart ached to smooth his hair back from his forehead. She steeled herself against backing down.

"There is no us. Apparently there never was."

"How can you say that?" he asked roughly. "After everything."

"Keep your voice down. This isn't the time or place to have this conversation," she whispered roughly.

"Tell me where and when, and I'll be there."

She opened her mouth to tell him they would have to talk later.

"It's good to see you again, Meara," said a quiet voice behind her. Meara turned to see Alec's mother peering up at her, a small smile on her face. "I hope you are well."

Meara looked down at the diminutive woman and then at Alec. "I am, thank you very much."

His mother was giving Alec a speaking look now. "I am happy to see you two talking. I told Alec just the other night that his father and I had several issues to work through when we were dating."

"Mamma," Alec said warningly.

"And Valentina talked nonstop about you when she was with me," his mother continued, obviously ignoring him. "I won't pry, but I just hope that you both can talk sensibly so that there are no regrets later."

"It's complicated," Meara and Alec said at the same time, without looking at each other.

"So I've been told," his mother said dryly. "Complicated doesn't always have to be bad. Yes, Alec, I see you glaring at me.

I will go now." She patted Meara's arm. "I just spoke with your father, dear. He's very proud of you."

Meara turned to see her father across the room, talking to Kate. He gave her a small shrug, as if to say he was innocent. She turned back to Alec's mother. "Thank you. If you'll excuse me, I need to go work on my speech," she said woodenly. Giving her a small smile, she turned to Alec. "Goodbye, Alec."

He grabbed her arm, his eyes glinting. "Meara, we will talk later," he said softly. "I know you still feel something for me. I can see it in your eyes."

"Any feelings I have for you are irrelevant," she repeated quietly, before walking away.

SOMEHOW MEARA GOT through the evening. She had come prepared and only had to give a brief introduction before her team's video played. They had captured the essence of what the Angelo Foundation wanted to become, as well as all the significant success it had already achieved. The applause at the end had been thunderous. Meara purposely kept her gaze turned away from Alec, but she found herself drawn toward him at that moment. He was clapping with the others, but he was staring at her intently. It was as if everyone melted away and they were the only two people in the room. Was he thinking back to their time at the hospital and the moment they shared when they realized they were part of building something significant? Finally, she broke his gaze when Marco strode confidently to the podium. A moment of happiness overtook her sadness by watching her brother-in-law. He looked so proud, and she was hopeful she had something to do with it.

Tonight proved that she needed to leave. There was no way she could see Alec around every turn, especially if he was going to attempt to be friends with her again. Just thinking about that made her shudder. She would have to see him if she stayed. He was on the board of the foundation, and even though things hadn't worked out between them, she acknowledged he deserved to continue to be a part of it. For her, things were different. She was an outsider who could go back to her cut-throat corporate world and find a high-level job. It would mean leaving Italy and going back to the U.S. It would be difficult to see Kate and the baby as much as she liked, but it was better than the alternative of having her heart shattered repeatedly.

If only she had just left things alone. She had listened to Kate and others tell her how it was time to take risks and enjoy life. It had been safer when she had focused on her work and achieved the success that drove her. The firing had a been a low point, and she had been weak. Now she knew what it was like to have loved and lost, and she would not let that happen again.

Love.

Never again. From now on, she would protect her heart.

Suddenly, the empty chair slid out next to her. Kate sat down, smiling at her. "I have hardly talked to you all night! Stunning gown, by the way. How are you holding up?"

Meara smiled. "I was happy Marco was so happy."

"He's ecstatic, Meara. I'm sure he will tell you himself. I hope you don't mind, but Dad and I are going to slip out. He's had fun, but he won't admit it." She rolled her eyes. "But it doesn't matter. I want to get home to my son."

Meara nodded. "I think I'll go with you. No one will miss me once the dancing starts."

Kate looked at her wide-eyed. "But you can't. This is your night. You put this whole thing together! And everything is perfect. I'm so proud of you."

Meara looked around, blinking back the tears. "Thanks, sis. It doesn't feel like my night, though. It started with you, Marco, Teresa, and Alec. Everyone did the work. I just got a few things over the finish line."

"You did more than that."

She shrugged, still avoiding Kate's eyes.

"I've been dying all night. Speaking of Alec. What did he say to you?" Kate asked quietly.

"He said he wanted to talk."

Kate looked uncertain. "Maybe you should, Meara. You might not have heard him correctly on the phone. There may be stuff you can work out."

Meara finally met her sister's gaze. "I can't. He is just going to say he's sorry that things turned out the way they did. No matter what, he's such a nice guy, Katie. He probably wants to be friends and thinks we need closure because of working together. I can easily go my whole life without that conversation."

"He's probably right. You're going to keep seeing him around."

Meara bit her lip. Now was not the time to tell Kate she was going to leave. That discussion would have to happen later. And she owed it to Marco to tell him at the same time.

Kate shook her head in frustration. "I see I'm not going to change your mind." She stood, her eyes searching the room. "I haven't seen him for a while. Marco said he saw him escorting his mother out the door. At least you won't have to face it tonight."

At Meara's silence, Kate sighed. "I left Dad with a cluster of women around him. The man sure has the gift of the gab. I think I better go rescue them."

Meara laughed a little. "He's all talk with his complaining, but I'm sure he'll be happy to get that suit and tie off."

"Agree! You're coming for brunch tomorrow? Teresa and Stefano will be there, too. They slipped out early," she said with a grimace. "Honeymooners."

"Of course, I wouldn't miss it," Meara answered, kissing Kate's cheek. After the brunch, she would tell them about leaving. It was only fair to give Marco plenty of notice so he had time to find someone else.

After Kate departed, Meara stood as well, shaking her dress out. Kate had been right. Alec was nowhere to be found. He must have come to the same realization she had. Circulating for the next hour was tortuous, but Marco seemed to sense her discomfort. He kept her by his side, introducing her to several people. Smiling politely and answering questions was a good distraction. She and Marco continued to work the room.

As the dancing continued, Marco approached and bent to whisper in her ear. "I'm going to leave shortly, if you don't mind. I want to be home for the next time Frankie wakes up to support Katie."

"I am going to go check in with the staff, and I'll be right behind you," Meara answered. "The crowds have dwindled. They can close it down without us."

Marco looked at her, his eyes full of pride. "Thank you, *mia sorella* for everything. It was a wonderful night and a prosperous one. So many people want to be involved."

She nodded, glancing away, feeling guilty. Walking away, she checked in with her staff. They were young and happy to stay and mingle. They would ensure all the guests had left before signaling to the catering crew to begin cleaning up.

Meara sighed, walking out to the opulent lobby. She had told Cosmo that she would text him when she needed him but fully expected him to be hovering outside. As she walked out into the cool night, there was no sign of him and she pulled out her phone.

"Get in the car, Meara."

Her head snapped up to see Alec holding the passenger door open. He had lost his tie, and his crisp white shirt was unbuttoned a little. His hair was ruffled as if he had been running his hands through it, and he gazed at her intently.

"Cosmo will pick me up."

"I sent him home."

Her eyes widened. "What? That wasn't for you to do. It has been a long night, and now I just want to go home."

"You can as soon as we talk."

She looked at him now, a silent appeal in her eyes, but his face was impassive. He was bound and determined to have this talk. She might as well get it over with.

Getting in the car, she folded her gown carefully in before he shut the door. As usual, he drove through the quiet Rome streets with confidence. She turned away from him and looked out the window, rehearsing her goodbye speech to him. There was no reason to belabor points. Apologizing for not trusting him would be her one concession.

"Alec, this isn't the way to my apartment," she said, glancing around, coming out of her daze.

"I know."

"We can talk, but let's just go to my apartment. We are both tired. I'm not up for one of your adventures."

He continued to drive, and she took a deep breath and opened her mouth to again demand he take her home, when he pulled up the hill and was met by a security officer. A quick conversation had the officer chuckling and he waved them through the now open gate. Alec maneuvered the powerful car into a parking spot. He was around the car and ready to help her out seconds later. Taking his hand, she felt the familiar spark that leaped from her palm down her spine. That would never cease, and that's why she couldn't pledge some kind of friendship with him.

He continued to grasp her hand and she attempted to pull away, but he just tightened his grip. "Let me hold on to you, Meara," he said quietly. "Those heels are ridiculous. You'll break your neck on these cobblestones."

Since he was right, she stopped fighting and let him lead her down the path. The moon was full and cast a glow over them.

Realizing where they were, she took a deep breath. "Oh, Alec, not here."

"Yes, here," he said, pulling her gently to sit down next to him on the bench at the Borghese Gardens. The Eternal City lay at their feet, twinkling and glittering. "I thought a lot about where I wanted to talk to you, and I realized that this was the best place. Not only does it have the most amazing view, but I think it's when we both realized we were falling in love."

She put a hand up to her mouth, but the sound of her small choked sob came out.

He put his arm around her. "You're shivering."

Taking his jacket off, he put it gently around her gown. "I am sorry. I forgot you wouldn't have a coat."

She sunk into the jacket, warm from his body. "What do you mean we both realized we were falling in love?" she asked tremulously.

"Was it only me? I could have sworn that night you were starting to give me at least a small piece of your heart. It gave me such hope."

Her heart soared before starting to sink. "I...I don't know, Alec. Things have gotten so confused."

"Then we need to clear a few things up," he said quietly. "I take it from your remark tonight you overheard my conversation with my mother on the phone. You must understand this was not the first conversation we had about you."

Meara felt an uneasy feeling in the pit of her stomach. "Yes, I heard you. I didn't mean to eavesdrop, but I heard my name, and I stopped. It was wrong, but I am glad I did. I found out how you truly felt."

"How did you do that?"

"By hearing what you said to your mother."

He laughed dryly and turned toward her so he could stare at her. His eyes searched her face as if trying to determine what to say. Finally, he took a deep breath. "If I was going to tell a woman I loved her, I wouldn't tell my mother first. Or Stefano or anyone else who has asked. Besides, I didn't want her to pressure you or make you feel guilty for any of your feelings. Meara, I was bewitched by you from the first moment I saw you, but it was only after we began our adventures that I felt like I was seeing the real you. I felt you had come to trust me—at least a little. And that night that we sat on this bench, I felt your love as well. You can tell me I was wrong, but I do not think so."

She turned her head away, but he put a hand under her chin to draw her face back to him. "Meara Malone, you have captured my heart and my soul. I can't look out at this city—the city I love as well without seeing you around every turn."

Staring intently at her surprised face, his eyes glittered in the night light. "I need to know how you feel. Say it, Meara," he whispered.

She swallowed the lump in her throat. "Alec, I've loved you for a long time. Only, I've never been in love, and it scares me. Everything scares me, and I'm not used to anything frightening me."

He looked at her solemnly before slowly kissing her, savoring her lips. Finally, he spoke. "Tell me why you're so scared. And why do you doubt my love?"

"You said I wasn't a ready-made mother for Valentina."

"I did," he stated.

"But the thing is, Alec, I was beginning to think I could be, but when I heard you say that, I realized you didn't agree."

He shook his head. "That's not true. I was trying to say that I never wanted you to be that. You are a person who is entitled to feel the way you do. And though you didn't want to show me, eventually I saw your insecurities. You questioned yourself constantly around Valentina, yet I saw your tremendous ability to love. To even think that you would just be this ready-made, instant mamma to someone else's child is oversimplifying things.

I want you to be all in—to feel the desire to mother Valentina without any question.”

“Do you believe I can?” she whispered.

He nodded and smiled at her rare show of uncertainty. Then he winced. “I have had a lot of time to think over the last few weeks. I was so unfair to you, Meara. My ego and my own insecurities got in the way. You had every right to double check my decisions with another doctor. You did so because your capacity for love is so great. You’re a fierce warrior for those you love. I hope one day you can be that warrior for both me and Nia.”

“I can try,” she said simply.

He let out a deep breath. “Don’t you remember your introduction to *Star Wars*? Yoda said, ‘Do or do not. There is no try.’”

Her eyes widened before she finally nodded. “Then I do,” she said softly.

He gathered her in his arms and hugged her for a long time. How could she have forgotten how good those long hugs of his felt? It was like coming home, and a sense of calm flooded her.

“Let’s go home,” he said softly.

And for the first time in a long time, she realized she had a home.

“ALEC, I love our adventures, but one of these days you have to pick one that has some flat ground,” Meara grumbled good-naturedly as she clung to his hand, letting him lead her on the unstable path. He had suggested a sunset dinner, and she had dressed as if they were going out to a real restaurant, in a short dress with her usual heels. But now they had arrived at a garden.

“Where are we?”

He turned to smile, as always providing her with complete information. “*Giardino degli Aranci*,” he informed her. “We are on Aventine Hill, one of Rome’s legendary seven hills.”

Her brow furrowed. The Orange Garden. They talked about going there but hadn't done so yet. Smiling, she continued walking with him, admiring the orange trees that lined the path. Taking a deep breath, she sighed happily. It smelled like heaven. In fact, the last several months had been heavenly. It had been beyond anything she had ever dreamed of.

They agreed the night they reunited to take it slow. Alec said he would marry her that day if he could, but he understood Meara needed more time. They appeared at Kate and Marco's brunch the next morning as a couple. Marco's arm had tightened around Kate every time she appeared to want to ask questions. Meara could have easily explained. She had made up her mind that night that she wanted it all—Alec, Nia and their life in Rome. Seeing Kate flustered was more fun, though.

Finn, however, was a different matter. He had taken Alec's arm and gone for a stroll on the massive grounds, obviously wanting to know what his intentions were. They came back, laughing as old friends, and Meara rolled her eyes. Finn may think he was a protective dad, but he was also a big softie. He came over to her and whispered, "I like this one. Keep him around."

She continued her role at the foundation, and soon they would go down to visit the new clinic that was almost finished. The gala had been wildly successful, and now it seemed every day more people wanted to be involved. They were building something lasting that would affect many people's lives. Meara relied more on her staff these days. At first, they seemed confused about the change in her. She was relaxed around the office, smiling more and wanting people to enjoy their work. One by one, she had brought her employees in to ask them if they were happy, just as Marco had done to her. Her management style had completely changed, and therefore, the atmosphere in the office was lighter and productive.

And then there was Valentina. She had physically grown

since Meara first met her. Meara insisted that she wanted to take her shopping for new clothes. More importantly, she told Alec to stay home as it was important for them to do things together. Alec worried that Meara felt pressured to spend time with the little girl, but she didn't. She enjoyed Valentina's company. There was something so endearing about her innocence, and Meara loved seeing and hearing Valentina's excitement over the smallest object. Meara even bought her a new dress for Frankie's baptism, which was coming up in two days at the Church of *Santa Maria Assunta* in Positano, where Kate and Marco had married. Nia kept saying Frankie was her *cugino,* and neither Alec nor Meara chose to correct her.

Yes, things were good, and Meara felt like they could go on forever this way. Now standing in the garden with Alec, she gasped as they came upon a beautiful table set before her. It was in the secluded part of the garden, with a crisp white tablecloth, silver cutlery and crystal glasses sparkling in the lamplight.

"This doesn't look like any picnic I've ever been to," she remarked dryly.

Alec turned and grinned, leading her to the side of the table against a rail. A breathtaking panoramic view lay before them. The dome of St. Peter's glinted in the golden light, and the Tiber River was before them.

"This is so beautiful, Alec. Why haven't you shown me this area before?"

He put his arm around her, staring at the view. "I was saving it."

"Saving it for what?" she asked absentmindedly, looking at the view. "Oh look, you can see everything from here. So many adventures we've been on together."

She turned to smile at him, and then gasped when she saw he had gone down on one knee. Her heart slammed into her chest.

"Meara, I want to ask you to go on one more adventure. This one will last a lifetime. I love you even more each day. Will you be my wife, my partner, and my love? I promise our life together will be one magnificent adventure."

Meara nodded, speechless for once. He grinned at her and snapped open the blue velvet box he held in his hand.

"I've rarely seen you speechless," he commented wryly. Standing, he took the oval emerald from its white nest and slid it on her finger. "If you prefer a diamond, we will exchange it, but I kept going back to this because it matches your eyes."

"It's perfect," she whispered, admiring it in the glowing light.

She turned to him. "But, Alec, there's Nia. You really think I can be her mother?"

He smiled tenderly at her. "You already are. Remember a couple weeks ago when that boy pushed her down at the park? Before I could even get there, you were telling all the boys in no uncertain terms to be careful. When she got sick the other night, I have to say you were less than pleased with me for not taking her to the pediatrician immediately."

"She had a temperature!"

He smiled. "Yes, and we monitored it. A dose of medicine brought it down. And it ended up being a small cold. You were ready to fight me, though."

"What's your point?" she asked, making a face at him.

"You're already her fierce warrior. You will fight me, little boys, and anyone else who harms her. That's what a mother is, Meara. You don't have to know everything. All you need to do is care for her, be there for her, and love her. You're already doing those things."

"But I still do stupid things. At Katie's Easter luncheon, I let Nia eat way too much candy, and I'm sure that's why her tummy hurt that night."

He grinned. "Someday you will look back at that candy and wish every problem was so small. I promise you there will be joy, heartache, worry, and moments of panic. But I will be alongside you every step of the way. It will be a rollercoaster adventure of raising her."

"Alec, what about more children?" She asked uncertainly.

"What about them?

"You should have a houseful. You're so good with them. I still don't know if I will want more."

He kissed her for the first time, a long, deep kiss. "I am happy with just one. You forget, I see a lot of babies all day long."

"But don't you want more?"

He shrugged. "Not necessarily. If down the road it is something together we decide we want to pursue, we can. And you know there are other ways to have children. If you don't want to become pregnant, we can always adopt. Or not. What matters to me the most is we raise one child really well. The rest will fall into place."

He leaned his forehead next to hers. "A few months ago, I asked you to be all in and not just try. I need to hear it again, *cuore mio*. I need to be sure you're sure."

She flung her arms around him. "I do. Forever"

epilogue

"Nia, stand still. I promise I'm hurrying," Meara muttered, with hairpins in her mouth. She quickly took one out and stuck it in the small girl's hair.

Kate opened the door. "You're not dressed! Meara, you're getting married soon! Why didn't you have the hair and makeup person tend to Nia?"

Valentina lunged toward Kate. "*Zia* Katie!"

Meara grabbed her with one hand and stuck the last pin in her hair. "There, done! Now you can hug your *Zia* Katie, but don't rumple her."

Kate bent over to return the child's hug. "She looks adorable. But you are running late."

Meara grinned. "The stylist did her hair, but I didn't like it. Nia looked like she was fifteen years old. If you can take her, I'll get into my dress. I need you to button me, though, so come back."

Kate nodded, as she was already busy handing a basket of flowers to Valentina and leading her away.

Meara walked over to the immense wardrobe where her dress was hanging on the door. It had been fun to go to Milan for the weekend with Kate and select a dress to be made by a top designer. Meara had ordered a dress for Valentina as well. Never fussy, she knew what she wanted for herself. The cream gown was a V-neck sleek sheath. Its back featured a cowl that folded inward, tapering at her small waist, leaving most of her back exposed. She smiled. Alec would like that.

At the weddings for Kate, Teresa, and Ellie, they had all helped the bride dress, and it had been a flurry of activity. Meara was strategic in assigning everyone duties to keep them busy. She wanted this calm before her wedding to Alec. Standing now with the dress on, she waited for her sister to do the small covered buttons at the waist on her lower back.

"I'm back!" Kate said, breezing in, wearing a silky emerald green gown. Stopping abruptly, she quickly got tears in her eyes. "Oh, Meara. You look so beautiful." She studied her sister for a minute. "You also look happy. And there's just a calmness about you I've never seen."

"That's Alec," Meara said, turning to smile at her sister.

Kate shook her head and began to do up the small buttons at Meara's waist. "No, it's you. Sure, he has helped, but you have grown Meara. You know you are my older sister and you always seemed like you could do anything—move mountains if you had to. But now, it's like you have already scaled those mountains and you're just so…"

"Relaxed?" Meara said and laughed. "It's okay, Katie. You can say it. I don't think I ever thought I could be this way. And Alec does that for me. He grounds me. And Nia as well. Come on, weren't you the one complaining I was going to be late?"

Kate laughed and handed her a large white bouquet, its stems gathered at the base. "Okay, let me just pull myself together. You're going to be amazed at how beautiful it looks down there."

Meara's heart skipped a beat. She couldn't wait. She and Alec had originally planned on a small wedding, but as they added up the amount of family and close friends, it had gotten larger. Margherita generously offered the lemon grove, but she and Alec decided the wedding should be in Rome. It was where their story began and would continue. After looking at several venues, both old and modern, they had gone back up to the Borghese Gardens to sit and think about it.

"*Mio Dio*, why don't we just have it here?" Alec finally said, smacking his forehead. "Why didn't I think about it before? It's perfect, and there are weddings here all the time." After debating several options, they decided on the Secret Garden. Nearby, a tent had been constructed for the reception and dinner.

Now today it was already her wedding day. Following Kate out of the room that had been set aside for them to dress, she joined her father, who gave her a soft kiss, his eyes filled with tears.

"Not now, Daddy. We have to take a walk," Meara whispered serenely. They followed first Valentina and then Kate down the white carpet that had been created as a makeshift aisle. She almost laughed out loud at the big clumps of rose petals that Valentina had dropped in heaps. Their practice apparently had not taken hold.

Meara raised her head to see Alec gazing her way. He looked so handsome in his black suit and emerald green tie. His eyes were already full of tears, which made her smile even more. Marco stood next to him, his arm carefully on Alec's back to steady him. As she got closer, she saw Valentina in her tiny cream-colored dress, clutching Alec's hand. Wasn't she fortunate? She was going to say I do to both the loves of her life.

THE PARTY WAS STILL GOING ON LATER that night, and Meara sat down with relief in a chair next to Kate, Teresa, and Ellie. "Why aren't you guys dancing? Do your feet hurt as much as mine?" Meara slipped off her rhinestone encrusted high heels and breathed a sigh of relief.

"I told you to bring another pair of shoes," Kate said and laughed. "You and your shoes! We were just here talking about all the weddings and how much change has happened over the last two years. Marco and I kicking it off, of course," she said smugly.

Ellie sighed. "If you and Marco hadn't gotten married, I wouldn't have come here to decorate your cake. And that means Lucca and I would probably never have met." She smiled, watching her husband, who was bent over, holding Valentina's hands and attempting to dance with her. He finally picked up the child to twirl her around to her delight.

"And if you hadn't met Marco, then Lucca would never have thought of me to help Stefano learn how to be on camera," Teresa said, smiling at her husband who was standing across the room, his gaze steady on her.

Meara laughed. "Okay, I'll join in. If you hadn't gotten pregnant or started the foundation, then I probably wouldn't have met Alec."

Kate raised an eyebrow. "Probably?"

Meara smiled, watching her husband talking with Marco. "Somehow I just can't imagine that not happening," she said softly, her gaze intent on Alec. Nearby, her eyes were drawn to Nico, who was sitting at a table, long abandoned by its occupants. His chin was in his hand, and he was twisting his wineglass solemnly.

"What's wrong with Nico? I've never seen him not smiling."

Kate shrugged. "He's been that way for the last few weeks. He won't say anything about why he's so serious. He should be thrilled that he's been able to travel to the U.S. to learn more about crop management. He came home so enthused and then just lately Marco said he's been down in the dumps. Margherita hasn't even been able to get it out of him what's wrong."

"It's a woman," Meara speculated, raising her eyebrows.

"Really? Do you think?"

"I'm going to go ask him," Meara said, standing.

"Meara," Kate yelled after her, but she ignored it. It was hard to see someone so miserable on the happiest day of her life.

"Where are you going with such determination?" Alec stopped her, gripping her around the waist.

She grinned, putting her arms around her husband's neck. "I was going to chat with Nico. He looks miserable," she said. "But now I'm distracted." She gave him a small kiss, realizing with a burst of happiness that she could do that for the rest of their lives.

"Are you ready to leave soon?" he whispered, his eyes glinting. "It's time to get this honeymoon started." Her heart raced, and her back tingled from his hand running up and down her bare spine.

"Where are we going? You still haven't told me," she said, as he leaned forward to kiss alongside her jaw. She tilted her head to give him better access. He got to her ear and paused, his breath making her tingle. "To our next adventure."

upcoming books

Looking for your next sweet romance from Italy?

Check out the next in the series—
Nico and Georgina's story: ***My Sicilian Promise***

E-Book Available Now!
Paperbacks available at Amazon or your favorite bookstore
Continue on to read the first chapter!

MY SICILIAN PROMISE: CHAPTER ONE

Niccolo Rinaldi touched the brim of his black baseball hat, pulling it tighter down over his forehead. He shrugged the lapels of his jacket over his shoulders. Never mind that it was a bright sunny spring day, he wore the dark leather jacket to give himself a shield of sorts. He ran a hand across his tired eyes and tried not to think about his churning stomach. He couldn't leave his post now after waiting several hours. It was almost time. Glancing at his watch for what must be the tenth time in ten minutes, he impatiently frowned. Where was she?

As if the universe were answering him, a vintage white Bentley purred to a stop in front of St. Paul's Cathedral. Niccolo stepped back guardedly. The newsstand proprietor glared at him, rolling his eyes. He had asked Niccolo several times if there was something he could help him with, but Niccolo had only shaken his head absentmindedly. No one could help him. At this point, that was the only thing he was certain of.

His heart pounded as the chauffeur stepped out of the vehicle to open the door nearest to the cathedral. Across the street, a mass of white emerged from the elegant car. The bride's hands smoothed out the billowing folds and ruffles of the wedding gown that seemed to envelop her slight frame. Standing tall, she resembled a figurine atop a wedding cake. Bridesmaids came running down the stairs to greet her. She pushed back the veil impatiently, which was held in place by a shining tiara. Her beautiful blonde hair was regretfully pulled back severely into a complicated knot behind her head.

Climbing the stairs carefully, she suddenly stopped and slowly turned her head and upper torso. Her gaze swept across the street, almost as if she sensed his presence. By now, he was within the safe confines of the newsstand. Even if she saw his silhouette, there was no way she would suspect it was him. From this distance, he regretted he couldn't see her spectacular eyes—a rich blue that darkened when she was excited or angry. He could never forget that color.

Frowning slightly, she turned back around, bending to listen intently to a flower girl who appeared at her side. Lifting her skirts, she began to climb the stairs again, her back straight with determination, the enormous train of her gown trailing behind her regally.

An older gentleman also emerged from the car, and Nico frowned as the man placed his top hat on his head determinedly and followed his daughter. Never had Nico felt such loathing for a human being. Hatred was usually not in his character, but the darkness washed over him. It seared his soul, and if Nico wasn't already in such pain, he would have tried to find a way to hate the man more.

Photographers were now racing up the stairs to get photos of the gorgeous bride. The cathedral's bells were pealing across the London sky as if the most fabulous event was occurring. Only for Nico, it was the worst day of his life. The only woman he had ever truly loved was about to marry another man.

"Are you going to buy anything or not?"

The newsstand operator was clearly frustrated with him. Digging into his pocket, Nico pulled out a large bill and handed it to him.

"My apologies. Thank you for allowing me to occupy your stand," Nico said formally. Glancing one more time at the cathedral, he walked slowly away.

The man shouted after him, "Hey, for this, you can stand here all day, mate!"

Nico ignored the vendor's offer. There was nothing left to see. Georgina would be someone else's wife by the time he got back to his hotel.

～

TWO MONTHS LATER

"How's one of my favorite brothers-in-law?"

Nico turned in his chair as the beautiful brunette sat next to him. Her wide grin wasn't the only evidence of her happiness. She practically glowed. And why not? She was happily married to Nico's brother, Marco, and they were ecstatic new parents to a baby son, Frankie.

"Just wonderful," Nico answered dryly.

Kate gave him a joking frown. "You look just wonderful," she responded sarcastically. She elbowed him teasingly. "What gives? Why so glum, chum?"

He rolled his eyes at her teasing. "I just don't like weddings," he explained through gritted teeth.

"Uh, sorry, *mio fratello*, but I saw you dancing the night away at the last few weddings—not only mine but also your brother and cousin's. So, it seems as if only this wedding seems to be a drag. Aren't you happy for my sister and her new husband?" she asked mockingly.

Nico glanced over at the crowded dance floor. Kate's sister, Meara and her husband Alec were dancing as if they were the only two people in the room. Meara, a tall, stunning redhead, was a force of nature and known internationally for her leadership in the tech world. She had left that behind and now was the executive director of the foundation Marco had started on behalf of the Rinaldi Family. Alec, who coincidentally was Kate's doctor during her pregnancy, was on the board of the foundation. The two had met as Meara took over the reins, but apparently, there had been some bumps along the way. Alec was a single father to his niece following the death of his sister. Meara, who never imagined herself being a mother, had needed time to adjust to the idea. From the looks of them throughout the day, the couple was deeply in love, and Meara had grown into being a doting mother to young Valentina.

Watching the couple so immersed in each other made his entire body ache, but now was not the time to show it. Instead, he leaned over and kissed Kate's cheek. "Of course, I'm happy for Meara and Alec, *mia sorella*. I know the whole family is celebrating. Please don't let my bad mood ruin the evening."

Concern registered on her face. "Nico, I don't think I've ever seen you in a bad mood. I'm a great listener if you want to talk."

He sighed. "It's a long story."

She put her chin on her folded hands. "Isn't that interesting? I've got loads of time." To prove it, she kicked off her shoes and picked up a bottle of wine that sat on the table. Pouring herself a glass, she topped off his. "Spill it. Tell me everything."

Nico glanced around nervously. "My brothers don't even know the entire story. And it's a long one. Marco is going to miss you shortly and be stalking over here to claim you for the next dance."

Kate glanced around and shrugged. "He's in deep conversation with some of the company's board members. And he can wait. This is important."

Nico shook his head sadly.

"It's a woman, isn't it?" asked Kate softly. At his slight nod, she smiled a little. "I knew it. I bet Meara...well never mind that now."

"Meara knows?" Nico's eyes grew wide.

Kate smiled. "She was the first one to notice your... demeanor. She was on her way over here when her groom pulled her onto the dance floor. You're lucky she dispatched me instead. Meara would have already cracked you like an egg by now, shining a bright light in your eyes." Kate chuckled. "When we were kids, she could get anything out of me. I never stood a chance."

Nico grinned for a minute, leaning back in his chair. He had loosened his navy tie and slung his jacket over his chair. His black wavy hair was probably all disheveled from running his hands through it. Kate often told him he resembled his handsome brother, Marco. Marco was so striking he looked like he should be on the cover of a men's fashion magazine, and Nico didn't see any similarities. He glanced over at his other brother, Stefano, who was dancing with his wife, Teresa. Stefano's face had a lean, chiseled appearance, with a prominent jawline. Other than dark hair, Nico didn't resemble him at all.

Kate's voice broke into his thoughts. "What's her name?"

"George," Nico answered automatically. At Kate's quizzical look, he smiled a little. "Georgina. But I always called her George or Georgie."

"Are you in love with her?"

He shook his head. "It doesn't matter. She's married."

"You fell in love with a married woman?" Kate asked incredulously.

"No!" Nico responded loudly. Glancing around, he lowered his voice. "I fell in love with her when she was single. Two months ago, she got married."

Kate nodded understandingly. "Well, that explains your mood, I guess. Did you have a chance to tell her how you felt before…uh, the big day?"

Nico shook his head. "It's a long story," he repeated. "Maybe someday I'll tell you, but for now, it's not worth repeating." Standing abruptly, he held out his hand. "May I have this dance, *mia sorella*?"

Kate stood slowly, shaking out the folds of her gown. "You're trying to distract me. You Rinaldi brothers are famous for it. But just know that I'll be circling back at some point." She arched an eyebrow. "And I'm not putting my shoes back on."

He grinned and swung her out on to the dance floor. Pulling back, he smiled at her. "And I thought I was your favorite *fratello*? Forget Stiff Stefano. I'm much more fun and you know it!"

Kate's musical laugh rang out and for a moment, his heart felt lighter.

Get your Kindle copy of My Sicilian Promise!
Paperbacks available at Amazon or your favorite bookstore

273

author's note to the reader

Dear Reader:

Thank you so much for traveling to Rome to experience the Eternal City through the eyes of Alessandro and Meara. Rome has a special place in my heart. How can it not? To walk the ancient streets, history comes alive.

Thank you to my favorite Physician's Assistant, Martie, whose skills, kindness and compassion touch the lives of the tiniest babies and their families. And her mother Mary, my go-to for writing ideas.

If you want more…there is! Tour through more regions of Italy in this series: From Italy with Love. We'll travel all over, but we'll always swing by the Amalfi Coast to say hi to the family.

Grab some delicious Italian food or a gelato and enjoy more from Italia! Remember to sign up for my newsletter at Tessrini.com/newsletter to read a bonus chapter from *My Secret Positano.*

Cin Cin!
XO, Tess

about the author

Tess Rini has spent her professional life focused on non-fiction writing, from her journalism degree to her editing and writing magazine articles and content for local government. She has published one non-fiction book under a different name.

Tess was raised on a self-induced steady diet of Harlequin romances and so it was inevitable that she should try her hand at romance writing. The idea took off when she combined her love of Italy with her love for romance novels.

When not writing, she can be found relaxing in her Oregon home, traveling or cooking Italian cuisine (her specialty!) for her husband, four daughters and son-in-law. Keeping her company while writing or watching Hallmark movies is her adorable, but anxious, golden retriever.

Sign up for her newsletter at Tessrini.com/newsletter to read a bonus chapter from *My Secret Positano* and stay up on all the latest Italy news.

Website: tessrini.com
Or follow her on social
Facebook @tessriniauthor
Instagram @tessrininauthor